THE HOST

book 1 of 4 in The Host series

T. C. Westminster

WHAT PEOPLE ARE SAYING

Prolific author Jody Wenner says, "The Truman Show meets Black Mirror. I found myself reading faster and faster to keep up with the pace. If you like locked rooms, horror, suspense, and great characters all wrapped into one book, then you'll love THE HOST by T.C. Westminster!

"Super original concept, characters you will root for, and a really interesting read."

"Absolutely creepy, fun and fast-paced read!"

"It gave me Seven vibes with a hint of Patriot Games or something Clancy-esque," says Davin Roberts.

"The suspense is so damn delicious!" Kerri Jackson.

"A fast-paced, edge-of-your-seat, what will happen next, page-turner, Tori Westminster's The Host is the stuff nightmares are made of." Tammy Blakley

Copyright © 2023 T. C. Westminster

All rights reserved

The characters and events portrayed in this book are fictitious. Any similarity to real persons, living or dead, is coincidental and not intended by the author.

No part of this book may be reproduced, or stored in a retrieval system, or transmitted in any form or by any means, electronic, mechanical, photocopying, recording, or otherwise, without express written permission of the publisher.

ISBN: 979-8-9896901-1-4

Digital Art by: Cynthia Gold
Original Image Courtesy of Canva

This book would not have been possible without the unending support of my husband, children, and brother.

CONTENTS

Title Page
What People are Saying
Copyright
Dedication
Prologue   1
Day 1   3
Day 2   41
Day 3   69
Day 4   91
Day 5   132
Day 6   150
Day 9   166
Day 10   178
Day 13   181
Day 18   191
FBI Director Lucian Fenn   205
Day 19   214
Agent Mara Thornfield   232
Day 20   245
Day 21   256

Agent Grayson Holt	281
Day 22	298
Day 24	326
Day 1 Take 2	339
Epilogue	342
Acknowledgement	351
About The Author	353

PROLOGUE

Awake

Disorientation is the first symptom when you regain consciousness after being drugged. Vision is blurred. Up isn't there. Memory feels just out of reach. The world is entirely misshapen.

How do I know?

My name is Monti Cameron. After everything I've been through, I know.

DAY 1

Alone

What the hell!

2403

My head was splitting. The room seemed to be spinning even though I hadn't opened my eyes, and I was positive I was lying flat.

What did I drink last night? And how much?

I curled into a ball, hoping I could sleep it off, when another wave of nausea hit. It was unlike any hangover I'd ever experienced. I had to consider the possibility that the cause of my incapacity wasn't alcohol.

Did someone slip me something? Dammit! Who could have gotten close enough to my drink? What happened?

The conclusion was inescapable: sleep was no longer an option. New imperative: Excedrin. I forced my angry, rigid body into an upright position and sat there for a second, eyes clenched as I tried to orient myself. I gripped the edge of the bed, feeling like I was on a ship being tossed about in a storm. The sensation of having an ice pick buried in my temple didn't help the situation. I debated opening my eyes, but there was a case to be made for keeping them shut.

Everything screeched to a halt. The sheets in my hands were foreign.

This isn't my bed.

I peeled my eyes open and tried to focus, but the room was too bright. The light intensified the stabbing pain in my head. Recoiling, I released the sheets and shaded my eyes for a moment before forcing myself to narrowly open one in a feeble attempt to take in my environment.

This isn't my room.

Confusion took root in place of fear. Pain twisted my senses. For some reason, I still looked for my sheets, my bed, my Excedrin. Instead, I found a palatial suite that looked as though it had been teleported from a 1960s edition of *Good Housekeeping* magazine.

I sat on the edge of a king-size bed with an oversized pink-and-orange floral-patterned polyester bedspread. The twelve-foot ceiling had stained wood stretching from one pink-and-white striped wall to the other. The entire wall across from the bed had been substituted with floor-to-ceiling windows with a forested mountain view unencumbered by curtains. An orange suede armchair and a fluffy pink fainting couch sat in front of the windows with perfect viewing angles.

What is this place? Where is this place? I don't live in the mountains or anywhere near them.

"I live in Manhattan!

"Fantastic, now I'm talking to myself."

Where am I? How did I get here?

I lumbered across the expansive hardwood floor until I reached the longest, softest white fur rug I'd ever seen in my life. My toes sunk in, and I eased my aching body into the pink chaise longue to contemplate my perplexing situation.

The bowl of pink and orange potpourri on the end table assaulted my sinuses, compelling tears and making my nose run; it did nothing to help my pounding head. I tried to ignore it and instead gazed out past the meadow abutting the window and off to the right, where a forest sprung up out of nowhere. My eyes followed the tips of the trees until they met two majestic, snow-capped mountains ascending behind them in the distance. A river worked its way from the top of the mountain to a peaceful stream around the foothills. The prospect calmed me, and I flipped through the redacted files in my brain, trying to recollect something—anything—from the previous evening. My mind was still impaired from whatever I'd taken or had been given the night before. That wasn't helping.

Where was I last night? "Why can't I remember?"

Too much time slipped away before I recalled being at a charity event. For the life of me, I couldn't remember which charity it had benefited. I didn't have a good handle on the passage of time in that room.

"Why isn't there a clock?" *They had clocks in the '60s, right?*

Thinking back, I remembered music. *No. Wait. It's fragmented. Why can I only remember bits of the evening? What could I possibly have been slipped to cause this?*

I tried helplessly to piece the evening together. Bits of speakers droning, donors I met, people I skillfully avoided dancing with. I had stepped out onto a terrace for the cool evening breeze and a break from the chaos, and then . . . *nothing*.

Frustrated with my lack of recall, I tapped my forehead to jog my memory, resulting in a malicious, unmerciful pain, but it, unfortunately, didn't help me remember anything. I sank deeper into the muppet-like pink fluffiness and stretched my legs out over the length of the chaise longue, staring out the window.

"What am I doing? I don't belong here!" I scolded myself.

I couldn't abide even a few more seconds of self-indulgent pity; it was time to pull myself together and go home.

I heaved open the enormous bedroom door just wide enough to peer down the hall. With no one in sight, I walked silently down the long, bare hall, clinging to the right wall where the other doors were. Of course, my reasoning was flawed. The entire length of the left side of the hall—exactly like the bedroom—was twelve-foot floor-to-ceiling windows. But there wasn't a soul in sight. There wasn't even a landscaped yard; it was all untouched wilderness. No one could see me.

Paranoid, I kept an eye out through the inexhaustible vista for anyone who might catch a glimpse of me as I tiptoed down the corridor.

I have to find the front door.

Or a back door . . .

Any door that will get me the hell out of here.

14634

"Hello?" a man's booming voice sounded. It originated from the other end of the hall.

I froze.

"Hello?!" He called again, sounding closer.

Don't come this way. Don't come this way!

Moving quickly, I retraced my footsteps, but the voice grew closer. *I've got to get out of this hall!* If the man came down that hall, there were no turns, no other corridors; there was nowhere else to go. On my way out of the bedroom, I had checked all the doors. There were two: one to a linen closet and one to a second, smaller bedroom.

Before the owner of the voice could find me, I made it back to the pink-and-orange bedroom and silently shut the door.

Damn. No lock.

I waited, expecting it to take time for him to get down the hall. I sat on the floor and leaned against the door to keep it closed.

Slow, deep breaths. He didn't see me.

"Who's in there?" The distinctly British voice was on the other side of the door.

Don't breathe, Monti; he can't know you're here.

"Look, I don't know who put you up to this, but I'll pay you double to tell me who and help me turn the joke on them." He sounded oddly cheerful. "Are you listening? I know you're sitting on the other side of the door. I can see your shadow."

Think, Monti. What are the options with an unlocked door? A friendly tactic might be the best way to find out what's going on. I may have to take a chance. If he is a serial killer, claiming to be the victim of a prank is a singly odd approach to murder.

Upon opening the door, I could not accept the face that greeted me. "May I come in?" It was Henry Walker Beecher—one of Hollywood's most celebrated actors—in the flesh. He belonged on the cover of a magazine, not . . . wherever we were.

I stuttered back at him, "Um, I guess?" It was more question than answer. I gestured into the room, and he waltzed past me.

"What the hell are you doing here?!" *Ooh, that sounded like an accusation. But I don't need to add a sidekick to my crisis.* I tried to rearrange my face and avoid the combination of shock and annoyance. *Can I pull off polite interest?*

At the center of the room, he turned back to look at me. "I was going to ask you the same question, only slightly less aggressively." He spoke with irritatingly disarming charm. "To answer your question, I don't remember coming here. Then again, I was at a big do last night, and I don't remember much of that either. There could be any number of explanations. So, I ask again, who put you up to this?" He asked with levity in his voice, but something other than humor hovered behind his brilliant green eyes.

"Trust me, this is no prank, and I, most assuredly, am not here voluntarily." He seemed to catch the intensity in my voice, and his smile froze, but it didn't fade. Instead of responding, he took a leisurely stroll around the room.

The unwelcome celebrity looked like he was admiring the dated furnishings. *Well, that's weird. Why is he wearing flannel pajama pants and a worn-out Beatles shirt? And why are his feet bare?*

Watching a Hollywood immortal calmly take in the unnecessarily vibrant midcentury-modern décor made my neck and shoulders tighten. My hands curled into fists, and my headache sharpened.

"What is wrong with you?

"Nevermind. I don't need this, or you. I'm leaving." The words exploded from me with the force of a cork from a bottle of champagne, but his only response was to lift his hand, bringing my momentum to a halt.

"Are you serious right now?"

Henry Beecher—famed leading man—stood gazing out the

window at the mountain scenery. I opened my mouth to release a torrent of abuse when he raised his halting hand again, pointing it toward the bottom corner of the wall-to-wall window. "The scenery doesn't pan."

"Come again?" I had no idea what he was talking about, but he had piqued my curiosity enough that he effectively kept me from berating him as planned. The movie star theatrically poked the window. Before I could roll my eyes at his dramatic display, ripples spread across the pane as though the glass was a lake with a mountain reflection and his finger a stone thrown in.

"It's a screen, not a window." His hushed tone told me he thought it was a fascinating technology, not a disconcerting discovery.

"Huh?" I moved closer and pressed my hand flat against the window. It was unquestionably some kind of display. The image warped at my touch. "We aren't in the mountains? Then, where are we? What the hell is happening?"

"You aren't having me on then?" His laid-back tone shifted to concern, but he made no sense.

"What?"

"This isn't a practical joke?" he asked, apparently interpreting his British slang for me.

I backed up, looking at Henry instead of the freaky window. "No. This is not a practical joke. I have nothing to do with you being here, and I am not here by choice.

"Now, you can marvel at the wall . . . window . . . screen . . . whatever it is, all you want. I'm going to find the door." My feet slapped against the hardwood as I willfully stomped toward the hallway, and all at once, I became acutely aware that I was barefoot and wearing a nightgown. *Have drugs and a migraine truly distracted me that much? Un-freaking-believable.*

I paused in the doorway before deciding I was not leaving the house from *Ozzie & Harriet* in a satin negligé. I turned and obstinately marched into the walk-in closet, deliberately avoiding eye contact with my strange new companion.

35796

"Hey, how're you getting on in there?" Henry called toward the closet after me. "It isn't as though time is of the essence when being held against your will." His snarky comment barely registered; I couldn't believe my surroundings.

"Come here." The words were caught—strangled—in my throat. He couldn't hear me. I tried again.

"Come here." That time, I choked it out. It wasn't loud, but it was firm.

"I'm fine waiting out here, thank you." He was still joking around like it was a fraternity prank. I didn't particularly want his help or his involvement, but—stranger or not—he was apparently stuck with me, and he needed to see.

I took a breath and focused myself, calming my nerves just enough to get my point across; then, I stuck my head out of the closet and made unyielding eye contact. "Two minutes ago, this was unnerving. When I walked into this closet, it escalated to alarmingly disturbing.

"Come. Here!"

Henry's smile disappeared, and his jaw tightened as he made his way to the walk-in closet. As he strode in past me, I was instantly aware of how conspicuously tall he was. *Good grief, he must be six foot three or even four.*

I was so taken aback, I inhaled sharply when he passed, and he surprised me a second time. I had expected a movie star of his caliber to smell of high-end cologne; instead, I closed my eyes and smelled a warm summer day, sunshine, and clean, fresh air with the slightest hint of soap. *How had he managed to bottle the outdoors?*

Focus, Monti.

His Sasquatch-like bare feet thwapped against the hardwood floor all the way to the back of the closet, then he turned dramatically and glared at me like I was a flake. "It's nothing but a closet, albeit a dated one. Nothing sinister here." Said in the King's English, it sounded more condescending than I think he intended.

Or was it? Hard to tell, actually.

"No, you don't understand; it's not about the closet. It's about the clothes in the closet. They're all mine." I foolishly grabbed clothes from either side as though he'd recognize anything I held out to show him. "Every single item in this closet is mine. The same brand, size, color, and style." I pulled out my go-to green satin shell and waved it at him like a crazy person. "Nothing that I don't have. Nothing out of place. Everything hung in the same order even. These are all my clothes. But not." I threw the blouse at his feet and charged toward the door. *I'm not making sense. Why bother trying.*

"I'm confused. Either they are your clothes, or they're not. Which is it?" I turned to look at him. He folded his bulky arms over his chest and raised one eyebrow. I could sense he questioned my sanity. I questioned it right along with him.

I don't know what kept me from continuing to walk out of the closet, but I stayed and tried to explain myself. "I am telling you that someone went to a lot of trouble and found replicas of all my clothes. They didn't take the clothes from my closet but purchased identical copies and placed them in this closet. Then they arranged them the exact way I keep them in my closet at home. Not one item is missing."

I still sound insane, and my propensity for talking with my hands isn't helping my case. I've got to get out of here. That left eyebrow is still firmly situated above the right one. Yeah, he's ready to have me fitted for a straitjacket and a padded room. I don't need this.

"Why would anyone do that? It seems a bit excessive, don't you think?" Henry gently probed.

"You're right. It makes zero sense. But neither does the two of us waking up here in the first place. Neither does that window that's not a window in there." I pointed toward the bedroom with an exasperated huff. "Nothing about this morning makes any sense whatsoever."

"Quite." The eyebrow came down.

What does that mean? It doesn't matter. I don't need him, and I don't need to justify myself.

"Whatever, I am entirely creeped out by this place." I grabbed an outfit hanging on the rod next to me, "I'm going to find the door and get out of here. You do whatever you want." I curtly motioned for him to exit the closet.

His eyebrows furrowed. "You know we're far more likely to succeed together than in isolation." I didn't answer, only motioned toward the door again, and he walked out of the closet and shut the door, presumably so I could change.

I put on my favorite pair of jeans and the comfortable top I'd snatched. The jeans were stiff and didn't fit the same as mine did. Years of wear change the shape of clothes, I suppose. There was no time to ponder that; it was time to leave. I slipped on my favorite pair of cork wedges sitting by the door on my way out of the closet, same as I did most mornings, but unlike most mornings, the persistent Henry Beecher was waiting for me in the bedroom.

56967

We emerged into the hall, crouched over and tiptoeing like characters from one of Henry's spy movies. I don't know why. There wasn't any evidence of other people in the house. We'd probably both watched too many horror flicks. Sneaking around is what you do when trying to escape, isn't it?

"We don't need to bother checking the doors on this hall. There's a massive linen closet behind this door and another bedroom behind that one, but that's it," I whispered, waving Henry ahead, trying to expedite getting him to the end of the hall and finding the way out.

"I know." In his answer, he was so abrupt and matter-of-fact that I stopped and stood bolt upright. He glowered at me, unappreciative of my response. He stayed crouched—awkwardly trying to make his massive body as small as possible—and slowly lowered a flattened hand, signaling me to resume stealth mode.

I started to make a snarky comment—teamwork has never been a strong point—but instead, I closed my mouth, crouched, and continued creeping down the hall. *Remarkable self-control under the circumstances.*

When we reached the end, Henry turned around before I could see the next room through the open arched doorway. He covered my mouth with his right hand and had his left pressed so firmly against the back of my neck, I felt like a fox snapped in a trap.

"You are not going to expect what you see in there; don't make a sound." He whispered, waiting for me to acknowledge understanding before releasing his vise-like grip. I nodded, wide-eyed.

This man has definitely been in one too many spy flicks.

When my line-backer-sized companion stepped out of the way, I stepped across the threshold, and the room at the end of the corridor came fully into view. I gasped. Henry turned back. He didn't have to speak to offer reproach; his face said it all. I clasped my hands over my mouth, but the damage had been done; if anyone was there, they'd already heard me.

The space we entered wasn't a room exactly; it was an indoor garden. The hardwood floors gave way to a path of smooth stones leading to grass. The lawn wasn't even Astroturf; it was actual living grass. I reached down and brushed my hand across the tips of the blades. *Fresh dew.*

The crisp smell of apples drew me over to a tremendous tree with a twisted trunk erupting from the center; it had to be over forty feet tall. *How bizarre.* I quickly forgot my mission and wandered closer to investigate. At the base of the canopy, the tree split; someone had successfully grafted a pear tree onto an apple tree. As twisted and contorted as the trunk was, the canopy was tall and full of healthy leaves and fruit of two strikingly different varieties.

Who could have done something like this? And inside a house of all places?

"Wait. It's November. How is anything here in bloom? It should all be dormant."

I spun around to find a series of stone paths surrounding the flourishing tree, like spokes on a wheel, pulling my attention away from the indoor Eden. Lined with benches, each path led to its own grand, distant door. Another path encircled the room, touring raised garden beds and vines that climbed up between the doors.

The stucco walls were at least three stories high, and the top of the room was open to the sky. Fluffy white clouds drifted overhead, and the sounds of the wilderness outside could be heard echoing in from above: blissfully chirping birds, rustling leaves, rushing water, even the occasional woodpecker.

What a beautiful and peculiar space to have at the center of a home. I closed my eyes and stretched out my arms to let my senses drink it all in.

After a moment, a series of flower beds caught my attention on the opposite side of the immense room. There were large hedges with a variety of flowers, though they didn't seem like they belonged together. They were oddly familiar, yet I couldn't place them. There was a lovely white lace-like flower and a dark black bud with a black berry I didn't recognize. One hedge even had red leaves. They didn't coordinate visually in any way. Although, I did recognize the one on the end. It was an oleander bush. *What a strange assortment. If they have something in common, I can't put my finger on it.*

I was lost in my head, pondering the bizarre atrium-type room until I remembered that I was not a guest in a home. I jerked my head up and found Henry waiting for me to come to that precise conclusion. Without chiding me, he pointed to a large, ornately carved door hiding behind a trellis of English ivy. "Shall we?"

I didn't have time to respond or make an excuse for getting swept up by our surroundings. Henry was off and reached the door before

I even made it to the trellis that obscured its view.

"Argh!" he snarled. When I rounded the trellis, Henry was clutching his hand.

"What happened?" Henry held his wrist, his hand stretched open wide, a red imprint of the twisted, ornamental pattern on his palm.

"Something on the lever burned my skin. It's fine." His voice was strangely calm for someone with, what appeared to be, a chemical burn. He stretched out the bottom of his T-shirt and used it to cover the handle while he tried again. His shirt looked so old and worn that I didn't think it would offer much protection. "Locked." Again, his voice was steady, as though he was thinking through a puzzle.

Why is he so calm? This is worth freaking out over!

Henry looked around the room, surveying the multitude of doors that remained while I focused on the handle. There was a keyhole above it. "Why is the lock on the inside of the house? You put the key in the door to get in the house, not to get out." I bent over, my hands braced on my knees, looking at the toxic handle. *This is messed up.*

"Right then. We find the key." Henry marched toward the next door clockwise around the cylindrical room.

His stride was long; I wasn't in the mood to jog to keep up. "Where are you going? What are you doing?" I shouted after him and plopped on the ground, leaning against the front door, waiting to see if he made any headway. Watching, I noticed he was wearing sandals that he hadn't been wearing when we met in the pink-and-orange bedroom. *When did he find those? And where did he find shoes that fit? Those look like a size 13!*

Trying a steel door, that, too, appeared to be locked. Henry reversed course, this time moving counterclockwise around the room. He noticed me pop up out of my seat to join him and offered an explanation despite my lack of requesting one. "That looks to be the front door," he said, pointing to the ornate door we had started with. Without breaking stride, he continued counterclockwise along the path following the perimeter of the room. "It appears that someone has intentionally reversed the lock to keep us in. So, we'll find a key and get out of here."

I'd been jogging along the rocky garden paths to keep up, and not expecting him to stop suddenly, I ran into his rock-solid back. "Oomph. Sorry." I backed up and peered around his broad shoulder. His hand thrust the handle downward. To my surprise, the second steel door opened.

105871

Fluorescent lights blinked on automatically in the chilled hall. There were no manufactured windows along the bare concrete walls that connected seamlessly with its arched ceiling. The short passageway slanted downward ever so slightly, giving the sensation that we were falling in slow motion. A plain, solid door was at the other end, nothing like the decorative doors we'd encountered already. Henry looked back at me before opening the heavy steel door as if seeking approval. I nodded.

Why am I even following you? I should be looking for another way out.

With my endorsement, he shouldered it open.

One after the other, fluorescent lights flickered on from front to back, accompanied by an industrial buzz. We stepped into the long warehouse-type room lined with rows of shelves like a bulk store stocked floor to ceiling with goods, momentarily forgetting why we'd opened the door in the first place. We simply marveled at what we'd found.

The floor, ceiling, and walls were poured concrete, not the elaborate Andy Warhol-era recreation we'd encountered in other rooms. I rubbed the goose bumps on my arms; the space was probably fifteen degrees cooler and had noticeably lower humidity than the rest of the house.

We walked through, scanning the rows of dry goods: canned food, boxed food, jarred food, cleaning supplies, bathroom supplies, paper goods, light bulbs, other household replacement parts, you name it. The aisles seemed endless. The end of every unit was labeled, making it easy to locate whatever you were looking for.

"You could live for months on what's stored in here." I was bewildered by what we'd stumbled upon.

"Years," Henry corrected.

I quit being impressed when I looked at Henry's face and connected the supplies with our predicament. We both put an end to our admiration and separated to look for the key.

I scanned the rows on my left. There was a shelving unit full of replacement parts: light bulbs, filters, a plunger, and other ordinary household things. On the bottom shelf, tucked way in the back, I found a small tool bag. Sticking out of the top of that tool bag was an extra-long flathead screwdriver. *Hmm.* I pulled it out and began slapping the handle in my palm. *It's not a key, but it couldn't hurt to offer.*

"Will this help?" I waved the orange-handled screwdriver out into the aisle for Henry to consider. *Not really feeling it for Team Henry. But if it helps . . .*

Henry grabbed the screwdriver from my hand and was out the door in one fluid motion. "Perfect!" he muttered, already halfway down the hall.

He sure is swift for such a bulky man.

So, what? He's prying his way out through a ten-foot door? And with a screwdriver, no less? He's insane.

I, at least, felt helpful finding a potential means of opening the door with the poison handle. However unlikely it was to succeed.

On my way out of the concrete hall, I noticed that Henry didn't walk in the direction of our hopeful exit. I lingered in the steel doorway and observed for a minute. He poked his head through door after door off the sprawling garden room until he apparently found whatever it was he was looking for and ducked in. He reappeared moments later with a yellow-seated stool in one hand and the orange-handled screwdriver in the other, advancing toward the front door with determination.

Here goes nothing.

I met Henry at the door. He grunted as he pried at the hinges with the screwdriver. "What's wrong?" I hesitated to ask; he seemed frustrated.

"Well," he grunted one last time before he gave up and lowered his tool. "The pin should slip out of the hinge with relative ease, but someone has welded a stopper to the bottom of each of the three pins, so they can't be removed. They've been tampered with." He examined them each one last time to make sure they couldn't be taken out before he moved on.

Henry knelt by the door to pry at the lock. The bulge of his biceps looked like they might tear the seams in the sleeves of his T-shirt. Having watched some of his films, it was obvious he worked out. But, seeing him up close, in person, he was more like a real-life manifestation of Paul Bunyan.

He grunted as he tried again without making progress. "Can I help?" *Why did I ask that? I have no skills that apply. Nor am I a team player.*

"Do you know how to pick a lock?" He leaned his arm on one knee and looked at me as if wishing rather than expecting I had a hidden talent that would save the day.

"No." *Do normal people know how to do that?*

"Then, hold this." He positioned the flathead screwdriver at the edge of the wooden door near the lock and carefully placed my hand on the middle of the shaft.

What in the world? I wasn't literally volunteering.

"Don't move," Henry warned in a low rumbling tone. Then he lifted the stool with both hands, pulled it back like he was swinging a baseball bat, and came down on the head of the screwdriver as if hitting a grand slam in a World Series. The screwdriver wedged through the wood straight through to the lock.

Thoughts spewed from my mouth before I could contain them. "That. Was. A-Mazing! We're getting out! Do it again!"

Flushed with excitement, I placed the screwdriver an inch from the edge, ready for another swing from my muscle-bound accomplice. Henry raised an eyebrow, significantly less optimistic. He lowered the stool and took my hand, repositioning the screwdriver at the edge of the door where it had split from the initial blow. Then he raised the stool to swing again.

Another blow. Straight through to the lock. I bounced in place.

We can do this. Well, Henry and his mountains of muscles can do it; I'm hardly holding the screwdriver.

The process was tedious, interminable. Each scrap of wood shaved off took intense effort and precision. More than that, it didn't remove much more than a sliver of door with each swing. But eventually, we—or rather he—chiseled through enough of the door that we were able to completely remove the handle.

"That is the most ludicrous way to open a door . . . " I chirped, unintentionally letting my thoughts escape.

Henry put his hand in the tiny hole he'd carved out of the door, and a mischievous grin spread across his face. "Ready to go?"

Bursting, I replied, "Are you kidding me?"

What's he waiting for? Now is not the time for games.

Henry flung the door open and stepped forward, only to be obstructed by a wall of solid concrete.

What? That makes no sense. What's happening? Who . . . ?

Henry rubbed his nose as he thoughtfully inspected the wall he'd run into. I, conversely, shoved him aside and furiously pounded on the concrete, trying to break through.

"It has to be a door." I felt myself wilt.

I have to get out.

Henry backed away, carefully evaluating our situation, while I leaned against the rough concrete slab, a dungeon wall hiding behind the door we'd spent hours working to open. I forced myself to swallow the panic that attempted to overwhelm me.

Panic isn't profitable. I have to feel it later.

I pressed my hands and face against the cold, damp concrete, allowing myself a silent moment to sulk before turning around to face Henry. His eyes were calculating. *He's figuring a way out, isn't he?* "What are you thinking?"

"That door." He confidently pointed to the steel door to the right of the one we'd just opened. "Of the eleven doors, most of the others are open and decorative. That's the way out."

When and why did you count all these massive doors? Whatever, I don't care. His tone suggested he knew what he was talking about. The steel door was plain and standard in size, while most of the others were grand in scale, material, and their carved patterns.

It looks like a utility room.

"Back to this one, huh? Worth a shot, I suppose." I walked over and jiggled the handle. "Still locked." I waved a hand, yielding to the locked door, then put my hands on my hips.

The steel material of the door wouldn't allow us to chip through it like we had the first one. "So, how do we break into this one?" *Maybe my tenure on Team Beecher should be coming to an end. I need to sort this one out myself.* I hung my head, letting my hair and its untamed waves fall over my face, and mumbled. "Can we pry it open? Steel bends, doesn't it?" *I'm being overly optimistic.*

I turned my head and side-eyed my muscle-bound companion through my unkempt locks. *He's built like the Hulk, but even he can't bend a door. Or can he?*

He must have overheard me mumbling. A single eyebrow raise and smirk were a definitive "no." Or so I thought. Humoring me with a sigh, despite my combative attitude, he put the screwdriver between the door and the frame and pulled. Hard. I jumped upright to watch. The handle of the screwdriver cracked and snapped off. "Careful there; you're lucky it didn't slice through your hand. I think the screwdriver has had enough of you."

Henry dropped the remnants of screwdriver onto the stone path. "I'm going back to that warehouse-looking room to see if I can find more useful tools." He was halfway there before he'd completed his comment. I stayed put, leaning on the door, pondering how to get it open my own way.

Face and body pressed to the door, I dragged my miserable hand across the cold, unpainted steel, trying to feel the freedom on the other side. I heard a heavy thunk and felt a jolt inside the door. *What was that?* I reached for the handle, but before I could touch it, the handle turned. I stared, my trembling fingers hovering over the depressed handle, not expecting the door to open . . .

But it did.

Not a way out, but a chilled, dimly lit room with concrete floor, walls, and ceiling. It felt like a damp, cramped cavern that had no place in a home. The ceiling was low, and the room completely bare. Bare except for a book carelessly tossed on the floor in the far left corner.

"Whiskey Tango Foxtrot!"

I hovered in the doorway. The hairs standing upright on my arms and the back of my neck told me I had no business in that room. But I couldn't stand not knowing why the door had opened and why there was a random paperback in an empty concrete room.

Who would throw a book in the corner like that?

I scuffed across the floor to reach my goal, unsure exactly why I was rushing. My stomach churned like I'd made a horrible mistake, and I needed to turn around. The scraping sound of my shoes reinforced my error with each step I took.

I made it to the book and picked up my prize the second I reached it. The yellow cover read, *The Kind Worth Killing* by Peter Swanson.

Ominous.

Something in the back of my head told me to drop it and run. I took a step back but only managed one. A page had been torn from the book and tucked back into the middle. I slipped the page from its resting place to see why it had been removed. There were hesitant yellow highlighter markings over a passage.

> "And to take another life was, in many ways, the greatest expression of what it meant to be alive."[1]

The book slipped from my fingers and slapped against the concrete between my feet. The torn page fluttered across the room as I backed to the wall behind the open door. Square concrete protrusions that I hadn't noticed before in the poorly lit compartment thrust into my back, and a smooth piece of glass hanging from the wall clipped me in the back of the head.

I jumped and turned around to see what had startled me. The wall wasn't elaborate. The open door must have blocked my view. There were plain concrete slabs evenly spaced over the entire fourth wall of the perfectly square room. They each had a cone-shaped glass vase with an iron mount fastened to the left side of the slab. Some had flowers, some had greenery, and some were empty. Many of the concrete squares had a simple brass plate affixed to the center. It seemed that the ones with plates also had foliage in their vases, but I didn't stop to check. I couldn't stop. I was operating on a self-preserving autopilot. Drifting through the room, looking through someone else's eyes.

Each plate I saw had the same set of numbers at the top, hand-scratched into the soft metal.

—*25 12 24 12*—

Some kind of serial number? I didn't see any with a different number. Below the number, they consistently had a first name—each one unique—and below that, two years separated by a dash.

"That's funny. Those look like birth and death years."

I took a step back for a more holistic view of the wall, stumbling over the book I'd dropped—*The Kind Worth Killing*. I looked at the title on the cover and then back up at the wall. All the names, the years, the cut flowers as if to memorialize them.

"Holy shit! They're dead people."

"It's a crypt!"

I regained control of my body and my senses and bolted out of the room, slamming the door behind me right as Henry reappeared with supplies from the other room. "Don't go in there!" The words barely audible as I tried to catch my breath.

"What?" His forehead was creased with confusion.

"Don't go in there. It's dead people." I tried to calm myself down. It wasn't working.

"Slow down. What do you mean, don't go in there? It's locked. We're trying to get out that way." He reached around me, trying to open the door. But it was locked again.

How?

"I don't know what happened. It has to be an automatic lock. It opened. I went in. It's another room. It's a crypt!" I backed away. I planned to be far from that room if the door opened again.

"I'm getting out of here. Now! I refuse to end up in there!" I gestured at the creepy steel door as I moved down a random stone path toward an alternative.

Somehow. I'm getting out.

"You aren't making sense. It's locked. It's been locked." Henry jiggled the handle.

He's not listening. I'm moving on, with or without him.

Ignoring Henry, I jogged down a stone path to another doorway. Focusing on the crunching stones beneath my feet, I desperately hoped it was all just a nightmare.

Please be asleep. Please be asleep. Monti, you have to wake up!

The random door I had chosen led to a short hall with a ten-foot, elaborately carved mahogany door, much like the bedroom doors, at the end. It seemed as decent an option as any other; I turned the intricate iron lever and advanced. Barely inside the doorway, I stumbled over vibrant-orange and royal-blue padded mats. I recovered my footing and realized where I was. "A home gym. Are you kidding me?"

I frantically scanned the room. It was massive, like everything else in that place. The finely-striped white-and-navy plaster walls were lined with every piece of workout equipment imaginable. All 1960s vintage, same as all our curious surroundings, yet everything was in mint condition as though it had been frozen in time.

I ran my hand along a piece of equipment that looked like it had been used and maintained regularly but not in this decade—in another era entirely. Though every mat, every weight, every piece of equipment seemed to have sat untouched for decades, there wasn't a speck of dust on anything. It all looked ancient and brand new, all at the same time.

What is going on?

The treadmill faced a wall of floor-to-ceiling windows exactly like the ones in the bedroom and hall. I pressed my hand against it just to check. The image warped.

"Nope, not a real window either." *Are any of the windows real?*

At the back of the room, another door sparked hope. I squeaked my way across the vibrant, matted floor and checked to see if, by some miracle, it led somewhere useful.

"Figures," *a musty closet full of workout equipment.* I slammed the door, and it bounced back as if in retribution. I folded over, hands on my knees, and tried to collect myself.

"This can't be real. What is happening?"

My body began operating without me. A robotic function devoid of connection to cognition. A bright-orange plastic chair sat in the corner, waiting for some workout purpose that I could not possibly have cared less about. In my zombie-like trance, I yanked it off the floor by one of its legs and hurled it at the wall display masquerading as a window. All control I had was gone.

The pane flickered and turned black. It didn't even have the courtesy to shatter. It was wholly unsatisfying. I didn't know what it was made of, but clearly, it wasn't glass. My zombie state morphed into a frenzied, enraged tantrum. I retrieved the chair and wailed on the screen. Over and over, I funneled all the fear and anger I'd bottled since waking that morning into the collision of the chair and the screen. Each time I revealed a bit of mechanics, the slightest bit of satisfaction bubbled up, then seething wrath washed over it because there was no broken glass or freedom. The additional anger fueled more frequent and powerful blows. I couldn't feel my arms anymore. I thought I'd go on like that forever until finally . . . Henry caught the chair by a leg in midair.

Where did he come from?

He didn't say a word as he gently removed the chair from my white-knuckled grasp and placed it on the floor. Exhausted, trapped, unable to break through the fantasy portraying a window, I crumpled onto the padded floor. Henry poked at the edges of the mutilated screen and began carefully pulling it down. It didn't come down easily, but after painstaking effort, he got one section off the wall. While most of the house had a beautifully crafted, pristinely smooth plaster finish, behind the screen was a rough slab of poured concrete.

"Concrete?!"

Behind the door. In the crypt. Under the screen. More concrete.

"I can't. I just. Can't"

Lying on padded flooring that looked and smelled like my old high school gymnasium, I stared up at a wall that minutes before had a view of an idyllic mountain wilderness. Glaring back at me was a cold, asperous concrete slab mocking my efforts to escape. I wanted to cry; I had every excuse, but the tears just refused.

248269

I allowed my eyes to close for only a moment, at least I thought I had. But I must have passed out from emotional exhaustion. Maybe there were residual drugs in my system. I couldn't be sure.

When I opened my eyes, Henry had vanished. *Alone. I can work with that. Alone is good.*

I got up and stumbled toward the door. I tripped over the edge of the gym mat again as I reached the threshold. The moment I did, Henry poked his head back into the gym. My face smashed into his brick wall of a chest. "Hey! Watch it."

"Sorry, I was just coming to check on you. You took a little kip after waging war against the window. I thought I'd let you sleep for a bit while I looked for another way out."

I shot a disapproving glare at him. *I don't appreciate being left out.*

He smiled before continuing. "I checked out every door, every corridor, every room, every cupboard. There is no exterior door besides that locked steel one. There is no one else in the house. You and I are here, unguarded. And I can't find another way in or out." He pursed his lips, looking helpless as he waited for a reaction.

My throat tightened. "That's not possible," I screeched through clenched teeth. "There has to be a way in, or we couldn't be here. They didn't build the house around us." My nails dug into my palms as I tightened my fists, trying to resist the urge to shout at him or, better yet, to slap him. "And I told you, that steel door leads to a crypt. It isn't a way out."

Fed up with his condescension, I murmured, "I may be tired, and I may have been drugged, but I'm not stupid, and I'm not lying."

Calm down. Panicking isn't the solution; lashing out won't help, however satisfying it might feel in the moment. "This just isn't possible."

"Alright." He broke in on my conversation with myself. I couldn't tell if he'd heard me or not. "We'll assume your story is true. Although, I don't see how a door unlocked itself without any kind of a mechanism attached to it."

Why do you insist on being so incredibly frustrating?

I rubbed my pounding temples with my knuckles while he insisted on continuing. "I think this is going to take us being more methodical, and I'm afraid it's going to take some time to find a way out. Hence, the wardrobe and the supplies. I checked; my closet is well stocked, similar to yours." Surprised by the statement, I opened my eyes. Henry tugged on his cargo pants with a bandaged hand, indicating he'd found something to wear besides flannel pajamas. "It would appear that someone expects us to be here a while."

A slight whimper escaped from my constricted throat. "Is that supposed to make me feel better, Oscar?" *Chemical burns. Unlimited supplies.* "I'm sorry. I think I was just more in the mood for: 'Guess what? I found the door!'"

Henry laughed at my pitiful attempt at humor, and I stared at his bandages, feeling a twinge of guilt. *I'm not the only one having a bad day.*

"Hungry?" Henry's back was turned, and he walked away as he spoke, so I was positive I'd heard him wrong.

"What?" I called down the hall, not catching him until we reached the massive garden in the center of the house.

He turned and stretched his arms out wide, showcasing not only the bounty around him but also the definition between every single muscle in his gargantuan arms and shoulders. "Are you hungry?"

I looked around. *He's crazy.*

He could plainly read my thoughts off my face and stepped toward me, gently taking me by the hands and leading me around the garden. He'd spent some time investigating our surroundings and had decided to give me a tour, showing me what the garden had to offer. I needed to know where we were, so I followed my far too-chipper guide on his tour.

He started with the two raised beds to the side of the bedroom hall. "Here, we have all the fresh herbs we could want." He seemed remarkably eager to show me our options—given our circumstances—as he moved on to the other beds between the bedroom hall and the gym hall. "Moving anticlockwise, we have two beds of berry bushes: raspberry, blueberry, strawberry, and such."

He continued around the circular room, showing planter after planter full of fruit, vegetable, and flower. "Here we have Kestrel potatoes and yams."

"I suppose we won't starve."

Between the laundry room, the crypt door, and the fake front door were the beds of flowers. It was that odd assortment I hadn't been able to figure out. *Not mentioning that to Henry, especially before I can sort it out for myself. Hold on, is that hemlock? Why would anyone . . .*

"Come on, this way." Henry pulled me forward, yanking me too quickly to allow a good look or even to complete a thought. *I'll have to go back and check it out when he isn't around.*

He progressed around the room until we reached the last of the beds between the kitchen and dining halls. "Over here are our leafy vegetables like lettuces. And we're back to the beginning. Honestly, any kind of garden food we can want all planted around the gnarled tree in the middle. I don't know how they've kept it all in bloom in November, but I don't plan on staying long enough to figure it out."

"I've decided to call it the conservatory."

His last statement caught me off guard, and my mocking tone came out before I could restrain it. "Hang on. The conservatory? Like Professor Plum did it in the conservatory with the wrench?"

Henry chuckled. "Something like that." He took me by the shoulders and steered me out of the "conservatory" and down the hall to the warehouse-like room we'd found earlier in the day. "What we can't find to eat in the garden is plentifully stocked in this massive larder in non-perishable form."

"We're calling this warehouse that we could live out of for years a larder? What is that even?" *He's legitimately off his rocker.*

"Do you have a better name for it? It has lower humidity and temperature than the rest of the house; it's full of dry food, goods, and meats. Granted, it has things I'd put in my pantry at home, and it has things stocked in insanely large volumes. But what would you like to call it?"

"I was asking what the word meant. Not arguing the designation. What is a larder?" I shook my head at him. *It's almost like he doesn't even speak English.*

"Oh. Well, then." He stretched his arms out and gestured around the room. "This. This is a larder."

I sighed and mumbled. "Looks like a giant pantry to me."

He stared me down, daring me to disagree. "Fine. The larder." I said it in an exaggerated tone, but I didn't disagree.

He smiled triumphantly and continued, "We also have every cut of meat imaginable in the commercial-size freezer." He opened up a massive deep freezer I hadn't noticed at the front of the "larder" on the left. It was chock full of frozen cuts of meat. He was right; we had everything we needed.

"So, we're well supplied until we find the way out." Henry seemed satisfied with his discovery. I was furious that we'd been equipped with provisions for an extended stay. For the moment, I forced myself to be content with eating lunch.

Henry selected some ingredients from the larder and picked some from the garden, and I reluctantly followed along as he brought them to a kitchen that turned out to be just as fully stocked as the rest of the house. Henry proceeded to cook a meal for us. *This can't possibly turn out well!* I didn't imagine many A-list celebrities could cook, but I found it interesting that this one wanted to try.

A FEMA disaster erupted in the kitchen as Henry foraged for all the kitchen doodads he needed. Utensils hit the floor, cabinet doors were left open, and pots and pans were strewn over the counters. More than once, Henry stood to find his scalp intimately acquainted with an open cabinet door. The entertainment factor alone was more than worth the risk of inedible food.

The comedy of the kitchen scene took my mind off our

circumstances. That is until Henry opened the fridge. "Bloody hell!" He pulled a beer bottle out and held it by the cap with two fingers as though it was contaminated, brandishing the bottle over the pudgy yellow refrigerator door for me to see. The label said, "Hogs Back Garden Gold." It had a peculiar picture of a hog with a farm on its back.

"This is my favorite beer. In fact, it's pretty much the only beer I drink when I go back home. If that isn't altogether unsettling?" He looked up at me, then back at the bottle. "And that's aside from the fact that bitters do not belong in the fridge." He replaced it as though disposing of a bomb, closed the door, and returned to his cooking efforts like it had never occurred.

Well, you're turning out to be a bit of a puzzle, aren't you, Mr. Beecher?

While he cooked, Henry distracted me with stories about growing up in the English countryside with his brothers. He was the youngest of four by several years. He told me how he'd sit apart from the others—watching as an outsider while the others played. My favorite story was of his two middle brothers tormenting the oldest.

"Mum often referred to David, my eldest brother, as a bull in a china shop." All four boys apparently shared Henry's tall, muscular physique. Perfect for the rugby field; not so wonderful in Mother's small country kitchen. "The twins, Mark and Andrew, took great pleasure in teaming up and tormenting David. Andrew would use his fingers to imitate horns while stomping his foot like a bull." Henry reenacted the scene despite having a ten-inch chef's knife in his left hand. "And Mark would hold up a red mac and wave it in front of David like a matador."

"A red what?" I interrupted.

"A mac.

"A mackintosh.

"A raincoat."

He smiled at me and tilted his head, almost in pity that I didn't know what a mac was.

"Mark waved the red *raincoat* like a matador, and it infuriated David so much that he would run at the twins and inevitably break something. This happened regularly, perpetuating the idea that he was a bull in a china shop. Mum never found out. I always kept to the corner watching, enjoying, but never getting involved."

Who knew that after a morning like we'd had, Henry could have me laughing for a solid thirty minutes with his stories while he made omelets from powdered eggs and fresh garden vegetables. When he finished, my sides ached. I was rather impressed; I wasn't a people person.

We took our plates from the kitchen into the dining room to eat. Behind the unreasonably long Formica table with a ridiculous number of blue pleather chairs was yet another floor-to-ceiling window façade with a breathless view that made me feel like we were at the foot of Grand Teton in the Wyoming wilderness.

I'd never eaten powdered eggs before. I couldn't say that I ever wanted to again, but Henry had actually managed to make them somewhat palatable. As we sat and ate our powdered omelets, I realized that it didn't appear to be noon as I had expected. The sun was setting over the mountains. I pointed to the sunset with a fork full of omelet. "I don't think we woke up in the morning."

He assessed the image thoughtfully. "If this is the only way we can keep time—and I have yet to find a single functioning clock—then you're right. We woke late in the day." I shifted my focus to the clock on the wall over the sideboard table. Like everything else, its oversized copper starburst design had a distinct *Partridge Family* vibe. Initially, I hadn't paid any attention to it. But once I did . . . *The second hand is perfectly still. And silent.*

I stood to investigate; Henry interrupted my movement, not bothering to look up from his plate. "There's no mechanism." He continued digging into his meal; I continued toward the clock.

Why hang a clock without working parts? And how could you possibly know that from over there?

Henry finished chewing his bite before he added, "I checked when I investigated the house earlier."

Mind reader?

I lifted the three-foot copper monstrosity off the wall and turned it over. Someone had scooped out all the mechanics and left a hollow shell of a clock behind.

"Why go through all the trouble? What does it accomplish?" I wasn't talking to Henry. I wasn't even sure I'd said it aloud.

What time is it? Why would someone not want us to know? None of this makes any sense.

After dinner—not lunch, it would seem—battered by the events that had besieged me in the short hours we'd been conscious, I resigned to sleep. On my way out of the kitchen, I blurted, "I can't deal with the house of no doors and no clocks anymore today."

"That's understandable. I think I'll stay up and investigate our surroundings some more before I turn in. See you in the morning?"

He smiled warmly as he asked the question.

I felt obligated to respond. "See you in the morning."

I migrated back to the room I had originated from and slipped under the covers, trying to ignore the satin sheets and the pink-and-orange polyester comforter. I faced the wall, trying to erase the day's trauma, but I couldn't simply close my eyes and wish it all away. *That would be too easy, wouldn't it?*

After more than an hour of tossing and turning, I threw the covers off. My bare feet thumped on the floor as I resigned myself to searching for a sleeping pill. In the bathroom, I found a medicine cabinet containing a heavenly bottle of Unisom. I rolled it between my palms and looked in the mirror to examine my dark circles.

What a peculiar mirror.

It was old. An almost fragile antique with ornate gold trim. It stood out, seeming out of place in the pink-tiled palace of a bathroom. I ran my fingers along the flaking paint on the hand-carved frame. The silver backing pulled away from the glass in places, making my reflection darker than it would ordinarily be.

I fixated on the glass longer than I normally would. *Something's odd.* My reflection was off. *My face doesn't look real.* I leaned in. "Do I seem younger?"

"That's not right."

The circles under my eyes had vanished. I touched my face. *My hair is lighter.*

No. My cheekbones are higher. "That's not right either. That's not my face."

"That's my daughter!"

Pill bottle clenched in my fist, I sprinted out of the bathroom. I didn't know where I was going, but I couldn't stay there.

I made it down the hall and into the conservatory, panting, palms sweating. Henry was there, his back to me. I slowed to a stroll before he had a chance to sense my panic. He didn't believe me about the door unlocking or about the crypt; why would he believe me about the mirror? I collected myself and walked past in a forged calm.

Where do I go?

I slowed my steps, giving myself a moment to think. *Alcohol. Yes.* Alcohol was exactly what I needed. I shifted my aim and headed for the epic larder in search of an intoxicated escape.

Barefoot in the concrete larder, I searched its endless aisles. *Bingo.* Turned out there was a lot of it. An entire aisle, in fact. I grabbed the first bottle of red wine with a screw top I came across; I was not concerned with vintage. It had been a day.

Determined, I showed myself back to my pink-and-orange penitentiary with a full bottle and no glass. Henry's mouth fell open as I passed him in the conservatory. He looked as if he was about to ask a question, but I did not slow down or acknowledge his presence. He took the hint.

Back in my time vortex, I proceeded to take my Unisom and drink straight from the bottle. *Not half bad.* Even though it is never a good idea to combine sleeping pills and alcohol, I thought that if ever there was an appropriate moment to do so, a day like mine was probably the only one.

Setting the bottle of wine down on the nightstand, I noticed something that hadn't been there when I'd left minutes before. A book. It was a copy of George Orwell's *1984*. A disturbing choice in literature to have on a nightstand in an unnerving house. It had been left open, facedown.

I refuse to look!

Too much had happened; I wasn't reading from a psychological novel on top of it all. I took another long swig of wine, leered at the book, and pulled my knees up to my chest as I sat up in the bed.

Even with the wine and the sleeping pill, there'll be no sleep, will there?

I relented and picked it up.

Uneven yellow highlighter immediately drew my eyes to a passage on the page.

> *"Power is in tearing human minds to pieces and putting them together again in new shapes of your own choosing."*[2]

I hurled the book across the room, drank again from the bottle, and leaned back against the metal flourishes of the vintage headboard, clutching the bottle, hugging my knees, and staring out the window.

Not sleeping. Not here.

395617

DAY 2

Bleeding

Why didn't the Twilight Zone come equipped with drapes?

806482

The windows may not have been real, but the morning sun beaming in on my face felt real enough. *So tired.* I couldn't sleep in because the artificial sun invaded every corner of the room. I flung the covers onto the floor in protest and discovered that I had spent my night of insomnolence wearing my jeans.

Ugh.

I stumbled into the bathroom for the hot shower I so desperately needed, determined to avoid the menacing gold mirror. I caught a glimpse out of the corner of my eye, and fortunately, nothing but my own reflection looked back at me.

As I squeezed toothpaste onto my toothbrush, it gradually occurred to me that every item from my bathroom at home was, in fact, in the creepy pink-tiled bathroom. My same toothbrush and toothpaste, my exact brand and shades of cosmetics, even my same hairbrush and hair products were there, arranged precisely as I kept them at home.

By the time my gaze completed its tour around the bathroom and returned to my toothbrush, where it had begun, I had inadvertently squeezed the entire tube of toothpaste into a minty mountain over my toothbrush and into the sink. My hands shook at the disturbing realization that someone had been so intimately acquainted with my habits and the most trivial possessions in my home.

I can't think about that. Focus, Monti.

"What do I need right this second?"

I steadied myself on the counter, elbows locked, shoulders at my ears.

A hot shower.

I indulged in a shower at a temperature higher than any hot water heater should safely be set. I was thankful that this one apparently had a faulty thermostat. Afterward, I found the pair of white jeans I'd always loved and a black silk blouse with a white floral-outline. I slipped into the black leather Tieks that were perfect replicas of my favorites from home and placed precisely where I kept them in my closet.

Not getting used to this.

Pulling myself together—my hair and makeup done—always made me feel confident, even dauntless, at times. *Maybe that'll help me face the challenge of the day. Maybe not. Surely, it can't hurt.* I had done all I could, and I tentatively made my way out of the room in search of coffee and a plan of escape.

Down the hall, the second bedroom door was partly open; the room completely dark. Tempted to peek in, I paused in front of what I assumed was Henry's bedroom door and looked up and down the hall to be sure the coast was clear. Henry wasn't around, so I pushed the door open and peered into the blackened void. I couldn't see anything. As I considered my next move, strange sounds drew my attention to the distance beyond the end of the bedroom hall. I redirected my focus and picked my pace back up, moving toward the strange crackling and hissing; I stopped suddenly when I realized I had no idea what the sound was or who was making it. I wasn't even sure if it was Henry.

New plan. Creep up on the sound and figure out who's making it before they see me coming.

My approach was more or less stealth-like. I determined that the sound was coming from one of the halls off to the left of the conservatory. I crept along the outer wall so I wouldn't be spotted.

When I got closer, I determined that there was a second sound in addition to the original. *Is that . . . humming? Yes, someone is humming and . . . cooking!*

The tantalizing aroma of bacon wafted down the hallway and into the conservatory, calling to me. Lured into the kitchen, I abandoned my stealth mode and found Henry cooking bacon, powdered eggs, and pancakes simultaneously. My mouth agape at his culinary acrobatics, I stifled the urge to giggle at the sight.

"Good morning," he chirped with the chipperness only a certified morning person can pull off. "Hungry?"

What does he have to be chipper about? We aren't guests at the Four Seasons!

"Exactly who do you think is going to eat all of this? That must be a dozen eggs, a pound of bacon, and an entire box of pancake mix. And did you pick every strawberry from the garden to put in that bowl?"

My motherhood is showing. I'm glad I didn't tell him to eat all his vegetables. I definitely didn't get enough sleep.

"Well, we aren't paying for it. I don't feel bad about wasting our kidnapper's resources. And I actually consume more food than you might think." He tilted his head at me and smiled. "Also, I didn't know how powdered eggs would taste by themselves, so I made extra bacon and pancakes just in case." He had a point. I didn't care about rationing our captor's supplies, and powdered eggs didn't taste as good as they smelled. I smacked my lips at the unpleasant thought, suddenly less excited about the feast before me. Henry read the look on my face. "You at least have to try it."

"Fine." *I've made my kids try unsavory-looking food enough times. This, right here? This is karma biting me squarely in the ass.*

I sat on the stool Henry had battered to break through the lock the day before and digested my surroundings while he cooked. With robin's-egg-blue aluminum cabinets, bright-yellow Formica counters, and perfectly matching yellow appliances—refrigerator, stove, trash compactor—as well as complementary blue vintage minor appliances—toaster oven, mixer, and coffee maker—it was a coordinated masterpiece. A kitchen frozen in time.

My eyes roamed the kitchen, taking in the anachronistic splendor, landing on the counter to my left, where a red paperback appeared to be tucked under a stack of blue vinyl placemats. Henry was in his own little world, humming as he cooked, so I slid the book from its hiding place. *The Great Escape* by Paul Brickhill. I rolled my eyes. *That'd be nice.* A bookmark with sheep on a farm poked out toward the end of the book. *The weirdness never ceases around here, does it?* I certainly didn't want to read it, and I don't know what made my hands go through the motions of opening the book, but I did. Once it was open, I saw that a character's dialogue had been highlighted:

"*It's my duty to escape,*"[3]

"Are you kidding me with this?!" I was shrill as I waved the book at Henry. *What kind of a cruel joke is this?*

"What are you talking about? What's that?" He threw a blue-and-yellow tea towel over his shoulder after drying his hands and turned off the gas burner to come investigate. I held up the cover so he could read it, then opened the book, shoving it in his face.

"Did you put this here for me to find? Because it's not funny." Henry's face was stolid. *He didn't do it. Why would someone leave this here? How? It wasn't there yesterday, I'm sure of it.*

After gently extricating the book from my grasp, Henry placed it on top of the antique fridge. "Out of sight, out of mind." His voice —low and smooth, like soft caramel—soothed my inflamed state of mind. "Someone wants to get under your skin. Don't let them. We'll get out. First, we eat." He smiled and moved back to the stove to retrieve our meal, motioning me to head into the dining room. I didn't want to be soothed by the practiced tone of an actor. Someone was leaving taunting quotes to torment me. Yet, somehow, Henry managed to calm my enraged disposition.

Adjacent to the kitchen, I sat in the coordinating dining space straight out of an episode of *Leave it to Beaver*. Henry had set out the blue-and-white melamine plates for two. I admired the floral place settings for a moment before Henry caught me glaring at the counterfeit windows. They were taunting me. Henry crept up behind me, set the remainder of our meal on the table, and placed his hand gently over mine. "Please don't break this one."

"I'm beginning to hate that mountain scenery. Every time I see it, with the fake wind blowing through the fake trees and the fish jumping out of the fake river, I need to throw something at it." I had a firm grip on the neck of the frosted pitcher of orange juice Henry had made from concentrate. Even the orange juice wasn't real.

"It isn't real. It's just a reminder that there isn't a window. There are no windows." I spoke through gritted teeth, but I didn't raise my voice.

Henry's voice was as cool as the stream running through the mountain scene that infuriated me. "I understand completely, but would you rather be surrounded by concrete reminding you that there are no windows, or would you prefer the illusion?"

I hadn't considered that. We hadn't checked any more of them, but I'd venture a guess that there was concrete behind the rest of the displays, and if I destroyed them all, it would become cave-like. The more I thought about it, there weren't many light fixtures in the house at all; most of the light was from the illusion of natural light from the outdoors.

What do you know? Henry's quiet thoughtfulness is paying off.

He set the food out on the table, and we sat down to a powdered feast. Henry strategically seated me with my back to the window image. I tried to keep a smile from appearing. I was not successful.

1037951

"We didn't get a chance to introduce ourselves properly yesterday. It was. Hmm. Hectic? I thought a nice breakfast might be a good time to get to know one another a bit and discuss our situation if that's alright with you." He seemed genuine and empathetic.

Dreadful idea.

"I don't do talking about myself." *Sidestepping is a perfectly viable option.*

"I suppose it was my idea; I'll go first." He cleared his throat. "My name is Henry Walker Beecher. I'm an actor."

I snorted coffee out my nose; it burned!

"Is that funny?" he asked, honestly wondering why I'd laughed at him.

I choked. "No. I'm sorry. It's not funny at all." *My sinuses are on fire!*

It was freeze-dried coffee. It burned my throat when I drank it, never mind when taken through the sinuses. My efforts to subdue the excruciating pain behind my cheekbones did nothing to convince him that I didn't find the fact that he was an actor downright hilarious. I grabbed the cloth napkin and dried the coffee off my face and off my silk shirt and white pants. *Fabulous, Monti, what a slob.* I blotted at my plate, turning the happy-yellow napkin into an unappetizing shade of mud. *I give up; there's no salvaging these eggs or pancakes.*

"I'm sorry, it's just, I don't know if there's a person on the planet who doesn't know your name and occupation. I wasn't expecting you to introduce yourself like that. I was expecting you to tell me something I didn't already know. Of course, now that I'm saying all this out loud . . . Ugh. How were you supposed to know that I knew who you were? I'm a moron. Ignore me. Continue."

I let my head hang over the back of my squeaky pleather chair in capitulation. I closed my eyes, unwilling to look at the derisive face likely glaring back at me. I hadn't explained myself well, and continuing to dig myself into a hole would've made it worse.

I waited. No response.

Then, a quiet snicker. I lifted my head.

"What's so funny?"

He was stifling his mirth. "I'm sorry, you have to admit, that was hilarious."

He's right. I'm absurd.

"Laugh it up, Fuzz Ball." I threw my coffee-soaked napkin, regretting it instantly.

The napkin splatted against the window behind him. *Why didn't he duck? He's lucky I didn't aim straight at him.*

If I had allowed him to laugh long enough, I might have gotten out of talking about myself. That would have made the awkward interaction entirely worth it. Maybe I should have left it alone.

But he wasn't laughing anymore.

"Did you just quote *Star Wars*?" His face was scrutinizing.

"We're trapped in a perfectly preserved time capsule of a house with no windows and no exterior door, and you want to know if I'm quoting *Star Wars*?"

I've entered the Twilight Zone. What do I do with that? Do I laugh, cry, or be comforted that he recognized the quote?

"Sorry, you just caught me off guard. You're right. Down to business." He cleared his throat, straightened his posture, and began again with his thoroughly dignified British narrator voice. "As I was saying, I am an actor. I live in London, but I film in countries all over the world. It's easy to travel, being unattached." He broke eye contact and ran his fingers through his hair. For a split second, I wondered if he regretted his bachelorhood. But he pulled himself together too quickly for that to be the case, and I let the thought go. "I was in the US on tour promoting a film before the holiday release—you probably don't . . . I don't know if you follow things like that."

I just stared at him. I knew what movie he was promoting. He was a top ten Hollywood star. Everyone knew. But I wasn't about to say anything.

"Anyway, when I film with US production companies, I stay in LA, and we promote more heavily in the US. I was in LA at an event for *Captive Estate*—that's the film—when I was taken. And I woke up here. The rest, you know. His voice petered out at the end, and his eyes wandered around the room. They landed on me, and he waited for me to reciprocate.

Crap, my turn.

"Ah, well. I am . . . Ugh. I'm a recluse of sorts. I avoid people and society at large when at all possible. I spend most of my time working from my home office, collaborating with four different nonprofits. Well, one isn't a traditional nonprofit, but whatever. We don't need to delve into technicalities. You don't care about that, do you? They are all out to improve the world. That's what matters. Right?

"I don't interact with people often, or well, for that matter. That's blatantly obvious." I tried to smile, but I could feel that it was awkward, and it morphed into an eye-roll. I wiped my sweating palms on my coffee-stained pants.

This is a horrible idea. "My memories of the night we were taken have been slow in returning. I now remember that I was at a fundraiser for a charity I work for. We help children who've been victims of sex trafficking. One branch is dedicated to rescue, and I work with the branch dedicated to victim recovery and reintegration into society.

"That evening, though, is still incredibly fuzzy. I can't remember most of it with any clarity. And then I was, well, here. That's it. That's everything." I forced a half smile, calculating my options if he asked probing follow-up questions.

Don't ask anything personal.

"Do you have a name?" His head tilted, and his voice lowered like he didn't want to make me look foolish, but he was out of luck.

I closed my eyes and lowered my head. *I don't want to answer, but it's a fundamental social mores.*

"Violet Cameron. But everyone calls me Monti." *I've gone from not answering to oversharing. What is my problem?*

"Now, I know there is a story behind that nickname."

You're not wrong, Oscar, but I'm not in the mood.

"There is. I . . . " I took a slow breath in. When I opened my eyes, I spoke with all the calm I could muster. "Maybe I'll share the story with you someday. I can't manage right this second. Can we say that giving you my nickname instead of my legal name is a big step for me?" I pleaded with him internally, desperate that my exterior remained stiff & dignified.

"We'll call it a step in the right direction." His smile was mischievous, and so was his tone when he said my name in that James Bond accent of his. "Monti." I should have been happy he was dropping it. Instead, I felt like he was saving it as ammunition.

Henry redirected. "Yesterday, I took the opportunity to try every corridor, every door, every normal avenue a house would have for an exit. I got nowhere. Today, I think we should plan to look for the unusual. Do you have any thoughts . . . Monti?"

Logical and methodical, I like that. I do not, however, like the way you say my name. I glared at him to let him know, and he smirked back at me. A little black curl of hair fell into his face, and he pushed it back without a thought. It made him look less sinister, and I didn't appreciate that. I preferred to dislike him.

Focus, Monti.

"I was thinking about the ventilation system. Highly unlikely that's how they got us in here, but it might be a way for us to get out." I didn't want to take credit for the idea; I'd thought of it in my sleep. Nightmares about trying to get out disturbed the few hours I managed to sleep. *Not explaining that to Henry.*

"Excellent. While you tackle that, I thought I'd find a way up the wall in the conservatory and get out through the opening at the top. I haven't found a ladder, but there are plenty of materials throughout the house. If I can fashion one, it may be our means of escape."

He's right. There's a gaping hole in the roof! Why didn't I think of that?

"What about the tree? Why don't we just climb it?" *Let's simplify things and get this over with!*

"I spent several hours last night trying to work it out. If we climbed the tree, we'd be too far from the walls to get to the roof. Also, the tree isn't tall enough to get us out. If we were to chop down the tree completely—and I've found no axe to do so—it would not get us to the top of the wall to climb out. It's close to forty feet tall, but that isn't tall enough. The room is another story taller."

Huh, you spent a lot of time thinking about this. So, that's what you were doing in the conservatory last night.

I felt deflated and suddenly less ambitious about our day. Evidently, my face showed it. Henry firmly grasped my forearm. "We will find a way out. Don't get discouraged. They got us in. We'll get out."

He seemed empathetic and steadfast. *But he's an actor; he portrays emotions that aren't his own for a living. Then again, I seriously need to believe him right now.*

So, for that moment, I did.

1252036

We left the breakfast dishes on the table and the pans on the stove. We had agreed over breakfast that we would find our way out and leave a kitchen disaster for our captors. As we left to approach our tasks, I heard Henry humming again. *What is that song?* I couldn't make it out, and it was bugging me. I tried to get closer to hear, not exactly being covert.

He stopped abruptly and turned. "Um. Hello?"

I'd been caught. "What are you humming?"

Henry looked up, musing. "Hmm. I was humming, wasn't I? Huh. I think it was the Animals." He continued walking as though he'd answered my question.

I followed. "Wait, what?!" I squawked as I chased him down. "How do you hum animals?" He was so fast with those long legs of his.

Henry stopped and turned to laugh at me. "The Animals are the group that sang the song. They hit #2 on the charts in 1965." He tilted his head at me, disappointed that I wasn't aware of that bit of pop-culture trivia. I shrugged, still confused.

He raised that eyebrow again. "'It's My Life'?"

He waited; I shook my head. "'Don't Bring Me Down'?"

Henry grew impatient, but I was at a loss. "Come on. 'House of the Rising Sun'?!"

I gave up. "I'm sorry, Henry. I have no idea who you're talking about."

"Wow. When we get out of here, I have to introduce you to some quality music. The Animals were an international sensation in the '60s." He gestured to the 1960s prison we'd been cemented into. "And they sang a hit titled, 'We've Gotta Get Out of This Place.' I think I was humming it because my subconscious need to escape was finding a creative outlet."

I smiled at the idea.

Henry shook his head as he continued with his task of finding materials to build a ladder to get over the wall and through the opening in the conservatory ceiling. This time, he sang his song instead of humming it, louder and louder with each line. By the time he reached the end of the chorus, he was belting full voice across the massive chamber, arms outstretched for dramatic effect.

When he finished, he looked over his shoulder and grinned widely at me. "Monti, you know what this means, don't you?" I looked back, his meaning completely lost on me. The combined glee and mischief on his face worried me. "This is our song!" He continued singing boldly as he left to gather supplies, bobbing his head as he went.

What a goofball.

I shook my head at him and went to get myself an outfit sans coffee stains before searching for the largest vent in the house.
2908374

The bedroom vents were probably twelve inches wide. *I'm not a big girl, but I'm not fitting through a twelve-inch anything.* The bathroom vents had the same problem. While I searched, I finally had an excuse to investigate Henry's bedroom. The décor was vintage, just like the rest of the house: solid wood furniture with tapered legs, navy-blue paint over the pristinely smooth plastered walls, and wood plank ceiling. I was surprised to see that Henry had a twin-size poster bed as opposed to the king in my room. *How can he sleep? His feet must hang off the end.*

Noticeably absent of the pungent potpourri smell my room had, his smelled of baseball glove oil and old leather. If it was possible for a space to smell of nostalgia, his room had managed it. I walked by the twin bed, running my hand over the coarse polyester navy comforter that perfectly matched the walls. A large framed sketch of Nolan Ryan hung over the hand-carved headboard. *This has to have been a child's bedroom.*

Curiouser and curiouser.

A twinge of jealousy tugged at me; no bootleg window in his room. Complete darkness aside from the baseball-themed wall sconces on either side of the bed and a matching lamp standing beside the navy leather reading chair. The landscape view was across the hall from his room. No sunrise wake-up call for Henry. He could sleep in. *Then again, he hadn't.*

Back to work, Monti. Move on.

I went to the gym next and held the handle longer than I should have. I'd let the screen get to me before. I couldn't let it get to me again, so I lifted my chin and marched in triumphantly, careful not to trip over the edge of the mat a third time.

The home gym had small vents, too. That wasn't going to work.

Keep going—find a way out.

There were other halls off the conservatory that I hadn't investigated with Henry the afternoon before. The first one, next to the gym, had a library at the end of it. Floor-to-ceiling bookcases brimming with books and a sunken sofa in the middle created a room I could get lost in for days. I plunged headlong into perusing the reading material before reminding myself to stay on task. Unfortunately, those vents were too small as well. I took one last deep breath of the marvelous, musty smell of old leather and paper before moving on.

I followed the path around the edge of the conservatory, and the next hall had a room at the end that appeared to be a retro mini theater with all the bells and whistles. It had an old film projector with two reels on the side hanging from a high gold-leafed coffered ceiling. There were three levels of reclining seats upholstered in red velvet down the middle of the room with a carved gold letter affixed to the end of each row, even though there were only three of them. The walls were covered in a lush red carpet, and mini chandeliers gave it the perfect finishing touch of the retro theater image. *No faux windows to torment me.* A candy and beverage bar at the back was decked in rich red velvet and lavish gold trim. *How unbelievably bizarre.*

Responding to my entrance, plush red curtains at the front parted automatically, a full-size theater screen descended, and a menu appeared. The dichotomy of ultramodern technology installed in the picture-perfect retro theater was startling. I looked up again, and the reels on the projector were frozen—a façade covering a modern digital projector. The space was mind-bending.

The menu before me wasn't from any streaming service I'd ever used. It listed hundreds of thousands of movies and television series. There were options to sort them alphabetically, by release date, by genre, by actor; the options seemed limitless. There appeared to be everything from old silent films up through Henry's new movie. It hadn't even been released to theaters yet. *How is this possible?*

I was perplexed, but I couldn't let it distract me. There was nothing in the room that would remedy my immediate dilemma. I had to continue with my task. I looked for vents large enough to fit through and, not finding any, was about to move on when a return on the other side of the theater caught my eye. It was near the steps on the wall furthest from the door, and the vent cover blended in so well with the wall that I had almost missed it. It was only about twelve inches high, but it was probably two feet wide. *It'll be tight, but I think I can fit.*

Butterflies filled my stomach. I suppressed the feeling. *Don't get ahead of yourself.*

Motivated by the possibilities, I sprinted back to my room with a mental to-do list: *1. Tie my hair back, 2. Get a screwdriver, 3. Escape through the vent.*

If I was climbing through a ventilation system, the last thing I needed was wild, almost waist-long hair getting in my way. Henry didn't ask what I was doing as I ran by, but he did seem to appreciate my enthusiasm.

The second time I breezed by, he laughed, watching me simultaneously braid my hair and jog across the conservatory to retrieve a screwdriver from the tool bag in the larder. *Go ahead, laugh, Sasquatch; I'm on a mission. You climb your wall. We'll see who gets out first.*

Screwdriver in hand, I raced back to the theater to begin. Down the hall, through the door. I jumped over some steps down the side of the theater. Realizing I was a little overexcited, I took a breath to slow myself down.

In. Out.

In. Out.

Ready.

I pried the cover off the return. The vent looked dark but clean. I'd never been claustrophobic, but somehow, I felt like I was about to crawl into my own grave. I swallowed, tossed the cover aside, put my arms out in front of me like a diver, and squeezed my way in. It was wider than I had expected, but my rib cage was still cramped, forcing shallow breathing. There were a couple of inches above my head and back, but the pressure on the sides of my ribcage in the darkness gave the feeling that the house itself had gotten a hold of me and was squeezing me—an intentional act to let me know it would not let me escape.

Focus, Monti. You're losing it.

My pace was snail-like—inching my way through—pulling my body with my fingertips and toes because I couldn't move anything else in the cramped space. Every movement constricted and plodding.

Ow! I'd sliced a finger tip on a sharp connection point. It didn't matter, I had to keep moving.

Distance was difficult to judge, but I estimated that I'd gotten about fifteen feet when heat came inexplicably blasting through. It made no sense; it was a return. Air should have been pulled from the room into the ventilation system. It shouldn't have had heat blowing through the vent into the room. *Someone reversed it.*

"What do I do now?" *If I continue, what will I find? If I give up, will there be another way out?*

I have to press on.

The heat was intense, an industrial level of heat and force. *If I pass out in the vent, Henry knows I'm in the theater. He'll find me. But . . .*

There's no way he can fit in here and get me out.

I pushed the thought from my mind. Dwelling on the negative wouldn't get me out of the house any faster. I had to keep going.

Why is this vent so long? How long are air vents, anyway? I felt like I had long-since crawled beyond the length of the house. Exhausted and sweating like I was in a sauna, my hands lost traction and slipped as I tried to pull myself forward.

Weird. There's a light up ahead. Why is there a light in an air duct? Can it be the center of the heating system? Seems the wrong place for that. Maybe I can reach the attic, better yet, the exterior of the house.

I stretched and pulled myself forward, slipping and struggling as I went. As I sweat through my clothes completely, it became even more challenging to move; my wet clothes became heavy and adhered to the metal, and I lost my grip on the vent entirely. The light grew brighter, and I forced myself to slither closer.

There's another grate.

My body stretched to its limits in a desperate effort to reach the grate at the end of the shaft. The tips of my fingernails barely scratched it. I wiped the sweat off my hands onto the ceiling of the vent and made one last attempt to pull myself the last few centimeters until I jammed my fingers between the bars. I grabbed the grate and yanked on it with my body's weight.

I'd made it.

Instantly, as if in response to my touch, the heat and the light turned off.

Wait. Is this a game?

Is someone taunting me?

I pulled myself closer and felt around the vent cover. It wasn't a cover at all. Heavy iron bars had been welded there, and they didn't budge. The light, it appeared, was to give me hope. There, so I could see the end, and then whoever had deposited us in that house took it away so I'd realize the vent was not a means of escape at all.

It's a cruel and sadistic feint.

I cried out into the darkness and tried to kick at the sides of the vent, though the cramped space wouldn't even give me that relief. Lying there for a moment of rest after my struggle, it occurred to me that not only was the heat not blowing, but there was no longer airflow through the vent at all. *It's getting stuffy. I'm going to pass out if I don't get moving.*

I pounded the heel of my hand on the metal grate one last time before I began to back out. It hadn't been easy on the way in. But, backward was worse. I tried to be logical, focused, even clinical about my situation. Freaking out and getting emotional wouldn't get me out of the vent. I analyzed my difficulties, trying to overcome them.

My knees were in my way. My feet couldn't feel the way my hands had on the way in. My shirt rode up, but no matter how hard I tried, I couldn't get my arms down to unbutton it and get it off.

The whole vent was slick because I had sweat the entire way in, greasing the length of the vent. I was barely able to maneuver over my wedge shoes to leave them behind. I had taken them off on the way in because they were the wrong choice in footwear for impersonating John McClane, and I needed better traction. My clothes were torn from every angle by parts of the vent; it turned out that the seams of the vent were pointed toward that light, and they were razor sharp. So, I was on the slicing leg of the journey, getting nicked and cut at almost every junction.

I'm getting nowhere fast, and clinical thinking isn't helping. I'm shimmying my way through a pitch-black, slimy cheese grater. This isn't working. I can't do this on my stomach.

I struggled and grunted, and I rolled onto my back. *This is a little better.*

I'd hardly made any progress squirming my way down the vent—my arms still pinned overhead—before I yelped and swore out into the abyss. I'd been skewered.

Somehow, I'd managed to wedge a sharp piece of the aluminum vent into the meat of the outer edge of the back of my thigh. I shifted in an attempt to carefully maneuver off the shard, but the vent was too tight. *How did I impale myself in the first place?* I tried to roll off, but somehow, I seemed to sink the ragged strip of metal further into my flesh.

My howl echoed through my aluminum prison. I braced myself on the sides of the vent so the fragment couldn't dig in any deeper while I tried to catch my breath, but each shallow gasp sent a dagger of pain up my leg and deep into my hip. *I have to get off. Think, Monti.*

The piece of metal has to be attached to the vent . . . feels like it's dug in up the length of my thigh. Maybe I can reach down, feel it.

Ahhh! Nope. That didn't work. No room to pull my arms down.

Needing a new tactic, I shifted my weight a little left, a little right, a little up, a little down. Argh! Every angle so I could feel exactly where it was. I bit the collar of my shirt, dizzy with pain. *Don't pass out. Focus, Monti. Stay awake. I think I feel how it got me.*

You can back off it, Monti. Lift and twist to the left.

I can do this. Can't I?

Three deep breaths. Don't pass out. One. Two. Three. Up, back, aaahh, rotate to the left.

I was off the metal shard. Resting my forehead against the side of the vent, I gave myself a second to breathe before I tried to navigate the rest of the way out.

On my side, my injured thigh turned upward; I tried to maneuver myself further out of the vent. With my arms still pinned over my head and my left leg throbbing—bleeding all over the vent—I couldn't make the forward progress I needed. I fell over onto my back.

No!

I'd moved forward a few inches, just enough so the shard that had impaled my thigh was perfectly positioned to skewer me in the ass like a Fourth of July shish kebab. *How in the hell did I do that?*

I had apparently bent the shard vertically when twisting myself off the first time, so when I landed on it the second time, it shivved me deep in the ass. *Did that hit bone?*

I knew what I had to do. I just didn't want to do it. I had to bend it—to flatten it, really—in the process of backing off this time. *I can do it. No problem.*

I screamed without restraint as I pulled myself upward and let my weight rest on the shard, bending it and flattening it as I slid off it. I could feel my blood flowing freely along with the shard, further lubricating the surface of the vent. I couldn't focus on that; I had to get out.

Once free of the metal, I barely gave myself a moment to rest. I was afraid if I stopped, it would be for good. I pitched and rolled onto my stomach before I backed out, making sure not to stab myself with the ragged strip a third time. *That would be just like me.*

Slowly and carefully, I worked my way out of the vent: angry, hot, bleeding, and thinking. Plenty of time to think. *This vent can't be a normal part of the house's ventilation system. It has to be some twisted attempt by my captors to mess with my mind. Its sole purpose to consternate and demoralize me.*

But do I tell Henry? What would telling him accomplish?

I had no idea how long it took me to get out. In the slippery blackness, I couldn't discern time or distance. If I was honest with myself, I didn't truly believe I'd get to the end of the vent before I passed out. I pushed on, one inch at a time, knowing that the moisture making my journey slick and challenging was no longer my sweat but my blood. I assumed every inch would be my last.

When I fell out of the opening at the end of the vent, I collapsed over the theater steps. I closed my eyes, eternally thankful for the stiff commercial polyester carpet in my face that had replaced the stifling aluminum vent. As I rested and tried to catch my breath, I lost my sense of time.

4564762

Henry barged into the theater, chuckling to himself, "I hope you had a better day than I did bec . . . " He must have caught a glimpse of me on the floor because he stopped short. "No, no, no, no, no." He was on the floor at my side in an instant. "Monti!"

I tried to open my eyes. I wanted to smile and relieve his concern, but I was so tired, and the room was blurry through my one open slit of an eye. I tried to look at him with that one eye, but I couldn't make out his face, so I gave up.

Henry was poking at me, checking my head and arms. *What's happening? I can't respond? So tired.*

He leaned over me, and I heard a strange squishing sound come from the carpet beside me. And for the first time since we had met, panicked tones and foul language spewed from Henry's mouth.

I managed to force out a whispered, "Sorry." *What am I even sorry for?*

"Don't you dare say you're sorry!" Before I could piece together what was happening, I was off the ground, and my wet leg felt a breeze as we moved swiftly out of the theater and down the hall. I couldn't focus, but I could have sworn I heard Henry mumbling and scolding me for apologizing along the way. *I'll have to ask about that later.*

I must have passed out as he carried me. I distinctly remember waking up to being stabbed in the leg. "What is wrong with you?!" I reflexively kicked, but I was apparently lying face down on the kitchen table and stubbed my toe. "That hurts!" I spat the words at him.

"So I gathered." There was a smile in his voice even though he seemed to be concentrating.

Stretched out across the table, I stared at the thick, unbroken trail of blood crossing the dining room from the entrance of the hall all the way to the table. The smell of iron was so strong I could taste it. Then, I noticed that my head was perched upon a pillow. I tried to lift my head enough to see, and I thought it was an orange one like the pillows I had noticed in the library, though I didn't spend enough time in that room to take notes on the décor.

Henry sat in a blue pleather chair, hovering over me with feverish intensity as he tried to stitch the gash in my thigh. *I'm still fully clothed. Did he rip open the back of my pants, or was that the vent's handiwork? I don't even care. That needle he's using feels like a barbed fishing hook.* "Aaah! Hey, now!" I flinched.

"Sorry. I'm almost finished, I promise." He seemed focused, yet he still couldn't manage pain-free or even minimal-pain stitches.

"You sure you know what you're doing?" I didn't know what was going on back there, but it was about as painful as when I was harpooned in the vent. My face was clenched so tightly I thought my eyeballs would retreat into my skull.

"Actually." He paused, focusing on a stitch. Or maybe, stalling. "I was a medic in His Majesty's Armed Forces."

"His what?"

"British Armed Forces. I was in the British Army and worked on the front lines, patching up wounded men enough to be transported to hospital. That was before acting, of course. I may not have the skill of a surgeon, but I do know how to properly clean and stitch a wound."

Not the answer I expected. I'd been teasing him to pass the time and distract from the pain, but he'd gone and shared an interesting and personal detail about his life. I began to unexpectedly relax.

"I'm sorry I didn't use the anesthetic. Your wound didn't need much debriding before I stitched it, and you were out cold when I began. I thought I could get it done before you came round" I was developing an appreciation for being trapped with a person who had life skills until it dawned on me how he'd worded his apology.

"Wait, you said, 'didn't' use anesthetic, not 'couldn't.' Why?"

He didn't answer right away, and I chose not to press. *Maybe I don't want to know.*

"Thigh is done. Let's tackle your um . . . Hold still, please." I heard a tearing sound and felt hydrogen peroxide pour over my bare ass. I rolled over, covering my nakedness. He had no right!

"What do you think you're doing?!"

"Well, I thought I was cleaning and stitching your wound. Would you like to try?" With a coy smile, he offered the peroxide in one hand and the needle and thread in the other.

Jackass. Of course, I can't do it myself.

I was incensed with our captor for inflicting the injury, infuriated with myself for not being able to deal with it gracefully, and irritated with Henry for being interminably patient with me while I had a meltdown. *This is humiliating on so many levels.*

I rolled over and dramatically let the flap of my pants flop open while I huffed. He took a breath—his Sasquash lungs sucking all the breathable air out of the room—probably contemplating the risk vs. reward of making a comment; ultimately, he restrained himself.

"You mentioned something about anesthetic?" *Why would someone have anesthetic and supplies for stitches in their house? Better yet, why did you not use it? This doesn't feel right.*

"Oh, well, when I was in the larder looking for things to stack into a makeshift ladder in the conservatory—you know, to reach over the wall—I found an aisle marked with medical supplies. I took the time to inventory what was there. It's an extensive supply, really. Not just odds and sods from home or things you would find at the chemist. There are some real hospital-grade provisions. It got me thinking that someone must have thought we'd need them. At the time, I couldn't fathom what for. Then again, I wasn't expecting you to come out of the ventilation system short a liter of blood. I'm suspicious that I'm missing something. I didn't want to use anesthetic we might need later. The supply isn't unlimited." He seemed empathetic to my pain but more conscious about the unforeseen intended purpose for the medical supplies. I may have wanted to whine about the painful stitches, but after his explanation, I shared his concern.

"No worries. I've experienced pain before. I can manage." *Why did I say that? I don't share. Must be the blood loss.*

He chuckled and continued stitching up the meat of my ass. *Thank you for letting the comment go.*

"There, these will dissolve in a couple of weeks. Change the bandage every morning, and it should heal quite nicely."

When he finished, he closed my pants over my wounds as best he could. I lay there, resting on the table, staring at the nonfunctioning clock on the wall, forever frozen at 11:02. Not knowing how long I was there or even if Henry had left the room —he wasn't in my line of sight—I broke the silence. "Are you married?"

"No." He sounded confused by my question and perhaps by the emotionless monotone in which I had asked. Then again, he'd already answered that question earlier.

"Do you have K&R insurance? Kidnap and Ransom, I mean." I was still unmoved in my posture and unchanged in my tone.

"No. What are you thinking?" I couldn't see him, but I could hear in his voice that he was following my train of thought but waiting to see where I was going with it.

"Neither do I. There's no one at home with access to my accounts to pay a ransom. Why would these people plan an elaborate kidnapping of two people of means and not have a way to retrieve the funds? It doesn't make sense. And if we weren't taken for our money, what other possible purpose could there have been? I can't make sense of it." I completed my thought as it had taken form, in a flat monotone. I had no energy—physical or emotional—to devote to the delivery.

What can our kidnappers gain by keeping us here besides money?

DAY 3

Skive

Still in the Brady Bunch house of horrors?

Not a dream. Perfect!

10873491

Not ready to trust everything supplied to us by these psychopaths, I had opted not to take any of the controlled pain relievers in the larder medical supplies. Wisdom prevailed, and I decided my cocktail of wine and sleeping pills ought not be repeated either. Therefore, the stitches in my thigh and left butt cheek, as well as the minor cuts spread across my body, had burned and stabbed me throughout the night and were not conducive to sleep.

I was left with a hot shower and fresh bandages to appease me in the morning. They soothed but were an insufficient substitute for a decent night of sleep. There was a bottle of Advil in the medicine cabinet buried in the bathroom wall. Still, the dark and ever-increasing bags sagging under my eyes longed for real coffee —or better yet, espresso—hopefully, to be found in the recesses of the epic larder.

When I reached the kitchen, I half expected Henry to be preparing a five-course meal. But no, he was instead precariously perched atop a mountain of furniture in the conservatory with his face pressed against the wall. The haphazardly engineered mountain looked like it was about to collapse. After everything I'd been through the day before, Henry's two-story construction of chaos was too much. I waited until his head was turned the other direction and snuck past.

There was indeed coffee in the larder; unfortunately, there were no real coffee beans and no espresso. There weren't even coffee grounds, only the row of industrial-sized canisters of freeze-dried crystalized astronaut-style instant coffee we had already discovered. I was convinced they had been sitting on the shelf since the mid-1960s with the rest of the house. Nothing fresh for me, it would seem. No complaint; it was caffeine. I had sugar and powdered milk to go in my burnt-flavored caffeine, too. *It isn't perfect, but it is breakfast. I suppose our hosts aren't the most inconsiderate kidnappers.*

What am I thinking? I've officially lost my mind. Must drink the coffee.

I sat—half on, half off—a squeaky stool with its yellow pleather cushion at the vibrant-yellow peninsula dividing the kitchen and dining room, savoring the scent of my coffee first, knowing full well that it wouldn't taste remotely as good as it smelled. I wanted to enjoy the illusion of a good cup of coffee, if only for a moment.

Before I could open my eyes, something crashed onto the Formica counter in front of me. I was reluctant to open my eyes; the day had barely gotten underway. I hadn't managed to get a drop of caffeine into my system, and I hadn't taken a single one of the handful of Advil loitering in the bottom of my pocket. I did not want to look.

I slurped at my coffee, eyes squeezed shut.

Maybe if I don't move, he'll just go away.

Nothing happened. *Maybe he's gone.* I waited and took another long, slow, obnoxious sip. The pleather of my stool squeaked beneath me, punctuating the silence of my inaction.

The suspense was more than I could stand. I squinted and peeked out of one eye. Standing at the end of the counter, with his bulky arms crossed over his broad chest, left eyebrow raised, Henry patiently waited for me.

"It's too early. Can you tell me later?" *I'm whining. I hate whiny people.*

"Okay." He turned and walked away.

Wait. That's it?

I took a massive swig of coffee. It was so hot and caustic that I choked. "Wait a second, what is this?" I coughed again. Henry smiled at his victory. I could tell, even though his back was turned, because his ears lifted.

Manipulative son of bitch!

He turned and was at the stool next to me and seated in half the steps he'd taken to leave. He straightened his face as he handed me the object. "I was stacking furniture to get out of the conservatory over the wall, and I reached a climbing vine. I clocked a bud slightly different than the others. This was buried inside." He poked at the object in my hand. It was something mechanical. That was about all I could make of it. Concrete clung to the outer shell of the marble-sized device, but I couldn't tell what was inside.

"It's a camera."

Seriously. Couldn't give me a second to figure it out?

"It doesn't look like a camera."

"See this here?" He pointed at a minuscule reflective surface on one side. "This is a lens cover. At first, it looked like a bead of dew, but underneath is a crystal lens. See there? You can tell if you look really closely. I know it's small."

He handed it over, urging me to investigate. But I couldn't tell a crystal lens from a disposable camera if my life depended on it. I turned it over. The back was a blob of concrete with frayed wires hanging out.

"I had to rip it out of the wall. I don't think we'll be able to follow the wires. They're buried in solid concrete.

He only gave me a moment to digest the information before he continued.

"It was well concealed. I would never have found it if I wasn't right up against the vine. I could've had my face next to it and never have seen it. It was a fluke that I looked at it bang on. So, when I found it, I dug it out of the wall with a steak knife."

Not the news I want to start my day with.

"You're telling me this, and it is incredibly unnerving, yet your face is telling me that there is worse news. Out with it." I waved him on to give me whatever bad news he was holding back. He lifted the chunk of camera and concrete from my hand and placed it on the counter, then wiped his hands on his cargo pants, drying sweat off his palms, and fixated on the floor.

"I don't think this is the only one." He continued focusing on the floor while he waited for the news to sink in, occasionally peering up at me to see what I thought.

It's not the only camera?

Of course, it's not the only camera. Why would anyone go to such lengths to lock people in a house and not watch them? Watch. Us. I let out a deep sigh.

"You're right, of course." I did everything in my power to manage a deadpan voice.

I can't freak out. We're being watched. Apparently. I can't give the watchers the satisfaction.

Henry looked at me again, tilted his head, and scrunched his face. *What now? You look like someone about to tell me they ran over my dog. I'm done. I don't want to hear it.*

Henry pursed his lips. He seemed like he didn't want to be the bearer of bad news.

"Just rip the Band-Aid off."

With reservation, he walked toward the conservatory. I knocked back the last few ounces of my wannabe coffee and followed, taking two steps for every one of his. We stopped between the raised beds of berry bushes that sat between the halls to the bedrooms and the gym.

Standing side by side, we scanned the furniture tower Henry had built and scaled two stories up to dig the camera out of the wall. Out of the corner of my eye, I noticed Henry tossing one of the larger walkway stones between his hands. It was a palm-sized stone. Well, palm-sized for Henry's hands.

"Whatcha doin'?" It came out in a singsong kind of voice. *You're making me anxious here, Sasquatch. You about to crack?*

"Watch." He pointed to the sky over the top of the wall and backed up. Before I realized what he was doing, he wound up like a major league baseball player and pitched the rock over the wall.

It took me a minute to process what had happened because the rock returned, bounced on the grass, and landed between my feet. I stared at the sky and then looked at the rock in the grass. It had ricocheted off the sky and left a crack.

What in the world?

Henry dropped to the ground, legs splayed out in the grass, his head drooping in front of him.

It slowly sank in that the rock hadn't bounced off the wall but off the clear blue sky. That sky and the clouds slowly drifting above me had a crack in them.

More screens.

Nausea gripped me. I turned to Henry, undoubtedly with a panicked expression. He merely lifted his drooping head and lay back flat on the grass. "Right then. We aren't getting out that way, are we?"

Wait a minute. Why is he calm?

He sounded as though he was checking plan B off his list and was moving on to plan C. *Did I underestimate him? Does he have this all under control? Maybe I should give team Henry a chance.*

"Okay, Obi-Wan, what's the plan of attack?" *We can't let this stop us.*

Henry did not respond with a plan but with an eruption of laughter. *What is happening? Nothing about this is funny.*

"Are you having a nervous breakdown? Did you need me to get antianxiety pills from the medical supplies?" Having to be the house medic was a problem. I knelt beside him, mentally preparing for the task before me.

I'm not qualified, but I'll do what needs to be done.

He clutched his stomach, sat up, and wiped tears away. I grew suspicious that his laughter had less to do with his mental state and more to do with my social ineptitude.

"No. I'm fine. But I have to say, I needed a laugh. That is the second time you've quoted *Star Wars* in as many days, and I find that entertaining."

I was a little peeved. Maybe more than a little peeved. "And quoting *Star Wars* somehow makes me ridiculous?" I was vacillating over whether or not that was important enough to fight about. I'd been imprisoned, skewered—twice—and my every move was being watched. I didn't need to be mocked as well.

"No." Henry straightened his face into a sincere expression and rested his hand on my arm. "No, rather the contrary. I've rarely met a woman who could stay awake through *Star Wars*, let alone quote it accurately. You are a gem, to be sure. I found both the quote and your unyielding optimism brilliant." His smile subsided. "I'm sorry. I have no plan for the day."

"Ah. Well, if we aren't mocking me, then it's time we devise a plan of attack. What do you think?" I elbowed him playfully, trying to be encouraging.

"Sounds like we need to plan to plan." We both chuckled and flopped back onto the grass. I landed square on the stab wound in my ass. "Ahh!" I carefully adjusted so I wasn't lying directly on any stitches and proceeded to look up and admire the technological marvel above. *I suppose that explains why it's spring in here when it's November outside.*

Even with the crack at the edge, it was breathtaking. There was no discernible repeating pattern in the cloud movement; there were birds and a breeze. Somehow, rain had even sprinkled on us for a few minutes the day before. I couldn't find the seams; there was no evidence of the technology behind it all. *Who could have created this place?*

My mind wandered a bit as we lay there. From ways we could attempt to escape to the things that had happened to the questions of why and who. As I gently brushed my fingers across the tips of the soft blades of grass, my mind settled for a short time on the man lying in the grass next to me.

For some reason, he's been a steady calm in this storm of insanity, never wavering, constantly thoughtful, always looking for solutions. All I've done is react to everything I've encountered. I hate to admit this would be harder without him. Or, worse, to be trapped with someone who wasn't him.

He deserves more than the closed-off, hyper-protective nature of my personality. He'd get lonely, stuck in any house with someone like me. Let alone this concrete sanatorium. How can I at least try to make an effort? I haven't made a friend in years. I'm not sure I remember how.

"Montgomery?"

The word hung in the air like a day-old party balloon. A question. Not the statement I had intended. I wanted to reach out and scoop it back into my mouth the second it came out.

"What?" Henry was wholly confused by my irrational utterance, but he seemed intensely intrigued. He rolled onto his side and propped his head up on his hand. I closed my eyes and wished myself away. A less-than-effective tactic. "What is Montgomery?" he repeated. I could tell he earnestly awaited the answer even though he was stifling a laugh.

I took a deep breath and opened my eyes, deliberately avoiding eye contact, keeping my gaze firmly fixed on a perfect facsimile of an eagle soaring above. "It's my maiden name. It's what 'Monti' is short for." I hesitated before I forced myself to continue. He'd earned that much. "I got the nickname in college. I thought you might want to know." I closed my eyes again and hoped he'd accept the gesture and let me resume our blissful silence.

Hoping, unfortunately, does not make a thing so.

"Wait, your maiden name? Are you married? You aren't wearing a ring. You said no one could pay your ransom!"

I could not believe the Pandora's box I had opened with one simple word. I shielded my face with my hands, and he stopped. I hadn't prepared myself for the onslaught of questions.

A moment later, I felt Henry's breath in my ear. Then he whispered loudly, "Did you take off your ring because you have a mistress?"

His question was so unexpected and so close to my ear that I exploded with nervous laughter and jabbed him in the ribs with my elbow. I wiped the smile off my face and resumed my silence as quickly as my outburst had begun, surprising even myself.

I felt Henry get close to my ear again, so I gathered my strength against his humor and hot breath. "Did you get caught?" he whispered, unrelenting. "Is that why we're here?" That was it. I could not contain my laughter anymore.

I hadn't laughed like that in ages. I punched him in the bicep for making me come unglued. Though it didn't do me any good. It was like punching an overinflated tire. Henry found it hilarious that I had bothered trying. We sat in the grass and laughed until we couldn't see from the tears. It wasn't even that funny, but once we started, it couldn't be stopped.

"Ugh, I absolutely needed that laugh." Until I released all that energy, I hadn't realized how much.

"I thought it might be good for the soul." He wasn't wrong. Henry continued, "Thank you, Monti."

"For what?"

"For trusting me enough to share something personal." His mouth curled into a sincere half-smile. As his head turned away, his smile morphed into a melancholy glance at my left hand. He obviously wanted to know what had happened. His hand reached toward the divot in my ring finger before he caught himself and pulled away. I was surprised but relieved when he didn't ask. It was a topic I couldn't bring myself to talk about. I didn't want to think about it—hadn't allowed myself to think about it in years. I wasn't about to start.

"Alright, Oscar. Enough lyin' around. Let's get this show on the road. Is there something in that larder we can bust down a wall with? Or did you learn chemistry for one of your movies? Ooh! Can we make a bomb? What's the plan?"

I don't know what we're going to do, but I'm ready for anything!

"You do realize I'm not actually any of the people I portray on film? I don't learn every skill my character knows. Sorry to disappoint. I can't make a bomb, and I didn't come up with a plan in the last ten minutes. Real life doesn't resolve in 120 minutes." My shoulders sank; he'd knocked all the wind out of my sails.

Henry tilted his head. I could see the wheels in his mind turning again. "I was thinking, though. We've been at it reasonably hard since we got here. We're going to get burnt out. Something tells me that this guy, or these people, or whoever it is, they probably have more up their sleeves. I'd rather not be completely knackered and emotionally tapped when the next thing happens." I nodded slowly as he continued. "I think there may be an element of psychological warfare going on, and we need to take care of ourselves and each other." Henry waited for a response.

"You know, I think you may have a point. When I was in the vent . . . " I swallowed.

I don't want to talk about this, but he may need to know.

I let out a deep breath and tried again. "When I got to the end of the vent yesterday, it didn't seem to be part of the ventilation system at all but a fake escape route we were meant to find. There was a light at the end. And what I initially thought was another grate. When I reached it and realized they were welded iron bars, the light and the air turned off like someone was watching and purposefully taunting me. I felt like a rat in a maze or some kind of giant laboratory experiment.

"It was tight but still manageable on the way in, but all the seams in the vent were sharp on the way out. That's how I got sliced up. By the time I made it out, I don't know . . .

"Between that and, well, the mind games around here, and the books, it's all beginning to get to me." As I said it out loud, even though I didn't tell Henry everything, it was the first time I realized how much the house itself felt alive, like an active participant in our captivity. It had actually gotten into my head.

Henry gently took my hand. It made me smile slightly; his Sasquatch hand swallowed mine. "Wait, books? Plural?" He looked down at me, his emerald eyes scolding me for keeping secrets.

"Yeah, I don't want to talk about it."

"Right then. Well, I decree that nothing like that will happen for the rest of the day." His voice was resolute and uplifting. I looked up to find that he had his gleaming Hollywood smile on. It was slightly cheesy, but there was a reason he got the big bucks. I categorically could not keep myself from smiling back.

I hate that.

"I declare this *Star Wars* Day."

I scowled, and my arms flung out at him in reflex. "You can't declare this *Star Wars* Day. We already missed it; that was May the 4th."

I can't believe I said that out loud. No one makes me say things I don't want to. How does he? Once it was out there, I did everything in my power to look deliberate in my declaration.

Henry was on his feet and, in one swift movement, had me on mine as well. He spoke, taking two steps backward toward the theater. "I love that you know that. You're brilliant. Yes, May the 4th is officially *Star Wars* Day. However, we are essentially on an island. We have no way of keeping time or telling the date, and we need a break. It may be November, but I am declaring today our own personal May the 4th. We shall watch all of *Star Wars*. All day long. Do you accept my proposal?" He held out his hand as if helping me onto a boat.

I'll accept, of course. The question is, can I get some minor payback for making me blurt out more than I meant to? Maybe in the form of a little shock?

"That depends. Are you proposing we watch in order of release, chronological order, or Machete order?" His mouth dropped open, and his forehead lifted.

Perfect. He's speechless. Payback is mine. We can officially move on.

He covered the distance between us in one giant step. Our faces only an inch apart. "Marry me now."

Nope, not speechless. Too far. I've gone too far. Time to run.

If I hadn't caught the quiver in the corner of his mouth fighting a smile, I would have finished calculating which way to make my strategic retreat. I released the breath I'd been holding, and Henry's grin spread wide.

I relaxed, but only slightly, and carefully backed out of the uncomfortable closeness before we set off toward the theater. Walking ahead of me, Henry suddenly turned with raptness. "Which do you prefer, out of curiosity?"

"Machete order, obviously." I don't know what he was expecting me to say, but he responded on top of my answer.

"Obviously."

The second I opened my mouth to question his comment, a downpour broke from the ceiling overhead, complete with thunder and lightning. "What the actual . . . ?" We took off and ran for the theater hallway, every footfall sending stabbing pain up my thigh and even shooting up into my lower back. At least until Henry had grabbed me by the waist to help me keep up with his Neanderthal strides.

I slipped on the hardwood when I landed in the hallway, my shoes slick from the rain. Henry caught me by the elbow, and I almost took him down with me because his shoes were just as wet. Drenched and confused, we braced ourselves on the wall and turned back to view the strange phenomenon behind us.

It appeared to be a full-fledged indoor thunderstorm with clouds, rain, thunder, and lightning. I couldn't figure out how it had been accomplished. *The frigid rain is real. But it isn't falling from a sky. That is definitely a ceiling. The deafening thunder is shaking the walls, but where are the speakers? I don't see speakers.*

Blindingly bright lightning cracked across the ceiling. Soaked to the bone, I stepped back into the garden to look at the sky image again. Without question, it wasn't a sky; it was a production. A confoundingly realistic one.

Another bolt of lightning raced across the ceiling, and I jumped back into the hallway as thunder shook the room. I lost my footing and braced myself against the doorframe. Henry's arm flung out in front of my face. My eyes followed his arm and pointed finger to the larder hall almost directly across the conservatory from us.

The light's on. "Why is the light on?" *It has a motion sensor light; it only comes on when we enter the hall.*

A smoky smell wafted over, and the light from the larder hall grew brighter. Henry leaned down to my ear and gripped my shoulders tight enough that I shrunk back. At first, I didn't hear his single whispered word over the intense volume of the storm, nor did I connect it with what I was seeing.

"Fire."

Henry moved with such force that he almost pushed me to the ground, bolting out of the hall and through the conservatory into the rain. Finally, my mind attached his whisper to the intensifying light in the larder, and I raced out into the downpour after him.

Before I reached the threshold, I ran into a wall of heat. "Henry, be careful!" *How does he expect to put out a fire?*

If it spreads to the rest of the house, we have nowhere to go. We have no way out!

I stopped by the tree, physically unable to continue. I fought to immerse myself in my present crisis and push away flashes—memories of the other fire—that battled for my attention.

I can't think about that tragedy. I have to focus on this one. Focus!

I pressed the heel of my hand to my eye socket as I regained control of my thoughts and actions.

Think, Monti! How can you put out a fire? This fire.

Oh.

That's it!

I raced to the linen closet in the bedroom hall and grabbed two king-size blankets to smother flames. *I hope they invented fire-resistant fabric in the '60s. If not, this'll be a short-lived firefighting effort.*

Henry had found an industrial-looking fire extinguisher while I was busy retrieving blankets. It had apparently been in the larder all along. He worked on the largest portion of the blaze, and I tackled the smaller flames at the edge of the fire with the blankets, working my way toward the center where Henry was. The most dangerous part of the blaze divided us—the untended portion. In that space, flames went unchecked, and temperatures rose too high, too quickly. Glass jars of provisions exploded without warning. It was volatile.

The blanket melted under the heat of the flames, but it was effective. As I fought the rim of the fire, the smell was foul, like we had microwaved spoiled leftovers in old Tupperware for too long. I smacked my lips, trying not to smell the pungent odor, and, of course, the timing was perfect, and sweat dripped off my face and into my mouth, bringing with it a strange mixture of the Barbasol flavor of the fire extinguisher foam and the soot I had accumulated on my face. Worse yet, the foam and soot dripped into my eyes. But there was nothing I could do. I couldn't stop; I had to keep fighting. The fire wouldn't wait.

I tried to keep my attention on what I was doing, only glancing at Henry, further back in the larder, from time to time to see how he was progressing. There were moments when the flames were so high it was hard to see him over the flicking tips and the flying foam. When I did catch a glimpse of him, I broke his concentration, and the fire seemed to fight him back.

Back to work, Monti. We both need to focus.

It took almost the entire morning to put the fire out completely. We used up every bit of the fire extinguisher, destroyed both blankets, and hauled countless pots of water in from the kitchen to finally get the last of it smothered completely.

Eventually, there appeared to be no flames left, only piles of ash smoldering across the right side of the larder. We lost about half of our supplies: basically, all the boxed food, glass jars of food, and twenty-five-pound plastic barrels of flour, sugar, rice, and the like all gone.

Exhausted, sweating, covered in soot, we sat broken and drained on the floor. I finally asked Henry, "What in the world could have caused that fire? The lightning strike wasn't real; it was an illusion." *I'm too tired to think.*

"You're right; lightning didn't cause the fire. The lightning was a show, a distraction. I found this nested in a pile of burnt paper goods." Henry held out something small and black, dangling by a wire.

What is that?

"Our captors set the fire to intentionally destroy supplies. I've determined that they didn't intend it to kill us, or they wouldn't have set the ventilation system to suck out the fumes while we fought the fire. We'd have suffocated otherwise."

He was transfixed by the device he dangled in front of his face. His voice was detached. "You said you felt like a rat in a maze, that we're in a laboratory experiment. I think you got that one bang on." He flicked the tiny melted mechanism into a pile of debris and rubbed the back of his neck, leaving his head drooping in front of his chest as though his neck couldn't hold it up any longer.

I sifted the device out of the ash to examine. It dangled by two melted and mangled wires. I couldn't tell what it was beyond a melted piece of plastic. "They knew about the other . . . " I didn't finish my sentence. *Not in the mood to explain to Henry that our captors customized our torment to me.*

"The other what?" *He had to ask.*

"Well, if this is part of the rat maze, then all the more reason we need that *Star Wars* marathon of yours." I wiped the sweat off my forehead.

Henry looked at me, surprised. "You want to watch *Star Wars*? Even after all that?" He gestured at the piles of warped shelving, burnt boxes of food, melted plastic, and other general evidence of our exhaustive morning efforts to remain alive.

"Especially after all that!" It had been a hellacious morning; what else were we going to do with our day? I was not about to delve into cleaning up our firefighting maelstrom. And I was in no mood to be otherwise productive.

Henry came over and yanked me to my feet. His pull was so forceful that I was launched forward further than I think he intended, compelling me to brace myself on his muscular pectoral and quickly back away.

"You have soot on your face." He reached a hand up to wipe the soot from my cheek, but I pulled away before he could make contact.

Don't get close, Monti.

"I think I'll go grab a quick shower. Meet you back at the theater?" I didn't look back on my way out. *He's probably offended.*

"Me too."

Crap, he's right behind me.

"Showers, then *Star Wars*."

I nodded as I walked quicker than usual, trying to stay ahead of Henry. *I should've known that wouldn't work. He can walk at a snail's pace and pass me. So much awkward.*

When I finally made it to the shower, the events in the house washed over and engulfed me as the water poured over me; I couldn't make sense of what my captors wanted from me. *What's the point? Why me? Why Henry? Why these circumstances, this nonsensical place?*

I had to push it from my mind if our movie marathon was to have the relaxing effect it was intended to. So, I put on some comfy jeans and a faded t-shirt, tied my hair back, and did my damndest to lock it all away in the darkest recesses of my mind.

11204621

Squeaky clean and in the theater, I hoped Henry had forgotten my weirdness in the larder. I was so laser-focused on that fact that I almost didn't catch Henry's odd body language while we were picking out theater candy and drinks at the glittering bar at the back of the theater. "What are you doing?"

"Me? Nothing." He was standing at the edge of the bar, puffing out his chest, looking oddly like an animal trying to make himself look larger before a battle.

I kept picking through the curiously vast array of theater candy, peering at Henry out of the corner of my eye. "You're acting very strange. What's wrong with you?"

He let out a deep sigh, dropped his shoulders, and stepped toward the candy bar to grab a box of Jr. Mints. "I was trying to block your view of the blood stain covering the entirety of that aisle. I didn't want that trauma to darken the day." His head drooped. I'd foiled his plan.

I giggled a little and slapped his ridiculously large shoulder. "Don't worry. This whole house is one giant trauma. This room is no different. I'm fine."

With our snacks and drinks in hand and the blood stain out of sight, we debated over the virtues of the different seats available in the theater, landing on the center middle row, of course. The awkwardness slowly dissolved, and I relaxed into my seat.

As before, the theater had responded automatically upon our entry. The lush red velvet curtain had parted, revealing the descending screen behind it, and a catalog of films and television shows had appeared. Henry found palm-sized tablet remotes at each seat to make our selection. We goofed around genially, trying to navigate simultaneously and purposefully irritate one another. It was a trivial bit of fun after the stress of the last couple of days.

We did find *Star Wars* among the vast array of options, and I didn't know if he truly thought *Episode IV* was the best place from which to launch his marathon, but that's where we began, and we binged for the remainder of the day.

"What a great way to skive off."

He sounds happy with our marathon, but what in the world is he talking about?

"What?" *Is that something crass?*

"To skive. You call it playing hooky."

"Yes. A great skive." He laughed at me and settled into his seat. *I'm saying it wrong. I give up.*

We filled up on popcorn and candy, forgetting about lunch and dinner altogether. I felt sick, but it was worth it. We talked through every single film we watched. I can honestly say I talked more through those movies than I'd talked in the previous few months combined. I didn't even detest the abundance of conversation. *What is happening?*

We didn't come close to finishing all the movies. There weren't enough hours in the day. It's called a marathon for a reason. At some point in the wee hours of the night, Henry woke me to suggest I go and sleep in a bed. I was not so polite in letting him know I had been perfectly content sleeping right where I was. I may have called him a jackass. Truthfully, I don't remember. He probably meant well, but I was tired.

He was a gentleman and walked me into my room. I dropped on the bed, still clothed, and watched through one drooping eye as he walked out the door.

This could have been worse.

As soon as the thought traipsed through my mind, I knew it was crazy, but it was also true.

Henry makes all of this eminently more manageable. The sad thing is, I doubt he can say the same about me. I probably make it harder on him. Maybe I can be a better cellmate. It might just kill me to try.

DAY 4

Bones

I need to put something over that window.

Must. Sleep. In.

11206514

I pulled the covers over my head and groaned. *No use. I'm up.* Having surrendered, I began my day—spiritless as I followed the rhythms of my morning, realizing I'd seemed to have developed a routine in my concrete incarceration.

"How long will this last?" I whimpered. *This cannot become my life.*

Making my way toward the coffee pot, I ruminated on my routine predicament, assuming Henry was still asleep. After all, we were up inordinately late, and his room didn't have an inescapable twelve-foot sunrise wake-up call.

At the kitchen counter, I struggled to enjoy my imitation coffee sludge—not because of the flavor or texture, though drinking a semi-solid was a hurdle in the process, but because of a rhythmic clanking sound reverberating throughout the house. I closed my eyes, earnestly trying not to wonder what it was. Wondering about things in that house had become hazardous to my health. I determined to sit at the counter and drink my sludge, deliberately not finding out what the racket was.

Clank. Pause. Clank. Pause. Clank.

I can't take it. What is that man up to? I followed the metallic sound that made my teeth ache and tracked it out of the kitchen and into the conservatory. It echoed throughout the massive chamber, making it hard to pin down which hall it was coming from. I poked my head down each corridor off the curved garden wall and discovered that it was coming from the gym, almost directly across from the kitchen hall.

Leaning in the doorway, I sipped my coffee, watching and waiting to be noticed. He was on some machine I didn't recognize—the only gym equipment I ever used was a treadmill. From the looks of it, he was lifting more weight than that of a full-grown adult, maybe two. I couldn't be certain; it was not my element, and even if it were, the machines were too antique for me to recognize.

I idled in the doorway, sipped, and watched in fascination. The clank was the weights coming down after he lifted them. But it wasn't loud because he dropped them; he set them down in a completely controlled manner. They were loud because they were just that heavy. One last clank, and he sat up.

"Yes?" The word stretched like taffy being pulled, suggesting he had known I'd been watching for some time.

"I can't believe you are up this early, and I'm astounded that you're working out. Honestly, what is with you?" It came out far more accusatory than I intended.

I need to recover.

"Seriously, if ever there was an excuse to slack off, being in this place is the mother of all excuses."

At least he smiled at that. *I haven't completely offended him.*

"Routine helps me. It calms me, gives me focus. It provides space to think and gives me a sense that the world isn't completely spiraling out of control."

Ironic, given my rumination on routine this morning. I snorted. My scoff did not go over well. *Crap, there goes that eyebrow again. I seriously can't breathe without offending him.*

"I didn't . . . I meant . . . Ugh."

Sometimes, I wish people could hear my intentions rather than my words. I closed my eyes in an attempt at a do-over while Henry chuckled at my obvious struggle. I offered an awkward smile. "I was thinking about routine this morning, and it bothers me that we've been here long enough that I was developing one. That's why I . . . Ugh."

"It's okay. But I wonder what's going on inside your head sometimes. I think you must have captivating thoughts to share, but you keep them all to yourself."

He gave me a charming side-glance that I was sure I'd seen in one of his movies. *Which one?*

"I don't. Truly. I'm a painfully boring person. Nothing to tell." *Keep the curiosity to a minimum. Is he buying it?*

"Tosh. I find that hard to believe. But I'll leave it alone. For now." He smiled again.

That smile reeks of mischief. Time to change the subject.

"You said that routine gives you a chance to think. Did you happen to think up a plan to get us out of here? It's been a nifty visit back to the '60s; you're a lovely person and all, but I'm ready to go home now." Henry put a towel around his neck, moved to the next piece of equipment, and began setting it up.

"I have not managed to find an escape route in the few hours since I awoke." He slid an enormous black metal weight onto a long pole perched over a bench. "But I have been engrossed in a few thoughts." The towel slipped off his neck as he bent over to pick up another large metal weight with white letters imprinted on the side that read "45 lbs" on the top and "20.41 kg" on the bottom. "They aren't complete yet, and I don't think I'm ready to share."

He turned his back to me and loaded even more weights onto the bar. *How much weight can you possibly lift? Come on, Henry, we have escaping to do.* I was having none of it. I set my coffee mug on the padded floor, maneuvered over to the bench, and sat on top of the bar he'd overloaded with weights. Henry was unimpressed. By the look of him, he could have lifted me right along with the bar and the weights. For a moment, he seemed to consider the option. Thankfully, he opted not to. Instead, he picked up his water bottle and leaned against the next machine over. I hopped off my provocative perch and sat against the wall to listen.

Henry took a reluctant breath while he collected his thoughts. *You never speak until you have every word in place exactly where you want it, do you? Never afraid to let silence hang excessively and uncomfortably in a room. Get to it!*

"Two things essentially. The first is this house, how it's set up. It isn't sitting right with me. I can't figure out who built this place, or why, or even when. And the supply situation. They have us set up so we could live here for several years. The food, the household goods, even enough books and films to keep us occupied and a gym to keep us healthy." He gestured around the room. "It's unnerving. But that isn't the only thing that's bothering me.

"I've been thinking about why we were taken. I don't think it was for financial gain—they can't access our accounts. So, I considered why, out of everyone in the world, select us in particular? A variety of things crossed my mind, and it struck me how opposite we are from each other."

He's so distant. He isn't even talking to me, really; he's kind of looking past me. What are you looking at?

"I don't follow." My interruption pulled his focus back to me, and his eyes met mine intensely, rather uncomfortably.

"Well, on a fundamental level, we're opposite genders. Expanding on that, we're opposite builds. You're what? Five-one, maybe two, slender? And I'm—"

"Hercules?" I interrupted.

He smirked and continued. "It goes beyond the physical. You've mentioned that you live life in solitude. You work from home and avoid contact with society at large. On the other hand, I spend almost every waking moment with people. More than that, I spend most of that time in front of a camera; my life transmitted to the masses. What I don't willingly broadcast is sometimes captured without my consent and circulated by the media.

"You and I live our lives in contrasting ways. We live on opposite sides of the globe. We have markedly different professions. I think if we talked, we'd find that we grew up differently, too. I have three brothers; I'm willing to venture a guess that you don't."

I didn't answer. My face was affirmation enough. *Sorry, Henry, this is not a therapy session where I spill about being an only child.*

"You, at some point, were married; I never have been. The list is probably longer if we took the time to explore it."

"I don't understand how this relates to why we're here." *What are you rambling about?*

"You said yesterday that in the vent, you felt like a rat in a maze. I think you were on to something. This whole house, the way it's set up, the way we were dropped here, the camera, the lack of a ransom, the choice of you and me. I think it's a kind of diabolical social experiment. And someone is out there watching to see how we react to the various stimuli." He held his breath and nervously tugged at the bandage on his hand, waiting to see how I took the revelation.

I stared back vacantly, not entirely knowing how to take it. I wanted to deny the possibility and storm off, yell that it couldn't be true. *That's what one of those wispy women in one of Henry's movies would do, isn't it? I can't do that. It makes sense. Doesn't it? Not that anything in this place makes sense.*

"What the hell am I supposed to do with that?" It wasn't a response I was proud of, but it was the best I could do under the circumstances.

"I . . . I don't know. I haven't finished processing it myself. If you'll recall, I didn't want to tell you in the first place. Don't blame me because you were being pushy." He tilted his head down and looked at me through furrowed eyebrows.

I deserve that.

I leaned over the long bar Henry had loaded with weights and stretched my back. It felt good with all the tension I was keeping in my shoulders and neck. So, I stretched my injured leg out behind me in a shallow lunge and reached both arms across the bar until my fingertips touched the large, heavy discs at each end. Stretching my shoulders and back even further, I released an exhausted sigh, "Ugh! What are we gonna do?!"

As I stretched and moaned over our situation, the weights shifted in response to my touch. Henry hadn't secured them because I hadn't allowed him to finish placing all his weights on the bar. One by one, they slowly slipped off the ends. I let my head roll to the side to observe the weights as they finished sliding to the ground. I made no effort to stop them. I was not risking injury; they looked remarkably heavy.

Hmm. "Hey, those look completely solid. Are they?"

Henry squinted at me. "I suppose so. Why?"

"Because I think we can bust out of here. You know, a jailbreak." That was the point I'm sure Henry became convinced I'd officially lost my mind. He was too polite to say so, but his face spoke volumes.

"Uh-huh. How do you plan to do that?" He eyed me incredulously, but I wasn't going to let his reservation squelch my enthusiasm.

"Grab one of these and follow me!" I slapped one of the larger weights on my way out of the gym. It was almost two feet across and two inches thick, a forty-five-pound one. I knew I couldn't carry it, but Henry could. He grabbed it with one hand and followed me as I practically skipped across the conservatory and down the larder hall—lucky I didn't sprain my ankle in the process.

In the larder, the lights came on automatically, same as they always had. Well, all but one light that only flickered after the fire and the one that had completely stopped working. *Whatever. It doesn't matter; we're going home!*

I raced past the fire mess on the right—it reeked of burnt plastic—and headed straight to the back wall. I smiled proudly, my feet and arms outstretched at the emancipating concrete wall before me. I knew it was our means of escape. Henry stood behind me with the massive weight balanced on his shoulder, waiting for a revelation.

"Yes?" He was looking for more of a big reveal than I had provided.

"Don't you see? The larder walls, the floor, the ceiling, they're all concrete. I'd been searching for a sledgehammer or some kind of tool to break through the wall, but I couldn't find one. That weight is large and heavy enough, and you're strong enough to wield it. We can break through the concrete wall and make a hole to get out."

I was ecstatic. *We're finally going to escape. It might take a while, and it might be like tunneling out of prison with a spoon. But we will get out of here.* I was so happy I was shaking.

Henry, predictably, was completely still and thoughtful; he could be infuriatingly calm. *Why can't you just celebrate the win?* "Since you're the muscle of the operation, I'll let you contemplate without getting in your way." I knew if I didn't leave the room, I'd get antsy and drive him nuts. And watching him stand there silently staring at concrete was going to drive me nuts. I left to refill my coffee and grab a pear from the tree.

At the dining room table, I sat down haphazardly and almost missed the rigid pleather seat. I caught it with the edge of my injured thigh and jumped up, cringing in pain. Then I remembered I needed to sit, hanging half on and half off the seat.

I leaned back in my pleather chair with a squeak and watched two bucks spar in the distance of the fabricated landscape. I fought off the idea that it wasn't real and tried to embrace the tranquil scenery and allow it to calm me. I had almost reached a placid mental space when I heard a commotion in the kitchen behind me.

What now?

I moved too quickly, twisting out of my chair to see what Henry was up to, and I pinched my bad thigh against the edge of the chair. The shooting pain forced me to slam my coffee down on the table, chipping the bottom of my mug. I gingerly leaned forward to ease myself out of the chair before I dragged my sorry self into the kitchen to see what chaos was brewing.

Henry was rummaging through every drawer he could find. I knew the kitchen was oversized, but I didn't truly understand how much it contained until every drawer was open and he'd completely expelled the contents onto the counters.

"What on earth are you looking for?" *I'm afraid to ask.*

"Aha!" A heavy metal meat mallet waved in victory over Henry's head before he charged back toward the larder as though I didn't exist.

Intriguing; who cares if he's ignoring me. I abandoned my coffee and half-eaten pear to follow Henry on his mission.

"Wait for me. What are you doing with the mallet?" *Mountains of furniture and now a meat mallet . . . His escape engineering borders on fun; I am not missing this.*

I found him at the back of the larder with the meat mallet in one hand and the disc weight in the other. "What on earth are you doing?" *I have so many questions.*

Without answering, he placed one corner of the spiky side of the meat mallet up against the wall and held the handle with his right hand. He grabbed the weight with his left, pulled it up to his shoulder, and heaved it down onto the mallet. *Is he left-handed? Huh. I hadn't noticed that before now.* Small chunks of concrete chipped away under the blow. The anticipation of progress vibrated through me.

"Woohoo!" I jumped up and down.

Henry twisted back toward me, eyebrow raised. "It's naught but a small chunk."

"I'm sorry, I got carried away with our progress." I clasped both hands over my mouth, breathlessly waiting for the next blow.

"Progress? It's a tiny piece of concrete." He held up a pebble between his mammoth thumb and index finger for dramatic effect. "We have no idea if this will accomplish anything. Or if I can keep this up for any length of time. I don't want to be a pessimist, just realistic."

You're right. Again. Ugh, you seriously drive me up a wall. But at the moment, all I want are those herculean arms of yours to start swinging again. Get to it, Herc.

"You can do it!" I opted for cheerleader, jumping and waving my arms like a college senior holding imaginary pom-poms. If I couldn't wield the weapons of destruction, maybe I could motivate the man who could.

Henry lost his grip on the weight in an effort to hide his laughter. *Cheerleader was never my strong suit.* I didn't motivate; I was more of a distraction. Henry missed the mallet entirely, and a familiar clank rang through the larder. He'd hit the wall because he was laughing at my cheerleading efforts.

In order to catch his breath, he sat on the floor, arms over his knees, the meat mallet in one hand, and his other hand over his mouth. When his eyes caught mine, his expression changed from one of amusement to one of a kid with his hand caught in a cookie jar, slowly backing it out. Priceless to see on an adult's face; it was all I could do to keep a straight face.

"Sorry." He cleared his throat, pursed his lips, and stood back up as though I'd given him a scolding when I had done nothing but meet his eye.

Guilty conscience?

"Back to it then, shall we?"

He gathered his tools and went back to chipping away at the wall. I retrieved my pear from the kitchen in a new effort to avoid being a distraction. Henry made slow but steady progress, and I tried not to get excited, but it wasn't easy.

"So, why are you using the meat mallet with the weight? Isn't the weight heavy enough to break through the concrete?" The pear wasn't working. I simply waved it around as I talked. *I can't help it; I'm dying to know. What's with the meat mallet?*

"Well," he grunted between heaves. "The weight provides a great deal of force." He swung again; more chips flew. "But it's blunt." One more swing and Henry put his tools down, opting for a water break. "We're trying to break through concrete. Blunt force may work over time, but I only have so much energy to supply before I'm worn out. I want to use it as efficiently as possible. If I can focus the force of the blow onto a smaller space"—he tapped his finger on the pointy corner of the mallet—"all the force of the weight will be focused on that one spot. Same amount of work, greater result."

"Wow, is that another secret skill you learned before getting into the film industry?" *You are full of surprises.*

"No, that I learned from a role, Doctor Joseph Adams, engineering physicist. I played him in the psychological thriller, *Schrödinger's Parents*. He waved the mallet in victory as though he were once again Doctor Adams, the engineering physicist. "But I don't usually pick up MacGyver skills from films."

He picked up his tools and resumed hammering away. It looked like it would take a while, so I provided plenty of water, swept up debris, and made a hearty lunch. It wasn't the same as Henry's cooking, but he accepted it graciously.

It took hours to chisel away a twelve-inch circle that was fairly shallow. *Will it go faster once we break through to the outside? The wall will be weaker once we at least have a small hole all the way through.*

Breaking through to the outside? I can hardly contain myself.

Henry, on the other hand, didn't appear to have his hopes up in the least. After lunch, he sat resting, eyes closed, his head nestled in his arms on the table.

Hercules deserves the break.

I went to the gym and got one of the small five-pound weights to give it a try for myself. Maybe I could make some progress of my own while Henry closed his eyes for a minute after his morning labours. I positioned the mallet as I'd seen Henry do all morning, lifted my petite weight, and swung with all my might. I braced myself for the blow, but I was not ready for the shooting pain it sent down my hip and thigh, reminding me that I had been working hard to ignore that pain all day. I set my jaw and decided to ignore it and move forward with my task.

My dent was paltry compared to Henry's, but a few concrete crumbs bounced their way to the floor. My shoulders straightened, and my chest puffed with my contribution. I may have picked the smallest weight, but it was still challenging to swing, at least for me.

I wailed at the mallet and chipped at the center of Henry's excavation. I'm not sure how, with all the noise, but he must have nodded off at the table. He hadn't returned after lunch, and I'd been working for over an hour when my concrete chips started to change in consistency. *The concrete isn't holding together at the back of the wall.* I shifted the mallet to the edge of the hole and chipped away a little more. *Something isn't right.*

Henry finally joined me in the back of the larder. "Your leg! Get off your leg!" I flinched at his piercing, overreacting tone.

What's he so worked up about? It hurts, but I've been walking on it for two days.

"Henry, it's okay. It doesn't feel great, but I'm okay. I can do this." I kept swinging. Henry came up behind me and swiped his hand across my wound. "Ow, Henry! That DOES hurt!"

He thrust his fingers between my face and the wall; they were covered in blood. I turned to face him as he pulled his bloodied hand away. His eyes were wide, but his voice had returned to its former, irritatingly low and steady tone. "Your leg."

It took me a second to realize why I might have been bleeding. "Oh. Oh! I hit the chair wrong earlier. Don't worry about it." I dismissed the problem entirely. "It's fine. Look at this; something is weird over here." I turned back to show him the changes to the hole in the wall, but Henry was too distracted by my bloody jeans to look at the debris. Then he inexplicably walked away.

I continued to poke at the wall. The tricky part was that I was blocking the light, so it was hard to tell what I was looking at. I kept hitting the wall, but it wasn't chipping anymore. *What is going on?*

Henry reappeared with his hands full. "Hey, can you look at this, please?" *I need his help.*

A firm "no" puffed over my shoulder, then he squatted and proceeded to slice through the back of my jeans.

"What the hell are you doing?!" I pulled away from the scissors, fumbled, and almost dropped my tools.

"Take it easy. They're white jeans, stained with blood—completely ruined. You've torn your stitches. You weren't going to stop working to let me fix it; I'm improvising."

You aren't wrong. The words "thank you" began to form on my lips but never made it out. Before I could speak, I felt hydrogen peroxide pour down the back of my leg, and I lurched forward. *That's the end of that thankful thought.*

He fished a broken stitch out of my flesh, and I braced myself against the wall. "You can't flex the muscle. You're pulling the wound open."

I was ready to smack him, but I kicked the wall instead. "What am I supposed to do then?" *Are you serious right now?*

"Try to relax. I'll work as quickly as possible."

You're joking, right?

I rested my forehead against the wall and tried to leave my leg dangling. He set to work restitching; I hated that part. I punched the hole in the wall with my right fist to distract from the pain. It didn't feel as hard as I'd expected. I turned my head to look at it.

"Don't move." Henry's irritation escalated. "Almost there. Okay. Done!"

I stretched my neck, tilting my head side to side. My muscles had clenched because of the stitching.

Without anesthetic.

Again.

When I was through, my head was so close to the wall that my nose was practically buried in the hole we'd created. It smelled . . . earthy. Almost loamy.

I reached my hand in and brought a fistful of debris into the light. "Henry, look at this." He interrupted his cleanup efforts and indulged me.

"That isn't right. Concrete is gray. That is brown." We both stared at the mound in my palm. He poked at it with a bloody index finger. "That isn't concrete; it's dirt." Henry looked back at the hole and scraped more out of the wall.

"What do you mean, it's dirt? Why is there dirt in the wall?

"Scratch that. Don't answer."

I know why.

I just don't want it to be true.

It can't be true.

I closed my eyes and willed it away. But when I opened them, another fistful of dirt spilled from the hole onto the floor.

This is worse than the vent. Worse than the cameras. Worse than the ceiling in the conservatory.

Henry looked at me in commiseration and solace. All the air left my lungs. I backed to the wall and slid to the floor next to the piles of burnt debris. My brand-new stitches resting in a pile of ash. *It doesn't matter. I don't care.*

"Okay. It's okay. That's just this wall. It's not every wall. It's only this one. Clearly, they built this building into the side of a hill. That's all. We have to try the other side of the house. Or . . .

"I know! We have to try the ceiling. Let's try the ceiling!" I popped up off the floor, vaulted out of the corner, and climbed the closest shelving unit still standing after the fire, mallet and small weight in hand. Henry looked worried, but he didn't try to stop me. He rushed over and steadied the shelves as I scaled them like a lunatic.

I will not be defeated.

It was a good thing I'd scrambled up shelves topped with the few paper goods we had left. I swept the top shelf free of rolls of toilet paper and paper towels, satisfied that nothing would shatter or hurt Henry when it toppled down on top of him. It was liberating, clearing it off.

Standing on the top tier of the shelf, the smooth concrete ceiling was mere inches over my head, an awkward angle to work at, but I didn't care. I had some rage to work out, and I'd had a productive way to do it. I raised the mallet and the weight, and I pounded into the ceiling. Even though I made progress initially, it was much harder to wield heavy tools over my head than at a wall. I wore out quickly; my wrist hurt because the weight was heavy, and my leg and ass hurt because of my ridiculous wounds. I barely made a dent before I couldn't lift my tools anymore.

While I wailed at the ceiling, I didn't notice Henry reconstructing part of his ladder of terror in the larder. The shelving system wasn't sturdy enough to hold his weight, but his improvised scaffolding just might do the trick. He climbed up next to me the moment I stopped swinging. I couldn't lift my arms one more time. Without a word, he took the mallet from my hand and picked up right where I left off.

Thank you.

13071962

We took more breaks working on the ceiling than we had with the wall, and the hole was narrower, but by dinner, we'd gotten a slightly deeper crevasse than the wide hole we made in the wall. *Is that a good sign or bad?* Either way, Henry suggested we break for a meal, and I was too tired to object.

"Freeze-dried meat or pasta?"

He's tempting fate. I haven't told him that my grandmother was Italian. She'd roll over in her grave if she knew I was eating boxed pasta and astronaut meat. Everything in her kitchen was always gloriously fresh. Oh, the smells that wafted . . .

Stop it, Monti!

"Well, it's the only box that survived the fire; let's live a little; how about pasta? I'll forgive the jarred sauce if you get fresh basil from the garden." He smiled and started for the garden without complaint while I grabbed a pot to fill with water. "Wait!" I yelled before he was out of earshot, and he poked his head back into the kitchen. "I just remembered, there's poison ivy creeping through the herb bed. Be careful."

"I've noticed. Boy Scouts." He saluted me with pride and ducked back out the door.

As I filled the pot with water, I considered the oddity of an invasive plant like that taking root in an indoor herb garden. *Not likely.* I strayed back to the nursery my mother, Mary, owned when I was a child—*probably still owns, not that we've kept up.* A horticulturist by trade, she seemed to know everything about plants, even if she knew nothing about raising a child. *I wish I had paid more attention.*

I finally realized what was so odd about the flowers growing at the back of the conservatory and cut in vases in the crypt. *They're all poison.* Before that moment, I hadn't connected the dots; people don't tend to cultivate poisonous plants.

Mary had kept an oversized, creepy, hardcover book under the counter at the nursery. I would read it after school sometimes when I was bored and lonely. It had warnings and treatments for poisonous plants if children or animals touched or consumed them. All the decorative plants in the conservatory had appeared in that book. The black flowers and berries were part of the belladonna plant, nightshade. It causes paralysis of the heart.

One of the white flowers I finally recognized as snakeroot. That was the plant that killed Abraham Lincoln's mother. It was so toxic that people were known to die from drinking the milk from cows that grazed upon it. *What in the world is it doing here?*

The other white flower was hemlock. *Hemlock!* The plant that infamously killed Socrates. An amateur gardener would recognize the oleander, but they might not know it can cause a coma and even death if consumed. Then, there was the castor bean bush. Farmers grow it to make castor oil, but you can also use the bean to make ricin.

What the hell?

What kind of person grows deadly plants and flowers for . . . What? . . . cutting them to leave in memoriam by people's tombs?

Lost in my thoughts, water spilled over the rim of the pot I was filling. *This house makes my head spin.* I emptied the excess water and put the pot on the gas burner, squatting to examine the ancient dials on the lemon-yellow stove top. They were completely foreign. *I miss my modern amenities.*

Okay, I can do this. Looks like I'm supposed to turn on the gas and light it by hand. So, where's the lighter?

"Hey! Monti!" Henry shouted from the conservatory.

What now?

"Monti! Come here."

Choices. Either follow Henry down the rabbit hole and find something inevitably disturbing or continue to figure out how to light the antique stove. Starting another fire doesn't seem especially appealing. I vote for Henry's distressing revelation.

14195273

Well, he's not in the conservatory.

"Monti." I heard him call again and looked around to gauge which hall his voice came from. The steel door to the crypt was open again.

"Don't go in there!" I shouted and waved my arms tightly in front of me as I ran toward the door.

"Come here. Have you seen this?" He sounded fascinated.

He's certifiable.

I stayed safely plastered against the wall outside the door. "I've seen that. Thank you. I am not going in again. Get out here! Shut the door!" The last place I wanted to be was in a crypt.

Henry stepped out and spoke softly. He bordered on patronizing; he was lucky—for his own personal safety—that he didn't cross the line. "I know this isn't the most pleasant room in the house. And I know I didn't believe you before. I am genuinely sorry. I apologize. However, I do think that looking around in here could give us some insight into the people who took us and into what is going on here."

He's trying to appeal to my rational side. Why does my rational side have to win?

"Fine. I'm not staying long." I entered, happy neither with the situation nor Henry's ability to talk me into it.

Stepping into the room again was equally as chilling as the first time. I looked around, taking in the dark void of the frigid concrete space. Henry had to duck for the low ceiling. It seemed like a habit, one he'd done so often that he didn't realize he did it anymore.

Someone had been in the crypt since I'd entered the first day. The book had been moved and propped up in front of the crypt wall, dead center in front of the graves, but still on the floor. I was frozen in place at the idea of our captor walking around without us knowing. Henry hadn't noticed the book yet, and I wasn't ready to bring it up.

He brushed his fingers over the foliage in one of the vases. "They're so fresh. I thought they were fake." I cringed.

Careful. I connected the flowers with the book and the dead bodies whose graves they adorned. I had to tell Henry. "They aren't just flowers; they're poison." I winced.

When Henry looked back at me, I eyed the book on the floor propped against a grave marker. I didn't want the reminder, but he needed to read—to understand—what we were dealing with. He opened the book and read aloud in his deep British baritone, making it noticeably worse than the first time:

> "And to take another life was, in many ways, the greatest expression of what it meant to be alive."[4]

Henry carefully set the book on the floor right where he had found it and focused his attention on the crypt wall. He had a remarkably placid calm that I thought it wise to mirror despite my growing trepidation.

He focused on the left and read the brass plates affixed the slabs. James 1968–2011. Hector 1973–2016. Phillip 1954–2003. Henry read one, and then I read one, alternating; we read the markers in no particular order. We tried to be respectful. Then . . .

"Oh, my goodness. Henry, look." I inhaled sharply and covered my mouth.

Henry came over and read the etching for me. "Mom 1947–1998." Then he pointed to the one next to it.

"Oh, man." I read that one. "Dad 1945–1998."

"'To take another life.' That's it. I have to get out of here." I scrambled out of the room, shouting back at Henry, "Forget dinner. I'm digging us out."

Henry chased after me, catching up in three long strides immediately outside the door. He grabbed my arm, but I twisted out of his grasp.

"Don't touch me!"

He stepped back and offered an "I surrender" gesture, both hands up. I stopped by the bench, barely willing or even able to listen; my arms were folded defensively. I was ready to bolt at any moment.

Henry began with the posture of a trainer herding a feral animal. "I understand that this is a nightmare. It is for me, too. But skipping supper to engage in hard physical labor on top of emotional distress is not the answer. You need to feed your body if you are to keep your strength up, and you need to give your mind something else to dwell on if you intend not to go insane. Quick supper, a little distracting conversation, and we'll get right back to it. You'll feel better, I promise."

He looked at me questioningly. Not knowing if I'd accept his reasoning. Frankly, neither did I. I walked across the conservatory, waiting to see if I would turn down the hall toward the larder or continue on toward the kitchen.

I surprised myself when I passed the larder hall and opted for dinner. I was physically and emotionally drained. *Henry's right. That's getting old.*

Looking over my shoulder, I noticed that he wasn't behind me. Henry had stopped to pick up the basil that I assumed he dropped when the crypt door had opened. Then he milled about the garden to pick a perfect mix of vegetables for a salad. *How much of his life has he spent in the kitchen?*

We made dinner. Though, I can't say I made much of a contribution. How hard is it to boil pasta? Then we sat down to our meal, accompanied by a rather nice bottle of cabernet and coated head to toe in concrete dust—like a haunted house that had been abandoned for a hundred years. The layer was so thick that Henry's ink-black hair was virtually white. We went to great lengths not to get any in our pasta and salad, but I don't know why. We'd ingested and inhaled more concrete dust throughout the day than the FDA or OSHA recommends, so what harm could it possibly have done to our food?

"You clearly have a talent in the kitchen, don't you?" *I have to give credit where credit is due.*

"I grew up cooking with my mum." The smile Henry developed as he invoked her memory was sweetly endearing.

"Aw. Do you get to cook often?" He cocked his head, visibly surprised I had asked a probing question.

"Careful, Monti, I might be inclined to think personal questions are fair game." I pulled back, rethinking my strategy. "I'm toying with you. Conversation isn't quid pro quo." He smiled impishly.

This will come back to haunt me, won't it?

"I do cook. For myself and friends mostly, but I've cooked for a girlfriend from time to time." He took a long, slow sip of wine, eyeing me over the rim of his royal blue-tinted wine glass, waiting to see if I would take the bait. I didn't ask outright, but I waved him on as I sipped my own wine. He seemed pleased that he'd captured my interest.

"I'm baiting you. There's nothing to tell, honestly. I've had somewhat serious relationships here and there, but I've never met anyone I ever considered marrying. I guess I just haven't met 'The One.'" I scowled at his last comment. I probably should have tried harder to keep my opinion off my face, but I absolutely could not.

"What?" My face had given me away, and now he wanted my opinion.

I hesitated. *Opening my mouth will ruin this perfectly good meal.*

He stretched his arm out across the table, palm up, making a "come here" motion. "Out with it."

I sighed and gave in. *What's the use fighting? He'll win eventually, anyway.* "Well, if you must know, you travel the world, you meet more people in a year than most people meet in a lifetime, and you genuinely can't find one single person you think is worth committing to? That strikes me as unlikely. Do you think you might be a tad picky or slightly unrealistic?"

I vomited my answer on him. I've never been good at conversing with people. And I was long out of practice.

I have to stop talking. "Forget about it. I take it back. I'm going back to work." I stood to clear the table.

"No. No, it's okay. I probably am being unrealistic." He motioned me to sit back down, and reluctantly, I acquiesced. "The truth is the person I'm waiting for may not exist. But I have to keep looking."

Curious. As he spoke, he wiped his palms on his cargos as though they were sweaty, and he looked at the floor. *I guess I hit a nerve.*

"We don't have to talk about this." I tried to give him an out. I didn't want him to be uncomfortable. I was uncomfortable for him.

"I don't mind. I've never actually talked about this with anyone besides my mum."

What? Why, then, tell me of all people?

He went on, "I wasn't particularly popular in secondary school. I didn't have a lot of dates. Any dates, in fact. I was shy and awkward; I was a nerd." An uncertain smile accompanied his last comment. I laughed internally at the idea of a shy and awkward version of the intrepid, self-assured, Oscar-winning star that sat before me. But as he spoke, the shy little boy seeped through. His posture sank, and his tone became increasingly unsure. "School was painful. There came a point when I wanted to be someone else—anyone else. That's when I discovered acting. I suppose that's a story for another time.

"Back to the topic at hand. When I was fifteen, I made a list of the qualities of the perfect girl so I wouldn't bemoan those who had rejected me." My heart broke for teenage Henry and for all those who had missed out on such an extraordinary guy. "I still have the list tucked away in my wallet." His hand absently brushed a pocket at the knee of his cargo pants. "The qualities I was looking for then still apply today. I'd rather be alone than settle." He tipped his head to one side and hunched over the table for another sip of wine.

What do I say to that? I'm certainly not going to venture any advice, and I don't dare ask more questions.

"Wow." It came out far more affected than I intended. *I have to recover. What do I say? What can I say?*

"So, you were a nerd, huh?" I tried to sound nonchalant. "I don't see it." Henry smiled back, and the tension eased.

"Fundamentally, it's about being seen." The satisfied expression on his face told me he thought he'd explained everything.

"Huh?"

"The women I meet, in the circles I run in. They . . . " He trailed off, searching for the right words. "People seem more interested in Henry Walker Beecher: Oscar-winning actor. The reality of Henry: mere mortal, tends to disappoint."

What is that supposed to mean? "I don't understand." I set my glass down and leaned on the table, trying to discern what he was getting at.

"I suppose I'm waiting for someone who can see . . . me. Just Henry." He shrugged. "Without the awards, and the films, and the cameras. Only me. Accept and want that." His shoulders drooped, and he picked up his glass again, staring at the garnet liquid as he swirled.

"Why would anyone prefer all the flash and pomp over getting to know the real you? It doesn't make sense." *You're much more than an action star.* "The Henry I've gotten to know here is far more interesting than anything you'd find on the cover of a magazine."

He looked up, tilted his head, and smiled as if he'd learned something about me that I didn't yet know about myself. I shifted in my seat, altogether uncomfortable.

I took the last sip of my wine and cleared plates from the table, removing myself from the awkward potential of conversation.

Once the dishes were clean and dried, we went back to attacking the ceiling. We kept to our pattern of trading out as we got tired, and after a couple hours of work, we'd reached a depth of about six inches.

Henry put down his tools and examined our results. "We should probably rest for the evening. I don't think we'll break through tonight, and we want to have enough energy to get a decent amount of work done tomorrow." We left everything there to pick up working in the morning and walked out of the larder side by side.

I'm so tired I could fall asleep right here. But I hate sleeping in this place; it gives me nightmares. Maybe I can coax some company out of him.

I jogged ahead and turned to walk backward. "The sun has barely set, so it's still early in the evening, a bit early to sleep. Are you ready to turn in, or are you up for a movie first?" After being isolated for so long, I was not skilled at requesting company.

Henry snapped the neck of his T-shirt, and dust puffed off him in every direction. "I'm coated in several layers of concrete, so my first order of business is a shower. But after that"—he contemplated for a moment—"sure, I'll watch a film." Smile lines creased the dust on his face.

"What?" *You're up to something.*

"Before we wound up here, I was on a promotional tour for my new spy thriller. The tour was meant to end with the summer premiere. I noticed that somehow that film was available to watch in the cinema room." He paused and side-eyed me, grinning. "What do you think?"

I stared back vacantly. "You want to watch your own movie?" *Haven't you already seen it?*

"No. Well, yes. Sort of. I mean. Why don't we have the premiere here?"

Okay, he wants to re-create an ordinary life activity in captivity. Is this weird or healthy? He seems excited, and we could use a bit of normalcy.

"Um, sure. How does a premiere work? We get cleaned up and watch the movie?"

Please don't be complicated.

"Yes, definitely showers. But we tend to dress up for a premiere. So, check your closet for an evening gown. Do you own one?"

Are you serious?

I nodded slowly in utter disbelief.

"Great, I have a tuxedo. I suppose we can forego the red carpet. I doubt the magic larder had one of those, even before the fire. I'll check it for champagne, though, and put that in the freezer for a quick chill and then see if there's anything that will work for appetizers."

This is getting to be a touch over the top for me. I need to give myself a profound attitude adjustment before I meet him back at the theater, or I will completely spoil his moment.

"Okay then. I'll grab a shower, find a gown, and meet you at the theater for showtime." I didn't sound nearly as excited as I should have, but I tried. I had to try harder.

"No. I mean, yes. I mean, get ready, but I'll pick you up at your door. We're going to do this right." He smiled and bounded back into the larder on his scavenger hunt. I shook my head, incredulous at what we were preparing for. Then again, after the week we'd had, he deserved his movie premiere, if nothing else. I needed to do everything in my power to make sure it was a good one.

16823614

After my shower, I braved the gold mirror and got my hair dry and into a dramatic updo. With long, wavy hair, it wasn't difficult to pile up on top of my head and make it look at least a little fancy. *Will Henry realize I'm overcompensating for a lack of enthusiasm?* I hesitated to admit that in the process of overcorrecting, I had actually started to enjoy myself. *I forgot this used to be fun.*

On my way into the closet, I found my favorite long dangling earrings in the jewelry hanger on the back of the closet door, exactly where I had them at home. I suppressed the nausea I felt every time I found replicas of my belongings in the closet. The thought of someone in my closet touching my things . . .

Stop it, Monti. Just stop.

I knew that if I walked to the back of the closet, I'd find several suitable evening gowns that I wore to various charity events. I pulled out the flashiest one and held it up. I'd never worn it in public, not once. I preferred simple things; I've never liked sparkles or lace. Solid colors and straight lines were more my style. It seemed like that particular gown had always been in my closet, but I couldn't remember why.

A floor-length opalescent gown with more sequins than any dress of mine should display and sections of translucent cutouts; it was so not my style. Some designer must have given it to me, hoping I'd wear it in public and be an unwitting ambassador for their brand. There was no way I'd ever purchase something so attention-grabbing.

I slipped it on and evaluated the effect in the floor-length mirror. *It does fit like a glove. It even makes me look slightly taller.* I turned to see the back. *It looks flawless. But there's so much sparkle. Exactly what you're supposed to wear to a movie premiere, right?* I looked at the front again to verify one more time. *Yep, this is the one.*

I slid into equally flashy opal stilettos and applied the vibrant red lipstick I was never brave enough to wear because it was so dramatic next to my ghostly pale skin tone and my long dark hair. But dramatic was the evening's goal.

When I pulled it all together, I flounced out of the bathroom with manufactured confidence. Henry was waiting in the hall by the bedroom door like a gentleman—patient, not hovering. I was taken aback by the sight of him—an oversized caricature image of a James Bond action figure. To date, I'd only seen him dressed casually. He was always clean-shaven and well-kept. But, wow, he cleaned up well—tuxedo, shined shoes, bow tie, and even a cummerbund. Broad shoulders, his hair perfectly placed.

Did he manscape his eyebrows? I won't dare ask.

He checked his cuff links one last time before he offered his arm. "My lady."

You certainly do know how to do this right. Don't you, Oscar?

I took his arm, and we glided down the moonlit hall. *This is strange; it feels like a date.* A surreal moment: it was the first time he truly seemed like the movie star that he was.

I don't know when or how, but it's inescapable: I am going to completely ruin this moment that is clearly important to him.

With that thought lodged in my brain, I unintentionally let out a long sigh.

"What's wrong?" It was sweet of him to ask, but that was it. I'd managed to put a damper on the evening.

We stepped onto the conservatory path, moonlight streaming down from above; it was almost magical. The stone path wasn't a recipe for success with stilettos. Henry stopped by the bench in front of the bed of raspberry bushes and let me recover my footing.

"It's nothing. I didn't mean to sigh out loud. I'm just not especially good with people. I figured that things like this must be important for you, and I'm bound to find a way to ruin it." I couldn't look him in the eye, so I tried to adjust my shoe.

He held one of my hands for stability. When I finished with my shoe, he gently held a finger under my chin until I was willing to lift my face and meet his gaze. "This? It's nothing but a bit of fun to take our minds off everything that is happening to us. It's not about me. You can't ruin it. Enjoying this film with you is the point. D'accord?" He smiled; it was genuine. It wasn't his big acting grin.

I eeked out a smile in return. "Okay." He repositioned my hand around his arm, and we continued our trek along the uneven terrain. "So, you speak French too, do you? Is there anything you can't do?"

He smiled again—"Preferiresti l'italiano?"—and winked. "We should have thought about different footwear for you. This is treacherous." He looked down as I struggled over the stone path, my free arm out for balance—about to fall over. I wanted to make a witty comment on his ridiculous and unnecessary ability with languages, but I was focused on reaching my goal.

On the whole, I'm dependable in heels, but the stones were too round and varied in size, and the conservatory too far across. Of course, I had picked the dress that was long and narrow and only had a pair of five-inch heels that matched.

My ankle turned.

"Nope, we're done," Henry decreed, dropping my arm and scooping me right up off the ground. "That's better." He carried me, jogging the last five yards across the conservatory, acting as though I weighed nothing at all.

I didn't have time to react. He had a hold of me for what was probably only seconds. But I hadn't been that close to a man—to anyone—in years. My ribcage collapsed in on my lungs. I couldn't breathe.

I need to get my bearings. I need space.

When we got to the hardwood hallway, he gently set me down and offered his arm again. "Shall we?" His smile was wide and easy. It was remarkable what a calming effect he'd grown to have on me. Calming enough to avert the panic attack I had coming on. *Incredible. I've struggled to be around people for years. I can't fathom what's different about Henry.*

In the theater, he had a sprig of oleander set aside. Henry reached to place the flower in my hair. Recognizing it from the collection of poison flowers in the conservatory, I instinctively flinched and stepped back. There was a flash of hurt on his face before he smiled and handed it to me instead. *I've done it again.* I wanted to tell him it was poison grown to memorialize murder victims in the crypt, but I couldn't think how to fit it into polite conversation. And then . . . the moment had passed.

Henry escorted me to our preferred theater seats and then returned to the back, where he retrieved the champagne he had chilling. I got a head start and navigated to his latest movie via the tablet.

"Hey!" I jumped when he snapped at me from the back of the room. He put his hand up dramatically but continued in a more soothing tone. "Not so fast. This is an experience."

I made an exaggerated gesture of putting the tablet down, giggling under my breath. *So, we are, in fact, not just here to watch a movie.*

He brought down strawberries he'd picked from the garden and two glasses of Dom Pérignon. We sat and ate while Henry regaled me with stories from premieres he'd participated in and how each was unique. He shared fun things about the industry and some of the downsides as well. *How do you manage to do that without sounding like you're complaining?*

When we'd each emptied a couple glasses of champagne and the entire bowl of strawberries, he leaned in, his eyes piercing through me. "Thank you for sharing this film with me."

Intense.

"It's an honor to watch it with you. Thank you for sharing your stories."

With that, he put away the glasses and bowl and sat back down to start the show. I'd been looking forward to the movie's release well before we got stuck in that psycho ward. *Captive Estate* was a spy thriller in which Henry played a British double agent. It wasn't clear from the trailer if he was the good guy or the bad guy, and I'd been looking forward to the revelations in store, not to mention seeing how good Henry's attempt at an American accent was. *Maybe I'll tease him about it later.*

I was fascinated to watch the movie with Henry in person. He was the kind of actor that did all his own stunts. I think that's part of what made his movies so popular. There's something about seeing an actor's face in a scene when they do something incredible as opposed to being filmed at a distance or having an obstructed view of the character because they have a stunt double. As a result, Henry's films always brought massive audiences. Action, romance, fantasy, historical drama, he had done it all. *Captive Estate* was an action flick and promised to be thrilling.

I found myself contemplating how different it was to watch the movie since getting to know Henry. *It shouldn't be different. Knowing him doesn't change the character he portrays. Yet somehow, it changes how I see that character—strange.*

I'd met actors before through the charities I worked with. I'd endured idle chitchat on more than one occasion and listened to stories I had no desire to hear in order to raise money for the causes I cared about. That never changed how I viewed any of their films. This was different.

Have we become friends? Have I, in fact, gotten to know the stranger on the screen?

I cocked my head, pondering the man beside me, the man before me, and the differences between them. *Is off-screen Henry acting more or less than I realize?*

The movie ended long before my pondering did. When I realized it, I noticed Henry standing beside me, offering his hand.

Well, this is awkward. The credits looked like they'd been rolling for a while.

How long has he been standing there? More importantly, how do I recover?

I kept my eyes fixed on the screen. "I'm sorry, my family has a tradition. My father always said that a lot of people put a great deal of effort into making a movie, so the first time I watched one, I should always pay homage to the credits and watch all the way through to the end." I held my breath, waiting to see if he had bought it.

It was true, mostly. My father did say that, and my family did try to watch all the credits. We just almost never made it. They're always so incredibly long. Unless there's bonus material.

Henry, it would seem, did buy it. He offered an interested "hmm" and settled back into his seat to watch the remainder with me.

Why did I say that? I don't want to talk about my father or my childhood. What a ridiculous way to cover up that I wasn't paying attention. I was so distracted. I don't even know how it ended. I want to know how it ended. I didn't even figure out if he was the good guy or a baddie. Now I have to sneak back in to watch it later. Ugh.

The credits ended, and the theater lights came up automatically. Henry stood again and offered his hand. I smiled, and this time I took it. "Thank you for indulging me." *Fabulous. Now, we'll have to sit through all the credits if we watch another new movie. I'm screwed.*

"Not at all; what a great tradition." We walked to the back of the theater, and Henry picked up the glasses and bottle of champagne on the way out.

"What usually happens after the movie?"

"After the film, there's usually a big do." He smiled a broad, bright smile worthy of a Crest commercial.

I giggled silently. "A what? You might have said that once before. It made no sense then either."

"A shindig . . . A party." With the bottle and two glasses gathered in one hand, he still managed to effortlessly pick me up and carry me again. I wasn't expecting it and let out a faint yelp.

"You alright?" He had jogged across the conservatory and set me down in the dining room hall before I ever had a chance to answer.

"I'm fine. I think. I just wasn't expecting to be swept off my feet like that." He chuckled at the cliché and was still laughing under his breath while he poured two more glasses of champagne. Then he disappeared for a minute; I decided not to wonder where he went. I couldn't anticipate Henry, and it wasn't worth trying anymore.

I stood by the dining room table sipping my Dom, wishing the bones in my dress weren't so long and poking at Henry's field stitching in my ass. I set down my glass and fidgeted with the dress, trying to find a more comfortable position. I contorted myself, but every angle I found seemed to poke down into the flesh of my wound and pinch the stitches and bandages worse than before. The muscle aches from working over my head weren't helping either. I had to stop, or I was going to tear a stitch loose, and I didn't want Henry repairing those stitches like he had the ones on my thigh.

He's coming. Relaxed pose, quick!

I picked up my glass and leaned against the wall, pretending that I'd been casually looking out the window. The champagne was so cold that the glass was sweating. I wiped a stripe of condensation off the side and began to play with the glass in my hand. I let it slip between my fingers until I held it by the rim.

"I haven't told you how stunning you look this evening."

The handblown tinted champagne glass slipped from between my fingers and plummeted to the floor.

It shattered.

I'm a walking catastrophe.

"Here, let me get that." He set something on the table and jogged back to the larder for the dustpan while I went to the kitchen for paper towels. I've never taken compliments well, even when I was expecting them. That one was a bomb from out of nowhere; I was completely unprepared.

By the time Henry got back, I was mopping up champagne and staring at the sad, broken stem. I stood to take the wad of soaked paper towels to the trash compactor, and as we crossed paths, I casually remarked, "See, I told you I'd find a way to ruin the evening." My attempt at humor.

With my back to Henry and the dining room, I didn't realize how seriously he had taken my comment. He followed me into the kitchen. Resting a hand on the back of my arm, he responded, "You haven't ruined anything. This has been . . . This is a perfect evening."

I was stunned. Momentarily immobilized.

His hand slid down my arm and across the outside of my hand until his hand slipped off the tip of my fingers. Then he returned to cleaning up the glass.

My social ineptitude strangled me. I touched my throat, trying to alleviate the feeling. I swallowed it; I had to.

I found a replacement champagne glass and sat at the table in awkward silence. Henry put the dustpan away and pulled a second bottle of champagne from the fridge. This time, a pink Cristal.

"I put this in to chill earlier, in case the evening went well." He was obviously proud of himself for planning ahead.

He poured it into my new glass and sat next to me. Then he slid over the lime-green box with the wide black satin ribbon, he had placed on the table when I dropped the glass. Confounded, I asked, "Where'd you find this?"

It was a box of Norman Love Confections, my favorite chocolates. Most of the things in the larder were staples, not indulgences.

To make matters more unsettling, it was my favorite of Norman's many collections.

How was it not ruined in the fire?

Henry delicately tugged at the ribbon and lifted the lid. The decadent smell of dark chocolate wafted into the air as he pulled one of the brightly colored delicacies out of the box, and offered it to me. "A magician never reveals his secrets." I could not suppress a smile at that. A line delivered so flawlessly, there was no option but to forgive him for employing one.

"Dark, fruity chocolate. Divine."

But how do they know it's my favorite? I don't want to think about it.

We finished the champagne and every last one of the chocolates, not without feeling sick to my stomach. We proved incontrovertibly, however, that Henry's stomach was lined with lead. We talked a little and laughed a little, but as the evening wore on, I knew I was getting too close.

Don't do it, Monti. You can't.

I forced myself to backpedal. I laughed a little less. I leaned back in my seat. After Henry told, yet another, delightful story that I was dying to laugh at but didn't, I stopped smiling altogether. By then, I think he knew.

When we ran out of sugar and booze, Henry stood up once again and offered his hand. This time, it was not a question. "Off to Bedfordshire."

I nodded.

"Wait. What?" *I must be drunk.*

"Time for bed," he said with a smile.

"Oh. Okay." *I am unquestionably done for the evening.* "You throw a good party, Oscar." He gave a polite chuckle. I'd had far too much champagne and leaned heavily on his arm despite my efforts to walk on my own. *I don't remember the last time I drank so much on a mostly empty stomach. Maybe college?*

We didn't even reach the threshold at the end of the hall before he scooped me off the floor again. "You aren't fit for walking."

I tried to protest, but I was simply too tired. We'd had a long day, stayed up far too late, and drank way too much. I gave in. "If you say so." I clumsily took off my heels and gestured toward the bedroom hall with my stilettos. "Home, James." I attempted my best Audrey Hepburn impersonation, but I was too intoxicated to succeed. Henry smiled down at me, and after that, I couldn't keep my eyes open. Somewhere along the route, I dropped my shoes. *I'll get those in the morning.*

Henry rested me gently in bed. "You're going to regret it if you don't change out of that." His voice was soft as he backed away.

"I don't care!" *I sound so much grumpier than I mean to. I don't care about that, either. I just need sleep.*

A satin nightgown floated down on top of my face. "In case you change your mind, Mon Bijou." His voice drifted off into the darkness, and the door closed softly behind him.

I was exhausted. *Sleeping in my clothes just this once will be okay.*

Ugh. Something is poking me. Too many sequins. Why are strapless dresses so . . . so . . . structured? Argh. He's right. Why is he always right? "Damn, that man!"

I gave up and stood to get out of the dress, but in my state of exhaustion and inebriation, it took more effort to stumble out of than it should have. I somehow managed the task, got into the satin, crawled into the bed, and drifted off into a sleep from which not even natural disaster could awaken me.

DAY 5

Broken

Ugh. My head.

27315722

Wait. This is new. Have I finally managed to sleep past dawn? What time is it?

I gracelessly stumbled out of bed, threw myself together, and aimed my unresponsive body at the hall in hopes of caffeine.

I missed.

My shoulder hit the doorjamb on the way out. *Ow.*

I slept in. I shouldn't be so groggy.

I dropped my head to rub my eyes and was entertained to find my shoes, not where I had lost them along the hallway, but neatly placed side by side just outside my bedroom door. *Is he trying to be nice, or is he a little OCD?* I contemplated the possibilities as I slogged down the hall, hungover and amused.

All the way from the kitchen, I could hear the faint but familiar crunching coming from the direction of the larder. Henry, it appeared, was already up and back to work on the ceiling. I started a pot of coffee—extra large for the day ahead—and followed the sound to peek at his progress while it brewed.

"You're up early. How's it going?" I smiled as cheerfully as I could manage and examined the depression in the ceiling. *Whoa. You've been working for hours.*

"I'm not up early; you are up late. It's almost noon. Not a champagne person, are you?" He beamed down at me, no worse for wear.

"Blatantly not," I scowled. *I guess I don't need to hide my state of hangover.* "Making progress, I see."

"Over half a meter in. I've hit a second layer of reinforcement bar and gone round. I can't determine how thick this concrete is. I understand it's the roof, but this seems excessive." Already sweating, he seemed more troubled than he should've been so early in the day.

"Let me get you some water. You've been working hard," I called over my shoulder, waving away his concern as I walked away. "There has to be an explanation." I tried to sound lighthearted, but the second it came out of my mouth, I knew what I had said.

He bellowed down the hall after me, "I know there's an explanation. But am I going to like it?"

It's irritating how he bounds into each day in such a reflective and ponderous way. "He manages to ruin my morning coffee every damn day."

I returned to the larder and thwapped Henry with the water bottle —harder than I had intended—my irritation apparently seeping out. He caught his breath and drank while I sipped my caffeine. "Lay it on me, Doctor Doom." I sighed.

"What does that mean?"

He's genuinely confused. How is that remotely possible?

"Seriously?" I tried to rein in the sarcasm, but the exhaustion and hangover made self-control challenging. "You spend the wee hours of every morning thinking your deep thoughts while I sleep. Then you reveal that you've figured out something alarming before I can reach my infusion of coffee and prop open my eyelids. And then you refuse to tell me until I beg you. Just tell me already. Get it over with." *How can you not see how your thoughtful intellect ruins every horrible cup of coffee I try to consume in this wretched place?*

"Don't get shirty with me, mon puce. Truly, I don't have an answer. I'd tell you if I did. It's been nagging at me all morning. It was bothering me last night. I lost sleep over it. I was up before dawn and came back to work. Labor orders my mind, helps me think."

"Mon, what now?"

His green eyes twinkled with mischief as he took another swig of water and climbed back up on his furniture tower to chip away at the ceiling. Henry hummed while he worked, getting a Bon Jovi song stuck in my head. *This is no time to have "Livin' on a Prayer" as an earworm. I have to get out of the larder. Now.*

I darted back to the kitchen and cooked up some powdered eggs. *Better than Henry's? Nope. Faster though.* I was working up the courage to consume my concoction when I heard a clank followed by a cacophonous, reverberating crash. I didn't have time to pause before I heard an unearthly howl from Henry that formed a pit in my stomach. I dropped everything—plate and eggs flying across the floor—and sprinted to the larder. I ran so fast that I skidded down the slope of the larder hall, falling on my wounded leg. I recovered my footing quickly enough and scrambled through the door.

No!

Henry's jerry-rigged scaffolding had collapsed. I found him stretched out on top of the pile of mangled furniture. *What in the . . . ?* When I got closer, I saw that Henry was mounded in crumbled concrete and dirt.

I examined the ceiling above him. The hole we created had widened. Where there once had been concrete had become a darkened void barred by a two-layered grid of rebar. At the center of that void was dark soil and . . . *roots?*

Henry began to stir and groan, shifting my focus away from the ceiling. I had to think about him; he could've been injured. "Henry, don't move. You could have broken something. What hurts?"

Adjusting to an upright position, brushing the debris from his torso, Henry groaned again, offering a pained smile, "Everything."

I felt marginally better. *I guess humor is a good sign.*

"Do you think you broke anything?" I checked his arms, legs, ribs, insecure about what to do. *I'm not the medic. You fell far and hard. Something has to be broken.*

He grabbed my wrist and pulled my hand away from his head as I searched for bleeding. "I'm okay. The ceiling is more important." His voice was strained.

I don't think so!

"Hold on one second. You just fell a solid eight feet onto a pile of demolished furniture. You could have fractured ribs, punctured a lung, cracked your head. And you think the ceiling is more important? No. It can wait. Are. You. OKAY?!" I gave him the best stern-mom look I could muster.

Both hands went up. "You win. Yes, I'm fine. Nothing's broken. I don't even think I'm bleeding. I'm bruised and sore, that's all. Satisfied?" I eyed him skeptically, and he squinted back.

A game of chicken, is it?

"Fine." *I'm not convinced, but what else can I do?*

"I think we found the answer to your question." I pointed toward the ceiling.

Henry tried to look up. "What?" He flinched and grabbed his neck.

You can't turn your head? That's not good.

I sighed. *It's one thing to look at it. Saying it out loud is another thing entirely.*

"You made it through the concrete. I think I know why it's so thick and heavily reinforced." Henry struggled to his feet, stumbling over the rubble, still holding his neck. "No. Sit down." I put my hands on his shoulders; he didn't resist.

"Whatever it is, just tell me." He hung his head and clutched his neck, leaning against the iron back of a conservatory bench he'd brought in for his tower.

Dragging it out was cruel. I had to spit it out. "Henry, there's soil above the concrete. It isn't only soil. There's soil and . . . and roots." I took a breath and closed my eyes.

"Henry, we're underground." I had to sit down. Saying it out loud somehow made it real. I put my arms over my knees and buried my head between them.

What are we going to do?

A moment later, I felt Henry's intense body heat radiating beside me, one colossal arm wrapped around me, and his head resting on my shoulder. He didn't utter a word. What was there to say?

I hadn't cried once since we'd been taken. Not when I realized we'd been kidnapped. Not in the crypt or in the vent. Not in the fire. Not once.

We were buried alive with no discernible way out. There was no use holding back any longer.

I let go.

33926194

I don't know how long I cried. At one point, I realized that my shoulder was wet. *It's hard on you too, isn't it?*

Then, there were no more tears. There was nothing left. I was empty.

Drained from the buildup and the repeated defeats of the previous days, time began to blur. We could have sat there for hours or only minutes; I couldn't tell—nor did I care. We merely stared at the dirt and the broken furniture piled on the floor—a tremendous heap of failure.

After what seemed to me like hours of silence, I resigned. "Thank you for indulging me, Henry. I'm getting up now."

I lifted his arm from around my shoulder, surprised at how robotic my voice and movements were. It wasn't only the external. Inside, I was hollow. I felt nothing at all. I'd been that way only once before. My emotions expanding uncontrollably like overinflated helium balloons. Too many and too full. I was afraid they would carry me away. So, I let them go, remaining alone on the ground in vacant emptiness.

It's an illusion. The feelings aren't gone. Eventually, they come back. And they return with interest.

I slipped out of the larder vacuously. Henry stiffly made it to his feet and followed me. "Where are you going?"

I didn't answer. I wandered numbly. Drifting.

Reaching the tree at the center of the conservatory, my fingers traced the mangled bark as I circled it aimlessly; I wasn't sure why at first. I looked up at the ceiling, then high on the walls, and I began searching for the cameras; I didn't find any.

Round and around, I went, more intently with each pass. I squinted and searched.

They're there, somewhere. But I didn't see a single one.

I was wandering around a twisted maypole in a Stephen King novel. *Something up there is out to get me. I know it's there; I just can't see what it is.*

Henry must be watching me. I don't see him. But I can feel his gaze on my back, like the winter sun, warm but distant and unreachable.

"Are you okay?" He sounds worried but far off.

I didn't answer.

Looking, searching. Round and round. *Where are they?*

It's no use. Wherever they are, they're too well concealed.

That was it. The moment something in my brain . . . snapped.

"I'm done!"

I stopped and screamed toward the ceiling at the top of my lungs. Releasing every bit of the anger and frustration I had pent up since I'd arrived, in a single unstable explosion.

"I'm not playing your games anymore." I barely waited for a response. I wasn't expecting one.

"I know you're listening. I know you're watching." I stalked around the tree to another side where there might be a hidden camera.

"What. Do. You. Want?!" I threw my arms up in exhausted frustration.

Rain poured down from the ceiling as though I was in the Amazon; I looked up and held out my hands, catching the giant raindrops. *Unbelievable! Not the response I expected.*

"You don't scare me. I'm through with all of it!"

I paced around the tree, continuing my castigation to every side of it—in the rain—resolute that whoever was there got a good look at how determined I was. "I'm done being your science experiment. I am done being a rat in this sadistic maze. I am done trying to escape for your amusement. You want something to entertain you?

"Read a book.

"Find a hobby.

"Go to fucking Disney World!

"I am finished!"

I paced some more. "From now on, all I do is the bare minimum to survive. I eat. I sleep. That's it. Nothing whatsoever to captivate or amuse you. And it will stay that way until you let us out!"

Continuing around the tree, I looked harder for cameras, though it was far more difficult through the downpour.

"Do you hear me?!" Screaming made me hoarse, but I didn't care. All that mattered was getting my point across.

All at once, the rain stopped, and the lights went out.

They all went out.

Every window illusion, the sky illusion, every light in every room, everywhere.

I was disassociated in an expanse of blackness and silence. The sound of my exasperated breathing amplified. Water dripping from the plants pierced the umbra. Drip. Drip. Drip. In rhythm like the ticking of a clock.

"I think they heard you."

I would slap you right now. If I could find you.

"I have to congratulate you; that is by far the most effective thing we have tried yet."

"How can you say that?" My snarkiness dug into my tone.

"Well, now we know conclusively that we're being watched and that they're willing to control the environment in response to our actions. So, yeah. I consider it proper effective." I was willing to concede his point, though I didn't admit it. "Shall we play Marco Polo?"

His attempt at goofiness to disarm is infuriating. Or am I afraid it's effective?

He had been using the conversation to find me. I heard the crunch of his feet on the stone path and put my arms out to reach him. Being more than a foot shorter, my hands ran into his belly. "Hey now, watch the hands." He tried to be cute, holding my wrists between his thumb and index finger. I was not in the mood and twisted myself free.

"Do you think you can navigate to the dining room?" *Hopefully, one of his superpowers is a good sense of direction.*

"What's your thinking?" he asked, but he was already leading us somewhere. I followed on faith that it was a helpful somewhere.

"There are candles on the table, and I think the matches are in the sideboard drawer. Seeing might be a start." *Light is my first order of business. Do you have something better in mind? You're always two steps ahead of me.*

"Excellent. We should be at the hardwood transition momentarily. I hope it's the right hall." He half-joked as we cautiously moved down the hall and into a room, one tentative step at a time.

"Careful!" Henry grabbed my elbow. Our rain-soaked shoes and the polished wood floors were a slippery combination.

Whatever room we'd entered felt cavernous in the dark. The sudden screech of the chair I ran into told me we'd found the dining room.

"Wait. Listen." Henry's arms flung out in front of me, halting my progress.

"I hear it." A clock was ticking. "But there are no gears. How can that be?"

"We need to find candles. Now." The urgency in his voice escalated.

We split up into the blackness; I went rummaging for matches, and Henry fumbled for the candles on the table and pulled out chairs for us.

We lit the candles and removed the starburst copper clock from the wall. Even without gears, the ticking grew louder. I looked around. *It's coming from everywhere at once.*

Henry interrupted my musings about the sound with his own thoughts. "You were serious in your declaration, weren't you?" He searched behind my eyes, looking for something deeper than a facial expression.

"What? Yes. I'm sorry. It was selfish of me to do that without talking to you first. I just . . . I lost it. Having our lives controlled by strangers for entertainment was hard enough to tolerate, but discovering they had essentially buried us sent me over the edge. It was the only thing I could think to do to take back some element of control and maybe get them to let us out of here."

Henry nodded thoughtfully for a moment. "It's a good plan. But it will only work if we both participate." He pounded a fist on the table, startling me. "I'm in."

"Henry, I can't expect you to do this. Not making an effort to escape is a big deal. I can't get in the way of that for you." I laid my hand over his white-knuckled fist.

I can't impose my hare-brained scheme on you, Hercules.

"I would feel wretched if it didn't work." His fist opened and engulfed my tiny fingers. He looked at them as though I'd offered a small treasure. His mammoth thumb gently stroked my hand, and

I realized that offering my hand like that must have seemed like a grand gesture.

We're talking about escaping our personalized oubliette; we have to focus. I extracted my hand from his grasp and sat on it.

The ticking grew louder, and I raised my voice slightly to compensate. "Henry, I won't make you do this. You have to do whatever you need to in order to get out of here." *Will repeating myself help?*

Standing up, I went to the wine fridge next to the sideboard table for a bottle of water. The light in the fridge was out. *Crap.* I glared back at Henry.

Smug and self-righteous, Henry interlocked his hands behind his head and leaned his chair back on two legs. "Well, I think, for the moment, *this* is our method of escape. We need a united front, and we need to hope this works because I don't think they just turned off the lights; it looks like they shut off the power entirely. And since I've been through every inch of the house, I know we don't have access to the mains."

I slammed the fridge door closed and tapped the water bottle against my thigh. *Am I tapping in rhythm with the ticking? Stop it, Monti.*

"Wait, Henry. Access the what, now?"

"To turn the electricity back on."

"You mean the breakers? It doesn't matter what we call them at this point; we have no access. No power." *What we do have is a serious problem. What did I get us into?*

I flipped the bottle onto the table, landing it upright in front of my seat, and ran my fingers through my soaking wet, tangled hair—tempted to pull it out in a clump. *This is it. Noncompliance has to work.*

"The good news is," I announced with fabricated confidence, "we have enough food and water to last quite a while. The plants will supply oxygen. I suppose our first stop is to find more candles now that we're without windows, then clean up because we are covered in concrete mud.

"Then . . . what? How is this even going to work?"

I collapsed into a chair. *Why am I asking him? It was my idea. I just threw down a gauntlet without a plan, creating more of a problem than we already had.*

"Candles first, then plan, then execute the plan. Yes?"

Henry to the rescue. And not for the first time since we became stuck in the evidently underground house. "Secret Agent Man" *began playing in the back of my head.*

Lucky for me, Henry had already looked through every nook and cranny of the house and knew where the hurricane candles were stacked in the larder. *Could this house have originally been some rich man's bomb shelter? What had they been preparing for anyway?*

Whatever. I don't care anymore.

Plenty of candles and matches accounted for, we decided to cover some ground rules.

"So where do we start? Passive resistance. I guess no recreation. Not that most of our recreation is available without power anyway."

"Right. Good." Henry added, "We should probably keep the talking to a minimum, only what is mandatory to get by. The idea should be not to do anything that will be in any way entertaining to our captors, right?"

"Yes. We shouldn't move around much, either. Little to no activity. I think we should each stay in our own beds whenever we aren't eating or in the restroom, even if we're awake. It won't be fun, but hopefully, it'll be effective." I felt my face tighten. *That's a lot to ask.*

"Quite. Meals will be tricky. Without the sun, we won't be able to tell when it's day or night or whenever. I suggest that when one of us is hungry, that person should make a meal, and we both eat. Then, we stay on the same schedule, and we won't be alone one hundred percent of the time and go completely crazy."

I snickered at his suggestion.

"What?" he asked.

"I'm sorry. It struck me as funny. It's just . . . Well. It feels like you're always hungry. If we're shooting for minimal activity and you're proposing that you make a meal any time you're hungry. Well . . . We'll always be in the kitchen."

He laughed and leaned across the table. "I'll try to restrain myself." He flashed a Hollywood grin. "Though it's well past lunchtime, and I should probably get some nosh before I head to my Fortress of Solitude." He seemed to dare me to keep a straight face at the suggestion.

I could not.

We both laughed at Henry's endless need to consume before we put an embargo on all signs of joy, ate, and began our attempt at passive resistance.

We ate food from the fridge that would spoil—not so much to avoid wasting food that psychotic people had paid for but to avoid having to endure the odor of that spoiled food. The compost in the conservatory could only handle so much at a time, and the trash compactor was without power and barely held a standard kitchen bag. We needed to clean out the fridge and fast.

We attempted to eat in silence. We couldn't avoid the few snickers over the odd combinations of food and the portions mounded on Henry's multiple plates. As the meal went on and the silence set in, my posture sank, and my head got heavy. I propped it up with my arm on the table. Henry seemed to feel the weight of our circumstances as well. He held his neck as he finished his meal, drooping over the table in silence. He must have injured his neck in the fall more seriously than he wanted to let on.

We've comfortably enjoyed each other's company in silence before. This is different; it feels forced and out of our control. I may have chosen it, but it's one more part of the psychological beating we've taken in this place. This house has been a prison from the moment we set foot in it, but now the walls are closing in.

Silently—we finished our meal.

Silently—we cleaned up.

Silently—we each took a candle and walked down the long black hall to our rooms.

Only the ticking echoing through the blackened house kept us company. I was about to close my bedroom door behind me when I heard a whispered "goodnight." I didn't answer, but I couldn't contain the slightest giggle. We weren't managing the silence and minimal activity routine just yet.

I showered off the concrete mud that had caked in my hair and climbed into bed to wait out my self-imposed sentence. Slipping under the polyester covers in the darkness, I felt something poke at my arm. I pulled it out from under the sheet.

Another book.

An involuntary scream escaped from deep in my throat. I flung the book across the room, and the spine cracked against the door before it hit the floor. *Another lurid quote is not what I need to occupy my mind in my newfound stillness.*

Henry exploded through the door, almost dropping his candle in the process. "What's wrong?!" I shrugged and rolled my eyes, putting a finger over my lips.

Silence and minimal activity? This is not a good start. Henry nodded, putting a hand on his chest as he calmed himself.

He picked up the book open-faced between his bare toes. I wanted to scream at him to drop it. But I was too late; he was already reading.

The color drained from his face as he staggered to my bedside with the book pressed to his nose. Henry's candle lit the words on the page, while mine was barely enough to make out the cursive red font of the title over the black image at the bottom, *Grace Street* by Ella Dominguez. *I don't recognize it.*

He turned the book around to show me the highlighted portion. It was too far to read, so I dislodged the book from his hands and pulled it closer to my face.

"So, you don't get to say goodbye. Not now, maybe not ever.

*That's the beauty of this arrangement. I make all the
decisions and you're left to wander around in the dark,
waiting, anticipating and fearing my next move.
Only when I'm done using you and I've gotten
what I need will I let you go."*[5]

I gasped. The book fell to the floor, and I covered my gaping mouth. Yet, I couldn't take my eyes off the cover as it lay spread face open on the floor. My veins ran cold. Henry ran his fingers through my hair, and I didn't even register the intrusion of personal space. It didn't matter anymore.

We have to get out. Passive resistance has to work. There is no other option.

I looked up at Henry, his face blurred by my tears. He squeezed my hand and nodded.

We can succeed. We have to succeed.

40182474

The empty hours dragged on.

Tick. Tick. Tick.

DAY 6

Seeing

The ticking is louder. Is that my imagination?

Tick. Tick. Tick.

46758491

I can't sleep.

Tick. Tick. Tick.

The darkness was more disorienting than I'd anticipated. What felt like hours could have been minutes for all I knew.

Tick. Tick. Tick.

It echoed throughout the house.

I want to talk to Henry.

I can't. Don't give in, Monti. Isolate. Resistance.

We tried to stick to the rules. Stay quiet. Not do much. Only get up for meals.

Henry wants to eat every fifteen minutes. I don't know why he got so irritated when I brought it up.

I knew we couldn't tell how much time was passing. When I discreetly showed him that I hadn't burned through an inch of my candle since the lights went out, he showed me that he'd burned through five. *What is going on?*

I suppose if our body clocks are adjusted to different candles, it might explain his differing sense of the passage of time and his constantly thinking that it's time to eat.

Tick. Tick. Tick.

I can't sleep. Did I say that already?

Neither of us slept. I could tell from the bags under Henry's eyes. We didn't have to talk to know that.

Is this their way of getting us to fall in line? It can't work. We have to keep going.

Tick. Tick. Tick.

Is it actually getting louder, or is it just harder to block out? Either way, the longer I can't sleep, the more it's getting to me. I'm anxious. Irritable.

Ugh. My head.

Tick. Tick. Tick.

Following the stone path through the conservatory after a meal one night, or day, or morning, or whatever, I stopped. Henry walked on ahead.

I heard something. A noise. A noise aside from the ticking. Something coming from . . .

I don't want to know.

I stood in the path halfway between the crypt door and the bedroom hall. Torn. Torn between finding out and not wanting to know.

A scraping sound.

I hunched over and cautiously inched my way toward the door. *Or do I want to know?*

More scraping. I stopped.

I can't do it.

Maybe.

I took one more tentative step.

Nope. Definitely can't.

I backed up. A hand landed on my shoulder. I launched forward and let out a shriek, throwing my candle into the darkness.

It blew out.

"What are you doing?" Henry had materialized in the darkness behind me. "Why didn't you continue down the corridor after supper? Where's your candle?"

I put a palm to my chest. My heart beat so hard I thought a rib might crack. "I heard something."

"Yeah. We've had that infernal ticking for the last, well, however long it's been going on." He tried to soothe me, stroking my hair and arm. It didn't help.

I pushed his hands away. "No, there was a scraping sound coming from inside the crypt. Someone is in there!" I was angry and exhausted. The house I was trapped in was attacking me. I was terrified, ready to snap.

"Okay. Let's look." He took my hand and walked in the direction of the crypt.

I dug my heels into the stone path and yanked on his arm as hard as I could, leveraging all of my body weight. "I don't want to look! Are you kidding?!"

He stopped and analyzed me for a moment. His eyebrow raised. I heard the scraping again. "There. Do you hear it?" I pointed at the door.

The eyebrow came down, and his expression shifted from confusion to concern. "No. No, I don't. Are you feeling okay?"

"No, I'm not feeling okay." I let go and sat in the grass, rubbing my temples. "I'm telling you, I heard scraping on the inside of that door."

He walked over to the crypt, put his ear to the door, and listened. He waited. "I'm sorry, I don't hear anything."

I lay back in the grass, my hands covering my languorous face. "Don't be sorry. That's probably better than something on the other side, scraping to get out." He chuckled, somehow found my candle in the grass, and brought it over to me.

"We're going to have to go back to our passive-resistant silence, aren't we?" He smiled as he said it.

I don't want to.

"Yep." I sighed before getting up to walk to the bedroom.

We trudged back shoulder to shoulder. I leaned on him a little. *Why have I let down my guard?*

Tick. Tick. Tick.

Part of the way down the darkened bedroom hall, Henry's low voice rumbled at me, "There's something you should know. When I trained as a medic in the military, I learned that one of the symptoms of sleep deprivation is auditory hallucinations."

I looked up at him, realizing what he had said. I shouldn't have looked. We weren't supposed to give any evidence of talking to the cameras. We'd already spoken too much in the conservatory. He continued quietly, "As we lose more sleep, the hallucinations may become visual."

"Fantastic," I responded louder than I meant to. Louder than I should have.

"There's something else." As he spoke, I forced myself to look at the floor to avoid reacting further. I was so tired and fried that the likelihood of keeping a reaction from emerging was slim to none.

"I did research for a film a few years back; it was never produced, but the director and I spent a lot of time with the military talking about torture tactics. Your government uses temporal deprivation as a form of torture."

"What?" I squawked. *I have no self-control left. Is it because I'm tired or because of the pounding headache? Ugh.*

And you've lost me, Hercules. "Temporal, what now?"

"They remove all sense of time passing. You can't tell if it's been hours, or days, or minutes. When your body's circadian rhythm is offset to the extreme, it's a type of psychological torture. You can actually go insane."

"Let me see if I've got this right. Our captors are using military-grade psychological torture and sleep deprivation that will create visual and auditory hallucinations. And we're sticking with passive resistance?"

I'm not impressed with us.

"Right. I'm a brilliant mastermind, and we are going to die."

He gave me a half smile and a nod.

I tried not to let my attitude about the situation show in my posture, but it was difficult given the lack of sleep and the ever-increasing migraine created by the unabated ticking that seemed to grow louder with each and every passing minute—minutes that stretched into infinitude.

If I could just bang my head against the wall a few times, it might relieve the pressure building inside my skull. For the moment, I'm going to assume that's not the answer. Only time will tell if I'm right.

Tick. Tick. Tick.

Henry dropped me back at my room and left for his. *If the ticking doesn't make me lose my mind, the solitude might.*

I blew out my candle. Maybe I can mentally block out the sound and try to sleep. If sleep deprivation is the problem, then sleeping has to be the solution.

Tick. Tick. Tick.

I smothered my face with a pillow. *I need to scream!*

Maybe counting ticks will help, like counting sheep.

I'm not a naturally patient person. Never have been. Nevertheless, after a few false starts, one by one, I counted twelve thousand seven hundred and ninety-two ticks.

When I gave up on the idea, I did the math. In my head. If each tick was consistently one second on a traditional analog clock, I had counted for slightly over three and a half hours.

I am. Losing. My. Mind.

Tick. Tick. Tick.

It wasn't long after, or maybe it was.

I can't tell anymore. The ticking is so relentless, so grinding. My muscles are involuntarily contracting. My neck hurts. My back is contorting. My legs are cramped. Even my feet are curling up.

Tick. Tick. Tick.

I have to make it stop. I have to muffle the sound somehow.

I fumbled my way into the bathroom and stared into the creepy gold-framed mirror. *I look almost as bad as I feel.* In the reflection, I saw a claw-foot bathtub behind me that I'd never used. After all, I wasn't a guest at the Ritz, and we weren't there to enjoy the luxury. But the more I thought about it, water was an excellent insulator. *Will it make a good sound barrier?*

I filled the immense iron tub to the brim, stripped down, and climbed inside, spilling water over the edge and onto the pink-tiled floor—burying my head beneath the cocooning water. Only my nose was left above the surface to breathe. *Please! Drown the sound. Restore some semblance of my sanity.*

It wasn't enough to completely block the sound—that would've been too much to ask—but it did provide some relief, enough that

I was able to mentally block the rest of the sound.

I floated in the tub, resting away from the unremitting tick of the clock until the water grew frigid and my lips turned blue. I didn't realize it had been so long until the first convulsions of shivers overcame my freezing yet completely slack body.

I pulled the plug from the drain and wrapped myself in an enormous fluffy pink towel, with plans to refill the tub and repeat the process, when I heard my name in the distance.

"Monti."

Another auditory hallucination, like Henry talked about. Ignore it. Back to the bath.

"Monti!"

Wait. That's Henry! He's scared!

I threw on a robe, grabbed my candle, and ran. As I entered the hall, I saw that Henry's back was to me. He was stumbling down the hall without a candle.

What is he doing? It's so dark.

"Monti, no!" Henry crumpled to the floor, one arm outstretched into the inky darkness.

What's going on?

"Henry, I'm over here." I ran up behind him, grabbed his shoulder, and swung around to face him. I knelt, inches from his face, shining the light on him. His cheeks and bare chest were wet with tears; even his silk pajama pants seemed to have tear stains on them. "Henry, what's wrong?"

"I couldn't save you. I'm sorry." He fought for air. "I wasn't in time." He covered his face and sobbed.

What? I set down my candle and carefully pried his hands from his face.

"Henry. You were hallucinating. I'm here. I'm fine. Look. It's me." I tried to show him that I was okay. He didn't believe me at first, but then he gripped my biceps with his leviathan hands. *Ow. That'll leave a mark.*

"You're alright?" He didn't seem ready to accept that I was real.

"Yes. I am." I tried to release his painful clench. Once I got one hand off my arm, the other hand released, and his arms flung around me. He crushed me in a hug; the force resembled that of a boa constrictor. Every time I breathed out, the hug tightened, forbidding me from inhaling again.

Too close. Definitely too close.

"You were . . . I couldn't . . . I thought . . . " Without a complete sentence, the best I could gather was that he thought I was in danger, and he hadn't gotten there in time to intervene.

He's absolutely devastated.

Tick. Tick. Tick.

Time forgot us sitting on the floor in the hall. I didn't blink in the blackness for hours; I was certain of it. My ears sounded like they'd filled with water. All I heard was the muffled sound of my own breath and the flush of my blood through my ears as I waited. For what? I didn't know. I suffocated in his embrace, trying everything I could to focus on anything other than his statuesque and very naked torso pressed against me. I finally worked up the nerve and asked the question foremost on my mind: "You okay?" Tact was never my strong suit. *Was there a better way to broach the subject? We aren't supposed to be talking. He's obviously traumatized.*

All at once, he released me. It was like getting out of a corset that was too small at the end of a night of dancing. The instinct to take a deep breath in was irrepressible.

"Yeah."

That's all he said. He stood up and disappeared into the darkness of his room.

We didn't talk about it after that—like it never happened.

Tick. Tick. Tick.

49752397

Abandoned by time, we couldn't decide when to eat. I wasn't hungry anymore. At all. Henry was always hungry. He said both were symptoms of sleep deprivation. Both added to our irritability. Both added to the temporal disorientation—that's what Henry called it.

Tick. Tick. Tick.

What am I saying?

Henry came to my door and motioned his head for me to join him for another meal. *The mere thought of food is nauseating. The constant sound impaling my head has created a migraine that has me hanging over the toilet half the day. Food is not an option.* I waved him to go on without me.

I sat up in bed and clutched my pillow, willing myself into a zen state. Unfortunately, without sleep, I did not have the mental fortitude to deal with the undiminished, enduring, imperishable ticking.

Tick. Tick. Tick.

I buried the heels of my hands in my temples. *Not helping.*

My candle burned out. *Fantastic.* I reached over and struck another match.

I fixated on the match in my hand. *That's my hand. I know it's my hand. It's doing what I want. Why doesn't it feel like my hand?*

I lit a new candle and blew out the match. I turned my hand to the back and to the front. *It's like being in a virtual-reality game. What a strange kind of dysphoria. I'm controlling it.* Front, back. Over and over. *But it doesn't feel like it's mine.*

I flexed and flapped my hand around to get rid of the sensation. That reduced it somewhat but didn't get rid of it completely.

I feel high. I wiped my hand across my face. *It feels like someone else's hand. Unnerving.*

I haven't been to sleep. No one could've drugged me while I slept. I haven't eaten. No one could've spiked my food. I haven't had anything to drink in a while. It couldn't have been in my water. Am I dehydrated?

I had a bottle of water on the nightstand and reached for it. The hand that was not my own missed, and not by a small margin. I fell off the side of the bed, hitting my forehead on the sharp corner of the nightstand.

Momentarily, I was relieved of the stabbing in my head. My body relaxed on the floor for the few seconds I was free from pain. Then it doubled down, crushing my skull.

Tick. Tick. Tick. Stab. Stab. Stab.

The sound and the throbbing synchronized.

A few moments on the floor, then I forced myself back up, planting my hand on the nightstand that moments before had cracked my skull. My hand did not land on the solid wood of the nightstand but on a book. *Dammit, not another book! How did I not see it? Was I that distracted by my phantom limb?*

I rolled back into the bed and blotted my bloody head with the orange floral bedsheet, then dragged the book into the bed next to me. My vision was too blurry to be able to read. *That's for the best.* As I held the sheet to my forehead, it draped over one eye, and the title came into focus. *Damn.*

The cover read *I Have No Mouth and I Must Scream* by Harlan Ellison. I could see that out of the well-read pages, one toward the beginning had been dog-eared. *Now, I have to read it.* There, as expected, was a shaky highlight.

> *"Surrounded by madness, surrounded by hunger,*
> *surrounded by everything but death,*
> *I knew death was our only way out."*[6]

"That's it. I'm done with the books." I held our latest paper scourge open over my candle until the green paperback cover and the well-worn interior pages caught fire. Once it was thoroughly lit, I stoically walked it into the bathroom and left it in the sink to burn to ash. By the time I'd returned to my bed and got the sheet back on my forehead to stop the bleeding that had made it all the way to my shirt, Henry had barged into my room, looking for the source of the smoke.

"Are you okay?" He was hunched over, arms outstretched, ready to attack like a wild animal.

"Yep," I answered in a bored intonation. *I really can't deal with it all anymore.*

He searched the room, found the trail of smoke, and bolted into the bathroom. Impressive that he'd noticed the smoke so quickly without a single smoke alarm in the house.

"There's a book on fire in here!"

"Yep."

He left the book, returned to the bedroom, and studied my face, deeply concerned. "You okay?"

"Yep." *No. But I have to be.*

I don't think he believes me. But we have to return to our solitude.

Tick. Tick. Tick.

52491038

It has to have been days. Then again, no way to tell. We should have a meal. Or maybe I'm lonely. It seems like it's been a while since we've eaten. Henry will be hungry regardless.

I left my room with my candle and entered the hall, dragging my pounding head against the smooth plaster wall as I went. To my surprise, I saw Henry toward the end of the hall, already on his way to the kitchen. *Strange. Why didn't he come get me?* I lurched forward and tried to catch up, but he picked up speed.

"Henry?"

Is he hallucinating again?

As he crossed the threshold into the conservatory, he didn't turn left toward the kitchen but to the right and tossed his candle into the grass.

"Henry? What are you doing?" *Where is he going?*

I shifted into a jog and followed. My candlelight was barely enough to see where my next foot stepped, let alone where Henry was up ahead. I held my candle out as far as my arm would stretch to see up ahead. I could hardly make him out as he wandered behind the benches and looked back at me, almost as if checking to see if I was still following. *Bizarre. Why do you look shorter?* I strained to catch up.

"Henry?" He turned back, and I glimpsed a familiar smile before he ducked down the library hall.

What the Hell! Not Henry. "Paul!"

I sprinted down the library hall, grabbed the door handle, and dove inside.

"Paul? Paul!" I ran laps around the sunken couch, knocking a lamp off a side table in the process. There was no one there. He was gone. *Where did he go?*

"Monti? You okay?"

Henry had come through the door behind me.

"No." I dropped into a leather chair hard enough to send the searing pain of a red-hot poker up my thigh and into my ass. I didn't care. I was too busy forcing myself not to cry. I refused to make a scene.

"What's going on? I heard you calling?" Henry's face told me that he knew more was going on than I was about to tell him.

I stood up stiffly, painfully, and responded in a cracked voice, "It's time for dinner." I walked past him—without explanation or eye-contact—and out the door.

DAY 9

Linked

In the kitchen, we prepared what was arguably the last safe food from the now warm freezer—although as I looked at my plate and my slimy gray meat stared back at me, I questioned my judgment.

56362869

I wandered back to the kitchen, opting to refill my glass of water to better choke down my dinner. On my way past the fridge, I started coughing. Whatever mystery meat we'd been eating was fighting back; I lost my balance. I fell against the stocky yellow refrigerator, and a torn page from a book fluttered down from on top.

I retrieved the page from under the cabinet where it had landed and brought it back to the table for candlelight. Henry yanked it from my hand before I could read it. "Give that to me; you don't need to see that." Agitated, he crumpled it into a ball and stomped across the room, tossing it back on top of the fridge.

"What was that?" *I don't like reading creepy pages left for us, but now I'm curious.*

"Don't worry about it." The page disposed of, Henry resumed choking down his questionable meal.

"I don't need to read it. But I'd like to know what's going on." *New tactic: kind, gentle tones. It feels unnatural, but he's earned it. Is it working?*

He sighed and dropped his fork; the clattering echoed throughout the house. "The page with the quote from the first day of the blackout was propped up on display in one of the candelabras on the sideboard table today. I put it on top of the fridge so you wouldn't have to see it. Looks like I failed."

"You mean the one about only when he's done using us will he let us go?" I paraphrased, but the general idea was there.

"That's the one."

I smiled. *You're trying to protect me.*

As I ambled back to the kitchen to refill my glass of water, I wondered how else Henry had tried to protect me in the time we'd been captive. I was startled out of my musings by an intense mechanical thunk. My glass slipped out of my hand and shattered. I was more focused on the sound than the glass and looked back at Henry warily. *I don't know what that was, Oscar, but something's changed, and not for the better.*

I stepped over the broken shards and, by instinct instead of cognition, grabbed my candle, cautiously looking around. There was something industrial in the ceiling that had started working again. Henry was inspecting the ceiling as well; we couldn't ascertain what it was exactly. Walking around, following the sound, I passed a vent in the kitchen. It forcefully blew hot air in my face.

I have to tell Henry. I opened my mouth to yell; nothing came out. *What's wrong with my throat? Whatever. We aren't supposed to talk anyway.* I ran to find him, but Henry had already found a vent blasting hot air. *That's a sour look.*

It wasn't that the house was being heated. It was an industrial heater, putting off temperatures like a forge. *We're going to get uncomfortable fast.* Henry turned to me and stiffened his posture.

You're right; we have to firm our resolve. I returned an expression of solidarity and nodded. *We can do this.*

I hope.

We resumed our meal. It wasn't as appetizing with the rising temperature. Not that it had been appetizing to begin with, but hot food just wasn't appealing, with hot air broiling my neck. Henry looked disgusted; we forced it down regardless. We did not need to add the stench of rotting food in a roasting house to our affliction. By the time we finished the dishes, we were both drenched in sweat. *It has to be over ninety degrees in here.*

Candlelight guided our path back to the bedrooms; upon reaching my threshold, Henry produced a water bottle. The change in routine caught me off guard. He leaned down and whispered, "The temperature is still rising; I don't know how hot it'll get. You can't let yourself get dehydrated." I took the bottle and nodded.

Thoughtful.

I watched as he slogged off to his room, head and shoulders drooping. *The heat must be so much more oppressive for a man of his size. He looks miserable, but he won't complain. He hasn't complained once since we met.*

The first thing I did was not lay down or drink my water; I found light cotton shorts and a thin tank top to wear. Outfitted for the Sahara, I grabbed a washcloth, soaked it in cold water, and brought it to the bed. With the cold cloth draped over my eyes and forehead, I lay down and sprawled out over the bare sheets, abandoning the covers on the floor. It wasn't perfect, but it had to do.

The temperature continued to rise, and the heat didn't stop blasting for a second. It didn't cycle on and off; it blew hot, suffocating air constantly.

Tick. Tick. Tick.

Does this latest attempt at behavior modification mean that we're bordering on winning? Perhaps if we stick to our plan, we might even be freed. If that's the case, it'll likely get a lot worse before that happens. I have to steel myself and prepare for the increased malaise. If suffering means that we're winning the war, that's precisely the motivation I need to endure the battles to come.

58879301

The temperature continued to increase, and I lost consciousness.

Tick. Tick. Tick.

Henry woke me violently. "Monti! Monti!" Yelling and shaking me by the shoulders, he had lifted me into an upright position. I woke when he shook me, but he hadn't noticed. I was so disoriented. My head was still flopping around like a rag doll. He continued to try to wake me by splashing water in my face.

I gasped for air. "What are you doing?!" *That goes against every one of our rules about silence and minimal activity.*

"You were completely unconscious and unresponsive. You scared the living daylights out of me!" A shaking Henry forced water down my throat. I choked on it and spat it right back up at him. "You didn't drink the water I gave you. You're dehydrated."

Yes. I am. It is sweltering in here. "I did sweat, but keep in mind, you just poured water on me."

"New plan. Drink this. Wait here." It was not a suggestion. Henry shoved two bottles of water at me and left the room.

Sipping slowly from one of the bottles, I tried to regain my bearings. *I feel off balance even sitting up in the bed.*

Tick. Tick. Tick.

Henry eventually returned with a tray loaded down with over a dozen blue-tinted glasses from the kitchen, all filled to the brim with water. He also had twelve-inch taper candles that he had striped with Sharpie. He set the tray on the nightstand.

"I've divided these candles into twelve segments. I think our host has deliberately mixed together high- and low-quality candles. That's why they burn at dramatically different rates. We can't help that. We can still use them to create our own hours since we've been deprived of time. It's the best option we have. There's a limited supply, so we'll have to conserve them." He looked at me intently to gauge a reaction. Something about the way he stared me down made me think I was missing something, but I nodded anyway.

"We need to drink a minimum of a half-liter of water per hour in this heat to avoid getting dehydrated, preferably more. We'll use the candles as a clock; I've brought the tray for convenience." He'd thought things through. I sat up as he set the first one of his candle-clocks on the nightstand and set out half the glasses for me.

"You aren't going to like this, but for safety and to conserve resources, we need to stick together from now on. We're going to be bunkmates." He visibly cringed, waiting for my reaction. I looked at him, not comprehending. When I didn't respond, he proceeded to bring the tray around to the other side of the bed and distributed the rest of the glasses onto the other nightstand.

"Whatcha doin'?" I asked, confused.

He put the empty tray on the floor and actually hopped onto the bed, fluffing several brightly-colored pillows behind his back before interlocking his hands behind his head. "Like I said, I'm your new bunkmate." He smiled, sank into his pile of pillows, stared up at the ceiling, and let out a long, satisfied sigh. Then he closed his eyes and said, "I do believe the candle is at the first hour-mark; drink up."

Not a fan of this new plan. And I'm not interested in sharing a bed with this man—or any man. The goal is to not give people a show. What is he thinking? I drank a glass of water and curled up on the damp sheets at the absolute edge of the bed with my back to Henry.

It'll be fine; there is a chasm of space between us; the bed is enormous. I can pretend I'm alone.

Nope. I change my mind. This is not okay. He's far too close for comfort.

Tick. Tick. Tick.

I stared at the candle as it burned—not closing my eyes longer than a blink—and I watched it flicker and melt for the entire hour until it reached the next mark. I focused on how the flame flicker and ticking synchronized: Flick. Tick. Flick. Tick. Flick. Tick. Effectively unhinging myself.

When the wax finally flowed over the uneven Sharpie line, I sat up and drank the next glass of water. I was marinating in sweat. The bed squished when I moved. *I want to do laundry. I could get dry sheets from the linen closet, but why bother? They'd be saturated in minutes.*

I turned to see if Henry had noticed it was time to drink his water, but he'd fallen asleep. *After days of being unable to sleep, he's finally managed it. I guess the human body can only take so much. The addition of sweltering heat must have pushed him over the edge. I hate to wake him.*

I leaned over to poke him in the ribs, but his gray gym shorts were soaked with sweat, and his bare chest was so saturated that he'd left a ring of moisture on the sheet around him. He was sleeping in a pool of sweat. *Ew.* I did not want to touch him, but it was time to rehydrate. I reached with my fingertips and gently shook; my hand slipped right off his arm.

He squinted and peered at me through slits. I mimed a drinking motion. He gave an anemic nod and rolled over. He drank the entire glass in one gulp and flopped back down, closing his eyes again. With the ever-increasing heat, we were likely sweating far more water than we were drinking. *Not good.*

I shook him again. And again, my hand slipped off his arm; this time, my nails left a mark. *Oops.* He opened one eye, clearly not wanting to be disturbed. To avoid being overheard, I lay on my stomach next to him as close as possible. "Henry," I tried to whisper—*I am horrendous at whispering*—"I'm worried about the amount of sweat we're producing compared to the amount of water we're drinking. I think we need to drink more. The bed is soggy."

His head rolled toward me, and his other eye opened. He whispered back, "Fair point. Two glasses? It's hard to say how hot it is in here. I don't think I've ever experienced temperatures like this. Not even in a sauna."

"I think it's worth a shot. Maybe more if we need it." He nodded and rolled over for another glass.

I did the same. We lay on our backs on the hot, sopping bed and stared at the candlelit pattern on the ceiling. Without a thermometer or a clock—with no alarm to wake us—the rising temperatures were a serious danger.

Unexpectedly, Henry gently linked the tip of his pinky finger with mine. They were barely hooked together.

Why did he do that? I wanted to look over for something that resembled an explanation, but the whole point of passive resistance was to stop entertaining the watchers.

So, we continued staring at the ceiling, our fingers linked. After days of darkness, ceaseless and gnawing ticking, sleep deprivation, and loneliness, that tiny point of connection—an innocent gesture, seemingly trivial and insignificant—gave me strength and courage to persevere.

Tick. Tick. Tick.

61071465

Hours passed. We drank our water. One or both of us fell in and out of sleep.

Sleep. That elusive state we had longed for. Yet, when it came, it couldn't provide the rest we desperately needed. It was barely enough to stave off the symptoms of sleep deprivation. I wasn't sure if we were sleeping or merely rendered unconscious from the oppressive heat and humidity.

The ticking never stopped. Unyielding and interminable. We tried to ignore it, but it was no use. We couldn't adapt to the constant migraine that resulted. We sampled every over-the-counter medication in the cabinet. Nothing helped. More potent medications were available in the larder medical supplies, but neither of us was willing to trust our captors' provisions where Schedule II drugs were concerned.

Whoever was awake and noticed reminded the other that it was time to drink. We decided to force ourselves to eat, though neither of us wanted to. *It's just too damn hot.* Lack of nutrition would have been almost as big of a problem as dehydration. We didn't want hot food anymore, and there wasn't anything cold. So, we stuck with whatever fruit was left growing in the garden and the boxes of protein bars stacked in the larder, thankful they had survived the fire, however mushy they'd become in the heat.

After eating, we washed and refilled our glasses and brought them back to the bedroom for the hours between meals—*if you can call them that anymore*. Even the walks to and from the kitchen had become a laborious task.

By the end of the first day in the heat, the temperature had reached well over 110°. Henry estimated that we were at temperatures close to 120° by the second day, and it continued to climb. I didn't know what the human body could endure, but after three days of consistently rising temperatures—over 130° by Henry's projection—I doubted our odds for survival.

On the third day in the scorching heat, I dragged myself out of bed to cool off in the shower, only to find that the showerhead refused to produce anything but boiling hot water. An unrestrained scream escaped from deep within me. I grabbed the closest object within reach, a freestanding mirror from the bathroom counter. In my fury, I hurled it into the pink-tiled shower.

Tiny shards of glass ricocheted out of the shower at my naked body. I looked down and pulled a sliver of mirror from the flesh of my abdomen. I didn't care. The house, the whole situation, everything, it was too much.

Enervated and seething, I collapsed onto the bathroom floor in front of the sink. The shower ran freely with its scalding hot water, steam filled the room, and tiny slits of glass punctured my legs and lower torso.

Henry barreled in, stopping in the doorway when he spotted me on the floor. Looking confused, probably by the hot running shower and my naked, bleeding body slumped on the floor, he rushed in and turned the shower off. I don't know how, but he managed to avoid the broken glass with his bare feet.

Carefully averting his eyes, he grabbed the enormous pink towel I had set out to use after—what should have been—a nice cold shower and covered me with it.

"Are you injured?" Henry sat on the floor across from me against the oversized cast-iron tub. His voice tentative as he questioned.

Leave me alone. Curled up in the blanket-sized towel, I buried my face in the pink fluff. I couldn't think of what to do or say. I felt so exposed. I just wanted to hide.

"What happened?" I could tell he was trying to be gentle, but I couldn't look at him.

I buried my face and mumbled through the terry cloth, "They turned the cold water off. Only hot now."

I finally turned my face toward Henry as my body hung languid over my knees. His face told me he understood my demoralized state.

I can't do this anymore.

He leaned toward me and whispered, "This is a sign of success." His hand reached to touch my knee, but he seemed to read my expression. I did not want him anywhere near me. He'd just seen me naked. *Go away.*

I tried to focus on what he'd said. I'd been thinking along the same lines. The more obstacles they put in our path, the more our passive resistance bothered them.

We have to keep it up. I can't let them get to me. But can I do it?

I took a breath, nodded, and forced myself up. Wrapping the towel around myself, careful to cover everything and tuck the end in extra tight.

As Henry made his way out of the bathroom, I grabbed my washcloth and put it under the faucet exactly as I'd done a hundred times over the previous two days. Even the water in the sink was scorching hot. "Dammit!" I slapped my palm on the counter. Henry looked back.

I should've expected that. I have to stop reacting; that's what they want.

I mouthed the word "sorry" to Henry as I rubbed my pounding temple, left the washcloth on the bathroom counter, and schlepped out of the bathroom.

Time to clean some cuts and find some clothes.

DAY 10

Shaking

We languished in the sweat-soaked king-size bed for what we could only estimate was another two days.

Tick. Tick. Tick.

62719348

The extent of our existence was reduced to drinking hot glasses of water and forcing ourselves to eat on occasion.

The candle reached a Sharpie mark, and it was time to rehydrate. I touched Henry's shoulder to wake him, but he didn't stir. No surprise. He was dehydrated and exhausted. The heat had drained us both. I sat up and shook him more forcefully, but he didn't even flinch. That's when I got worried.

Forget about silence and minimal activity; something's wrong. "Henry." I shook again. "Henry!" I shouted, grabbing his shoulders and bouncing him into the mattress. He barely stirred.

I yanked the pillows from under his head and slapped his face—though hesitantly and softer than I should have. I had been tempted to slap Henry several times since we had met. It was not one of those times.

"Henry!" I shouted, terrified that he might never wake up.

I held my breath, waiting for a response. I was considering checking vital signs and administering CPR. *I don't know CPR. Can you do CPR from watching TV?* Finally, one eye slightly peeped open at me. Relief hit me in the chest like a brick. I slapped him—for real this time—for scaring me, and I flopped onto my back on my side of the bed.

Tick. Tick. Tick.

It was a while before Henry roused himself enough to get a drink of water. I was busy recovering from the heart attack he'd given me, and I was certain it would keep me wide awake for days.

Tick. Tick. Tick.

Incessant sound. Unyielding heat. Restless sleep.

Overwrought. Apprehensive. Wrung.

Tick. Tick. Tick.

DAY 13

Stealing

I didn't realize I'd been asleep until I awoke in the bathtub, being doused in steaming hot water.

64201561

"What the hell!" I screamed at him and flailed like a fish on shore. Our passive resistance certainly wasn't a roaring success.

"We slept through the night. The candles went out. I've been trying to wake you for more than ten minutes." His voice was shaking. He was on the verge of tears.

"Thank God you're okay!" He scooped me out of the bathtub; I felt the bandage float off my thigh. It didn't matter; trying to keep it stuck to sweaty skin had become a full-time occupation.

My tank top and tiny cotton shorts were drowned in sweat and hot bathtub water that he'd doused me in. I was not pleased. It was bad enough being saturated in sweat, but the piping hot water from the tub was unbearable. I was more concerned with Henry's half-naked body pressed against mine and that the water accentuated the fact that I hadn't been wearing a bra for days. I did not want Henry to notice. I was sure he already had, but I didn't need the reminder. It was too much closeness, too much familiarity.

Despite my protest, Henry carried me back to the candle-less, blacked-out bedroom. He seemed to have the navigation skills of a bat. After depositing me on my side of the bed, he fumbled around for matches, lit a new candle, and collapsed onto his side of the bed, obviously exhausted from the scare I'd given him.

"Hell's bells and buckets," Henry mumbled at the ceiling with an arm draped over his face.

"What?"

We can't survive this much longer.

Tick. Tick. Tick.

64201561

With no way to tell for sure, our best estimate was that it had been eight days in darkness and four days in the blistering heat; we decided it was time for a meal. I could tell by Henry's drooping face and the dark circles under his eyes that the last thing he wanted to do was get up. His head hung low; his feet dragged. The sweltering, oppressive heat was wearing on him. He needed to eat, and he no longer wanted to.

Trudging down the hall, I thought through exactly what we'd been consuming. *You're a big guy. You must have about fourteen inches on me, built like a bodybuilder. You probably need two or three times the number of calories a day that I do. I'm only five-two, maybe 120 when we started out. Who knows what I weigh after living in a sauna and surviving off protein bars and no sleep. With your mountains of muscle mass, you have to weigh over 200 pounds. You need way more than 200 calories per meal. I can live off it for a while, but you'll starve. I have to find something else and force you to eat it.*

As we walked down the hall, I gently leaned my arm against his, trying not to draw attention. Surprised, he tried looking down to see what I wanted without anyone behind the cameras noticing. I didn't look up while I talked and tried to whisper low enough not to be overheard but still loud enough for Henry to hear over the incessant ticking. "I think you're getting worn down because you aren't consuming enough calories. We need to find a higher-caloric option for your meals. The protein bars aren't cutting it." I kept walking.

I could feel his body move as he suppressed a laugh. "I'm fine," he floated down on a half-hearted breath.

He wasn't. His face looked like Jack Skellington. I couldn't let it continue. I looked him directly in the eye; damn the cameras. "We're finding more calories." Then I looked straight ahead and marched down the hall ahead of him.

In the dining room, I shoved Henry into a chair. He didn't resist and slumped into a heap at the table, closing his eyes. *Is he worse off than I thought?* In a whirlwind, I ran through the larder, searching for something that survived the fire and might suffice under the circumstances. *I need good nutritional content and a high volume of calories without making him sit down to a huge meal.*

Easy! Find a pot of gold at the end of a rainbow with my candle in the dark.

Sweat poured off my forehead, threatening to extinguish my candle. Quickly wiping it away, I turned down an aisle lined with large plastic tubs, each full of powder. *It's as promising as any other aisle.*

There were all sorts of things in the tubs. Shining my candle down the row, I found powdered milk, powdered eggs, powdered hot chocolate mix—we certainly didn't need a bulk supply of hot beverages in our Turkish steam room. Then I spotted it: "Meal Replacement Shake." *You have got to be kidding me! It is a magic larder. What apocalypse were these people preparing for?*

I grabbed the tub. *What does this weigh, like fifty pounds?*

As I tried to manage the oversized container, my candle toppled to the floor and blew out. I fumbled around for it in the dark.

Of course, with my luck, it had rolled down the aisle and halfway under a shelf. I groped blindly along the floor and under shelves. *Nothing but soot and dust.*

Wait a second, found it.

I managed to carry both the candle and the awkward tub at the same time while feeling my way out of the pitch-black larder, guided only by the hint of a flicker from Henry's candle in the dining room—which was down another hall and in another room.

The monstrous container of powder slammed down onto the table. I unscrewed the lid and pulled back the seal, reticent to peer inside. Willing or not, he was going to eat. It was an unappetizing brownish gray. *I hope that means chocolate.* I poked around for a scoop and found one buried below the surface of the powdery mix. I read the instructions, dropped two rounded scoops into a glass, filled it with hot tap water, and mixed it as best I could. I was supposed to use cold water or milk, but I was stuck with what I had on hand. I appraised the lumpy beverage. *I can't give it to him like this.*

When Henry had emptied the contents of the kitchen drawers onto the counters, looking for the meat mallet, there had been milkshake straws somewhere in the debris. I tried to visualize where they were and which drawer we had put them in. Leaning against the table, I closed my eyes, thinking back to that day. I conjured a mental image of the disaster on the counters, remembering how Hurricane Henry had been worthy of FEMA stepping in.

I chuckled as I reminisced. When we sorted everything back into its place, Henry had picked up the regular straws and the milkshake straws and joked that they were Monti straws and Henry straws.

That's it! They're in the small drawer in the corner near the trash compactor. I lit my candle off Henry's and dashed into the kitchen. Upon my return, I noticed that Henry hadn't budged. *That's not good.*

I dropped the straw into the shake—although generous to call the concoction in my hand a shake—and sat down next to Henry. Nudging him gently, I whispered in his ear, "You need to drink this." He barely lifted his head before giving me a sideways glance. He was neither impressed with nor interested in my offering. I gave an apologetic smile and slid the glass under his nose. He took a big swig and grimaced, then shoved the glass away, wiping his mouth with his forearm.

I fought the smile off my face and slid the glass back, pointing at it firmly. He was going to finish it if I had to hold his nose and pour it down his gullet. Henry squinted at me. He seemed to be assessing if he would win or lose the battle and if it was worth the energy of fighting. Fully engaged in our silent exchange, I put on my best mom face; I would not lose the fight. He couldn't afford for me to lose.

It was only a moment before he gave in and sucked the whole thing down at once. His contorted face confirmed that it was absolutely disgusting. I felt contemptible for forcing him to drink it, but I knew it was necessary. Once he got the last of it down, he gagged and shoved the glass away, almost knocking it to the ground. I caught it before it rolled off the table and brought it to the sink to wash before I washed and refilled our drinking glasses to bring back to the room. Henry rested his head in his arms. He looked so exhausted.

At the sink, I turned the faucet on. Nothing happened. At first, it didn't click. I turned it on and off again two more times before I slammed the handle off and hung my head over the bone-dry sink.

A single tear escaped before I squeezed my eyes shut and put a stop to that. Giving some lunatic the satisfaction of seeing me cry was not on my agenda for the day. I took a slow breath in and let it out just as slowly. The tear blended with the sweat that saturated my face; I wouldn't have to wipe it away. *Good, no cameras will pick up any evidence of emotion.*

Now to suck it up and tell Henry about the water. Even though I was infuriated, I couldn't let it come across on a camera. I stood next to Henry and took another slow breath in and out. *What am I waiting for? Get it over with, Monti.*

With no emotions, no empathy, no intonation, I spoke, "The water's been completely cut off now." I waited, expressionless, counting in my head to even my breath, suppressing my rage.

Henry rolled his head to the side and looked at me through one eye, oddly unsurprised. "I was waiting for that one."

What? Why aren't you thrown by this?

Henry easily translated my thoughts. "It was the next logical step." He tried to stand but was so fatigued that he had to steady himself on the table. "We'll have to ration the bottled water." I pushed him back into the chair.

"You're not going anywhere."

"I'll get the water. You can inventory and calculate our rations." *He's too tired to argue.*

Henry didn't respond but rested his head in his folded arms on the table. That was answer enough.

I stationed candles—one in the dining room with Henry, one along the path in the conservatory, and one on the floor in the larder near the hall. I hauled case after case of bottled water into the dining room and piled them on the floor and on the table, only stopping twice because I got light-headed.

Surely, this will last weeks.

As I got down to the last case, I plopped it triumphantly on the table and proudly leaned on one of my water-case towers so Henry could inspect my work.

Instead of congratulating me, Henry winced. "Is that it?"

I had schlepped stacks upon stacks of cases of bottled water across the Brobdingnagian house; it was quite an achievement for me. I'm a little person. "Yes, why?" Put off, I impressed myself a second time by managing a soft, even tone instead of biting his head off.

"I've done the maths. I was hoping there would be more. At the rate we're drinking water, we'll run out in about a week. And that's without using water for cooking, cleaning, brushing our teeth, showering, flushing toilets, or any other things that require water. If we cut our rations in half, we can stretch that to two weeks. And if we do that, we'll still want to reassess our resources in four or five days."

"Whoa."

I was not aware such large volumes of water could go so quickly. If it wasn't so stinking hot in here . . .

"Okay, half rations it is." I wanted to scream into a camera somewhere, but that wouldn't help our cause, so I forced myself to make no expression—my twitching eye didn't get the memo. *Focus.*

I counted out the number of bottles we needed to make it to our next meal and set them on the tray. It was a meager volume compared to what we were used to. They'd have to do. *Do I even bother with the tray?*

I tapped Henry on the shoulder with my elbow. "Come on, Hercules, let's get going. We have a great deal of nothing to get to." He gave a half-hearted laugh as he scooted out his chair, took the tray, and escorted me down the hall.

Tick. Tick. Heat. Dark. Dry. Tick. Tick.

67395082

The next few days were grueling. The temperature must have gone up yet another four or five degrees. I didn't mention it to Henry. I didn't want to draw attention to it if he hadn't noticed.

The increased heat and dehydration made me delirious.

I moved my shake-manufacturing process out of the dining room and into the kitchen. Henry didn't need to see it. It was bad enough that he had to drink them. Besides, I hadn't told him that I was using part of our rationed water supply to make them, and I couldn't tell if he'd realized it. We were both so disoriented and delirious. He hadn't actually seen me make the first shake. I was hoping he hadn't seen any of the subsequent shake mixes either, and I could get away with stealing water for them. I tried to drink one less ounce every hour to compensate, but it only worked when he didn't catch me.

There was absolutely nothing else going on in the entirety of our day, so getting away with it was a seriously stealth move. I spent an insane amount of my time thinking about how to sneak my water thievery past him. Losing my mind over it had become a real possibility.

At first, I tried not finishing my bottles of water. But Henry noticed right away. He notices everything. I should have anticipated that. I had to find a way to get the extra ounce out of my bottle without him seeing. But after he caught my first attempt, he got suspicious and started to watch me. Maybe I was paranoid. After all, there was nothing else for Henry to do.

I ended up with water bottles lined up on the floor by my side of the bed. I worked it out to where I would roll over to drink, wait until Henry had his back turned, and pour an ounce out of the bottle I was drinking into another bottle I had hidden behind the bed. When I wasn't fast enough, Henry watched me like a hawk to ensure I drank every drop. I was certain he knew something was going on.

During my insane water-thieving process, I discovered that plastic water bottles are conspicuously crinkly when there is nothing else happening, and you are trying to be stealthy to save someone's life.

I was. Losing. My. Mind.

Tick. Tick. Tick.

68273194

DAY 18

Blinded

We dragged ourselves to the kitchen for lunch on our fifth long day without running water.

69283157

The plan was to reevaluate our resources; the unfortunate truth was that I had to come clean about my water thievery. Not looking forward to the conversation, I was sluggish, trying to procrastinate our arrival as long as I could.

We were both haggard and dehydrated. My lips had cracked and bled so many times that I was thankful we weren't talking—it would've been a painful affair.

The fact was: there wasn't enough water. We had to tighten our rations. Henry had estimated that the temperature was hovering over 130°. Our faces were sunken in; our skin hung on our bones like wet clothes. We wouldn't survive much longer unless we increased our rations. Doubling down on limitations ensured our demise. Sleeping almost all the time, we faced the distinct possibility of never waking up.

Then there was Henry to factor into the equation. After a few days of his revolting protein shakes, he looked the tiniest bit healthier; his eyes weren't quite as sunken in, and the dark circles might have been dissipating. I was happy to keep sacrificing a portion of my rations to keep him alive if I could continue to hide the fact from him. But there'd be no sneaking any water thievery by him after a ration conversation. And there wasn't the slightest possibility he'd agree to take an extra portion at my expense.

We were almost to the conservatory when I bumped my shoulder into Henry. I'm not sure why I did it; it was quite unconscious. He looked down; I shrugged and smiled. He smiled and shoved me back. I didn't want to allow the moment, the closeness, but we had been through so much; it just happened.

We crossed the threshold onto the familiar stone path. By that point, we no longer needed Henry's dim candle in the blacked-out house. We'd walked the same route so many times, it was second nature. We knew every stone, every transition, every step.

The ticking that had been our constant companion, relentlessly gnawing at our brains, grew conspicuously louder. We looked at each other. Ticking boomed in the cavernous space, and then it slowly, deafeningly wound down.

Tick . . . Tick . . . TOCK.

After a prolonged moment of screaming silence, the conservatory ceiling flashed on. Blinding whiteness everywhere. After existing in dark for so long, it was excruciating.

Henry lost his candle. I dropped the tray. We both fell to the ground, shading our eyes. The crippling pain in my head came to a zenith in response to the sudden luminescent silence.

Our vision slowly adjusted, and we tried to absorb what we were seeing. The ceiling wasn't flat as we'd thought.

"It's a dome!"

A new image. No longer white. Not a sky. A crowd.

People in Times Square, New York, were gawking at a screen with a livestream of . . .

That's us!

Instinctively, I looked for a camera. But the clamoring voices drew my attention back to the crowd above. Realizing that we were also looking at them, the audience gasped and shrieked at our actions.

I felt my nails sink into Henry's skin before he carefully released my hand from his forearm and held it firmly in his own. He stood up and lifted me to my feet.

The angle from which the audience saw us changed. We jerked around to find where the second camera was hidden.

The extreme responses from the audience made me retch. *There have to be hundreds of people crammed into that plaza, staring at us on that towering screen. What is happening? They're reacting to every move we make.*

Henry and I were glued shoulder to shoulder, moving as a single unit. We looked back and forth from the wall to the ceiling. We made out the location our image was being captured from, but we couldn't see a camera. It was too well camouflaged. Without releasing Henry's hand, I grabbed a stone from the walkway and hurled it at the wall. From the projected image, I could see the stone approach the camera, but I missed, and unfortunately, didn't damage anything.

The image on the dome changed. It was another crowd in a plaza somewhere looking at another enormous outdoor screen that viewed us from a third vantage point in the conservatory. "That's Trafalgar Square in London," Henry whispered in my ear.

"I'll take your word for it," I responded, not knowing if he could hear me over the clamor of voices thundering in the room. I began to feel like we were in a modern version of the Roman Colosseum. Here for the entertainment of an unseen, all-powerful emperor and his insatiable crowds of millions.

We turned again, looking for the new camera. When we couldn't find it, we turned back to the dome. That audience reacted to our every move, too. Henry pointed to the bottom of the image. There was a number across the bottom of the onlookers in a bold white font.

69348016

The number steadily scrolled upward. Henry looked at me as if to ask what it meant. I shrugged, still uncomfortable speaking aloud—the latest development didn't make it any more appealing.

The image of the crowd changed again while the number remained at the bottom of the image, scrolling higher and higher like a possessed odometer.

The new location looked vaguely familiar. *Is that Australia?* I wasn't willing to venture a guess under the circumstances. But world-traveling Henry confirmed my suspicions, whispering, "This group is in the forecourt of the Sydney Opera House." The outdoor venue was overflowing with people looking up at a massive screen with . . . well again, us. The swarm of ant-sized people cheered when they realized that it was their turn to be featured. Henry and I flinched, and the masses instantly stopped in a unison response to our reaction.

Not getting used to the interactive portion of captivity.

We turned when we heard an unfamiliar language behind us. Apparently, the conservatory came equipped with surround sound. "Is that . . . ?" I asked.

"Incredible," Henry replied. A group had gathered to watch us on a massive screen in Tiananmen Square in China. It seemed that people from all parts of the world had gathered to support us. I was moved and overwhelmed.

The cities flashed by more rapidly after that, and the angles from which we were viewed changed even more abruptly. There had to be more than thirty cameras hidden around the conservatory. So many it was hard to keep track. Disoriented, the changing perspectives had us circling the tree, looking from the walls to the crowds of people on the dome in plazas located all over the world. China, Russia, Europe, Japan, the United States, the Middle East, South America, Africa, India, the locations seemed unending.

The single image split into a pie of five, and those five images rotated between gatherings in different cities around the world, each crowd reacting to our response to the overwhelming stimulation. An identical number—boldly imprinted in white at the bottom of each slice of the screen—steadily rose.

I can't watch anymore. It's too intense.

I covered my face to block it out, but the cacophony of voices continued to grow. I pulled my arms up over my head. With hordes of people in so many languages, I couldn't distinguish any of them. They gasped and shouted at us. Individuals trying to be heard over the thousands surrounding them. We couldn't understand what any one person said.

I covered my ears, scrunched my eyes, and fell to my knees. That drew an even more clamorous reaction. Henry knelt beside me and wrapped his arms around me. "Take a breath. Block it out. No response, just like we've done for weeks now. Slow, deep breaths." His tenderness and compassion only raised the volume and made their reactions more emphatic.

The New York assembly rotated back onto the screen; a single voice sounded above the fray, "We love you, Henry!" My barely contained emotions spilled over into a giggle, and Henry shook his head over my shoulder.

He must get more than his share of inappropriate admiration.

At least this time, it's helping ease the stress of our outrageous circumstances.

Henry tightened his boa-constrictor hug. With the entire world swirling around us, I felt I would fall into a void if he ever let go.

The volume dimmed.

Something's changed.

There was a heavy mechanical sound—like a harsh gear shifting. It instantly drew our attention back to the dome.

Text appeared over the still-changing images. The number had moved. It was no longer at the bottom of each image slice but underneath a line of text across the center of the entire dome.

we're all watching

69380991

The bold white letters emblazoned across all the images of people and then disappeared. I looked at Henry, shocked into silence.

if you don't play nice

69423979

It flashed up just long enough to read before it vanished.

i'll find someone to replace you

69492312

I couldn't help but gasp. Regretting it instantly, I covered my mouth. All five crowds on the dome universally shared my sentiment. I tried to keep myself from giving that bedlamite a reaction, yet I couldn't help but look at Henry for a response. He did his best not to react either and simply glanced at me out of the corner of his eye, reassuring me. He tightened his grip on my hand as another line appeared.

you wouldn't want that

69552397

Each line of text drew more gasps and a few isolated screams from spectators. When the line disappeared, the images of the masses did, too, though the chilling audio did not.

A final taunt in bold white inscribed over a blackened dome:

would you?

69610548

The last of the text disappeared. The haunting gasps and screams were silenced. The furiously scrolling number lingered in solitude for a moment, then evaporated.

69741390

Finally, the house woke from its dreadful nightmare. The dome reappeared as a sky with wispy white clouds slowly drifting by. The appliances hummed back to life. The ventilation system harshly shifted gears and pumped heavenly air-conditioned air into its rooms instead of the incinerator temperatures we'd been forced to endure. Light filled every corner of the house, and water flowed back into the barren pipes.

"Did we leave a faucet on?" *I hear water running.*

Henry and I looked around in wonder. *Everything seems alien after living in blackness for so long.* After a moment of adjustment, the gravity of the message sank in. It took all my strength not to break down.

I put my hand on Henry's arm. "I am so sorry for everything I put you through over the last two weeks, and it was all for nothing."

I was the cause of basically torturing you, and to what end? We didn't accomplish a thing.

"I can't in good conscience let them put someone else in here just so I can get out. I . . . I just can't." When I finished speaking, Henry removed my hand from his arm. I dropped my head in disappointment. *Am I alone here? Have I misjudged you?*

No, I haven't.

He firmly clasped my hand between his two mastodonic hands and waited for me to meet his eye. "Of course," he began in his low, rumbled tone. "We could never let someone else take our places in here. That would be unconscionable." My entire body relaxed in relief. I didn't realize how much tension I'd been holding.

"I think you're being a little hard on yourself. We've accomplished more than you realize with passive resistance. You made our captor talk to us. They spoke in the first person and singular, so it might not be a leap to say that it's one person. We can probably guess that they took us to gain that massive viewership out there." He gestured toward the dome.

"We now know that not only does someone know that we're missing, but everyone knows we're missing. Therefore, the whole world is out there working to get us back. So, anything we can do to help them find us will get us one step closer to freedom."

Fortified, my back straightened.

"Like ensuring they know we are completely underground," Henry continued a bit louder than the beginning of his speech and eyed an area of the wall where we had determined there was a camera. He went on speaking much louder than anyone would normally talk, "And the fact that I was taken from the Hollywood Roosevelt, and you were taken from where?"

I like where you're going with this, Oscar.

I opened my mouth to answer, but the power went out once again. And once more, the dome was black with white text:

play nice or be replaced
69748632

The text hovered for a moment before it disappeared, but the power didn't return.

do we have an understanding?
69801893

When the message finally left and the power came back on, the house returned to normal. I looked at Henry. I didn't have to speak aloud. *No hints.*

Standing up, I asked the question foremost on my mind. "What do you think he wants from us exactly?"

I had my suspicions, but Henry was the more contemplative of the two of us; he'd have the next twelve steps planned out before I got past step one.

"I believe he wants us to continue trying to escape for the entertainment of himself and"—he gestured at the array of cameras we had discovered yet couldn't see—"his surprisingly vast audience."

I took a deep, cleansing breath. "That's what I was afraid of."

Slowly walking around the tree, I looked at each position where we had noticed a camera had been observing us. *They're there; why can't I see them?*

"Okay. I'm going to make a suggestion. It's out there. But what if we, slowly and methodically, one room at a time, look at every inch of wall, floor, ceiling, and each piece of furniture for secret passages or any clue of a way out. It won't be fun, but it's the best suggestion I've got."

I completed my lap, reaching Henry again, and got close enough to whisper, hopefully undetected, "And it won't be entertaining at all while we figure out what we really want to do next."

Henry covered a smirk with his hand while I continued, "Before we get rolling on that, I am going to find out if the shower is functioning and take advantage of it because I feel disgusting, and I'm not doing anything like this." I held up the bottom edges of my sweat-soaked tank and shorts. "If psycho man doesn't like it, he can come in here and fight me. And if I find out there are cameras in the bathroom, I'm going to have murderous intentions when I do get out of here." I glared in the direction of one of the camera locations.

"Right then." Henry took hold of my shoulders and aimed me toward the bedroom hall, walking behind me as he talked. "We definitely both need showers and to do some laundry before we get started."

Of course, I had to clean glass out of my shower before I could use it, but it was worth the extra effort. *I've never needed a shower so badly in all my life.*

There was a lot of cleaning up to do before tackling any escape work for our newfound admirers. Living in the dark and under the conditions we had, the house was left in an impressive amount of disarray. We spent the entirety of the day doing laundry, cleaning, and generally putting the house back in order. While we did that, we tried to get used to talking again. An awkward affair. We'd worked so hard at being silent for so long that it felt wrong to speak.

Silence hung over the library like a fog for hours while we sat on the floor in the center of the circular sofa, folding a mountain of laundry. I didn't mind; it was peaceful. I was startled and mentally unprepared when Henry broke the silence. "Batman or Superman?"

The oddity of the question didn't even register before the answer spilled out. "Superman."

Why did I tell him that?

"Iron Man or Captain America?" he asked as though my answer was a window into my soul.

"Captain America. But he's not my favorite Avenger." *It has to stop. I'm still so tired; I have no filter. I don't want to talk about this.*

"Now that's interesting. Who is your favorite Avenger?" He put down the mass of pink and orange polyester he was folding and leaned in rapt with interest.

I looked up at the walls, wondering where the cameras in the library were. "I'd rather not discuss it. Who are your favorite superheroes?" *Why does it sound ridiculous when I ask?*

"We weren't talking about me. I asked about your favorite Avenger. I promise to drop it if you give me this one." He scooted over next to me so I could tell him in a lowered voice.

I gave in. I didn't have the energy or mental fortitude to argue. "Fine. Agent Coulson," I scowled. *He's going to ask for an explanation; I'm not giving one.*

He never asked. He smiled coyly and went back to wrangling a king-size fitted sheet. *Is he just happy that he dragged it out of me, or is he pleased with my appreciation for nerds?*

We continued in our awkward on-and-off silence, trying not to doze throughout our chores until the house was back in order, and then opted for a late dinner. Henry was thrilled to eat something other than a protein shake and vowed that he would never consume another as long as he lived.

71108139

After two weeks of physical and psychological torture, we should have gone to bed early and gotten the rest our minds and bodies needed. But no. It appeared that sleep deprivation impaired decision-making skills as well as motor function. We decided that we deserved a movie and some over-salted, over-buttered popcorn.

FBI DIRECTOR LUCIAN FENN

Zugzwang

News Channel 4 Studio 2a

"This is Aaron De Fiore, live with Lucian Fenn, the Director of the Cyber and Criminal Services Branch of the FBI. The first African-American to hold this position in FBI history. Your remarkable breakthrough in the race barrier is a story in and of itself, but if it's all right with you, we'll stick with the case at hand.

"Yes, Mr. De Fiore, my race has nothing to do with my occupation, my position at the agency, or this case. Let's proceed."

I'd accepted the interview in the far-fetched hope of making headway in the case. This task was not made easier when the network inflicted upon me an anchor overcompensating for his inexperience with exuberance, slimy hair gel, and artificially whitened teeth. *This will be an uphill battle.*

Mr. De Fiore removed his probing gaze from me and bore directly into the camera, addressing his acolytes in his signature rapid-fire speech. "Thank you for clarifying, Director Fenn. The Director and I have been watching live along with those of you at home, as the two captives—two-time Oscar-winner Henry Walker Beecher and reclusive philanthropist Violet Montgomery Cameron—have discovered for the first time that they are being watched, and not only that they are being watched, but that they are being watched by the entire world."

The unprecedented activity at the Guest House had delayed the start of our interview—a fluke any opportunistic reporter would have seen as career-making serendipity. This one was no exception.

My interviewer shifted his focus back to me as he continued but with a new expression behind his eyes. *What's he up to?*

I donned my standard G-man presentation. A suit, expressionless, stiff. That's how it had to be. He had no idea who he was dealing with. I'd been doing this job and saving lives longer than he'd been alive.

"Director Fenn, can you tell us what the FBI is doing to recover Hollywood's hottest commodity and the Mother Teresa of our generation? How close are you to success, and what is the FBI doing to find the man responsible for this crime, the man the public has taken to calling 'The Host'?"

Which question does he expect me to answer? Does he expect me to address all of them or any at all? This is precisely why I prefer to decline interview requests across the board.

I let silence hang in the air. At six foot two, I'd use my six-inch height advantage to intimidate and seize control of the conversation. I leaned in and instead answered the questions I wanted to answer.

"Mr. De Fiore, for the safety of the victims and the success of the operation, the FBI does not comment on ongoing investigations. What I can tell you is that we have our top agents working twenty-four hours a day to recover Ms. Cameron and Mr. Beecher. We have multiple teams working toward their recovery, tracing the live feeds, and tracking the unsub. In short, the full force of the FBI is behind this.

"As far as the moniker 'The Host' goes, I am aware that Mr. Beecher initially used the term, and it took off almost instantaneously. I can understand the desire to play on the idea that this individual is 'hosting' houseguests combined with the clever play on internet terminology, but at the FBI, we prefer not to nickname unsubs. It gives them power. We purposefully refer to an unknown subject as an unsub because it removes that layer of humanity. They are not media sensations. They are nameless criminals. Let's not give him any more than he has already taken and take back that which he currently has."

Aaron De Fiore leaned over the news desk like a snake ready to strike. He may not have been a suspect in an investigation, but my instincts said he was looking increasingly like one every minute. *I don't trust you, Mr. De Fiore.*

"Interesting thoughts, Director. Let's move away from blaming my innocent audience for giving power to this malfeasant and return to your lack of progress in catching him, shall we? You've had over a month at this point. Can you tell me what you've actually accomplished to rescue these poor people? Where are your results? With all the resources the FBI has dedicated to this case, why am I interviewing you instead of celebrating their homecoming right now?"

If I didn't know any better, I would have thought I saw a glint off his smile like a cartoon villain. *This is an ambush.* He had clearly set up the interview not for information but for sensationalism. The entire situation was insupportable.

"Again, Mr. De Fiore, the FBI cannot comment on ongoing investigations. We will release information as we can." *I can't give this hack the satisfaction of thinking he's gotten to me.* I kept a placid expression and collected my thoughts.

I glanced at the large monitor situated between us, though only for a second; no one would have noticed unless they had a trained eye for detail. From the closed-captioning, it seemed Ms. Cameron and Mr. Beecher were discussing their new reality. Seeing them, I knew what I had to do.

"Mr. De Fiore, I may not be able to comment on the investigation, but your viewers can help us bring this case to a close." De Fiore's eyes grew wide at my announcement. *Point, Fenn.*

Every anchor is hungry for an exclusive. This one leaned in greedy for his. "Yes, Director?"

I have his attention. Up until that point in the interview, my posture had remained stoic and stiff. For the first time, I shifted and fixed my eye directly on the camera before me. Not once had I given an impassioned address during an interview, but I had to sway the hearts and minds of the public. I had to save the lives of Ms. Cameron and Mr. Beecher.

"Each person paying to access the livestream of Ms. Cameron and Mr. Beecher's captivity is funding its continuation. If each supporter will turn off their computers, their televisions, their phones, and their tablets and stop streaming the coverage, their abductor will have no reason to hold them captive. He will release them."

Unaccustomed to making pleas to anyone for any reason, I felt my chest constrict. *Shut it down, Fenn. Feel it later.* I couldn't let the depth of my compassion for these victims reach my voice or face. It wouldn't have been professional or helpful.

"Your actions have a direct impact on the lives of these two people. You can either fund the person holding them captive by feeding him cryptocurrency to watch the livestream, or you can withhold from him that which he is looking for.

"Turn off your streaming devices, and help me get these people home."

When I finished, both Mr. De Fiore and I scrutinized the livestream feed, particularly the viewer count at the bottom, to see if I had gotten through to anyone. I was surprised Mr. De Fiore allowed the dead air, but the two of us were nearly as captivated with the number as his audience had been with the livestream.

The number did move. Slowly at first, but it unmistakably decreased. Reaching that audience was almost enough to make me smile on camera. Almost.

A moment later, my victory was intruded upon. "Director, do you believe it is incontrovertible that the act of individuals disconnecting their viewership will actually save Ms. Cameron and Mr. Beecher?"

I could feel my internal temperature rising. *Why is this man-child threatening the progress I just made toward saving these people? Bane that you are, you couldn't resist the opportunity to stir the pot!*

Yet, he continued, "I mean, even if you can convince millions of people to stop watching what is arguably the most captivating event we've had to watch in a decade, don't you think that doing so will put their lives in more danger and not less?"

He leaned back in his chair like a teenager mentally doing a mic drop. *Of all the unprofessional postures . . .*

I was the only adult left in the room. I not only had to protect the lives of the captives from the unsub but also from that headline hunter.

"No, Mr. De Fiore, I do not. Unlike you, I am a veteran, a seasoned professional. We do not give kidnappers what they want. Historically, it puts the victims at greater risk. If we continue to watch this twisted version of reality television, we give him attention and money. If we stop, no attention, no currency, no reason to hold them hostage." I stood firm, refusing to break eye contact. I was determined to win the battle.

"Exactly," Mr. De Fiore responded.

I blinked, but nothing more. I would not give anything away while I analyzed his countenance for explanation.

He continued, "If he has no viewers, no attention . . . no money coming in, he'll have no reason to keep them hostage, no reason to keep them around." He waited for my response with a mischievous smirk.

I feel the rug slipping out from under me. I could count on one hand the number of times I'd walked into something like that. It had been decades since it had happened. *Now I know I'm getting too close to this case, to these victims.*

Mr. De Fiore's smile resembled that of a Cheshire cat. "If he doesn't need them around, Director, isn't he more likely to kill them than to set them free?"

Steady, Fenn.

"Mr. De Fiore, wild speculation only puts them in more danger. The media and general public need to keep your opinions to yourselves and let the proper authorities handle the matter."

Mr. De Fiore postured as he pressed his advantage, swelling as he leaned in. "Well. You *can* handle things. I'm merely saying that if you're going to ask people to make a choice, they should know that a consequence of that choice might be that a world-class actor and a beloved philanthropist—whose safe return the world has miraculously united behind—might just wind up dead instead. So, maybe, just maybe, they might choose to keep watching so The *Host*"—he emphasized the name, getting the dig in—"will have a reason to keep them alive. If they are of use, he won't have a reason to hurt or to kill them." He waved his hand at me dismissively and concluded his diatribe, "I'm just putting it out there."

My patience had exceeded its limits. "Don't play with people's lives purely for the sake of ratings."

I glanced back at the live feed to assess the damage. The viewer number rose much faster than it had been descending moments before. It already surpassed the number displayed when the interview started by over 120,000. My hopes for a positive impact through the interview had been extinguished. I was battered, though not broken—not that I'd let my state of mind show on a live broadcast.

There's nothing left to do here.

Mr. De Fiore collected the papers from the news desk in front of him, straightening them triumphantly. "Director Fenn, I report the news. I don't play with people's lives. I tell it like it is. If we have good ratings, it's because I am unrivaled at what I do."

I silently groaned for his besotted constituency as he turned away from me and looked back into the camera with a self-satisfied smirk. "This is Aaron De Fiore here with FBI Director of Cyber and Criminal Services, Lucian Fenn, live with your Channel 4 news update."

I had never been so thankful for an interview to end. When the red light on the camera blinked off, I took a slow, cleansing breath to calm my temper before removing the microphone. The need to leave the studio weighed on me. I had to recover the ground I'd lost. I had to return to work immediately.

As I fished the microphone out of my shirt, I felt an uninhibited slap on my back. No one dared invade my personal space like that at the Bureau.

"Director, you were amazing! Thank you for such a great interview.

All I expected was, 'We can't comment on ongoing investigations.' But that? That was television gold. I am definitely looking at an Emmy."

I didn't respond; I couldn't respond. If I opened my mouth or moved a muscle, I'd have to add an assault charge to the list of problems I had to deal with when I got back to the seventh floor. I chose wisdom, stayed silent, and removed myself from the premises as swiftly as possible.

DAY 19

Nightmare

Surreal, returning to old routines.

72615082

Henry characteristically started his day in the gym and met me for breakfast after a shower. The house was clean, organized, and back to the way it had been almost three long weeks before. Well, there were a few minor changes: a little fire damage, a couple of gaping holes in the wall and ceiling, and a pile of broken furniture shoved into the back of the larder. There was a bloodstain in the theater from where I nearly bled out after the vent incident, the battered stool from our very first day, and one severely damaged window display from my mini meltdown.

Perhaps it isn't back to factory specs, but I'm proud of our modifications. They haven't gotten us out, but they're a testament to the effort.

I sat at the dining table eating my powdered eggs, drinking my freeze-dried coffee, staring at two bunnies playing under a bush in the fictitious window.

Is this really going to be my life?

Henry startled me out of my trance. "Today's the day."

"What?" I squeaked. His morning chipperness never ceased to amaze me in the midst of our bleak predicament.

His face told me that even he didn't believe what he was saying. He tried again. "Today is the day we're getting out." This time, he stuck the tip of his tongue out and closed one eye like an emoji. I'd never seen an actual human being make that face, but it seemed perfectly appropriate at that moment.

I tried to share his façade of enthusiasm for the cameras. "Well, you never know. We may find a trapdoor on the first go. After all, they got us in here somehow. No one beamed us in." I hoped the *Star Trek* reference would entertain him. Henry's face lit up, and he dug into his eggs with vigor.

I reviewed our plan. "If we go over this place inch by inch, we're bound to find whatever hatch we were brought through. We just have to be thorough."

He shoveled food into his mouth and gave me a half-interested head tilt, and for the first time since I'd known him, he spoke through a mouth full of food. "And what tools do you expect us to use for this endeavor?"

Appalling manners, Oscar. It must have something to do with the introduction of an audience. I'll forgive. No, I won't. But I'll ignore it.

I slid our trusty mallet and a couple of dinner knives across the table. Henry looked at me like I'd come unglued.

C'mon, you know it's, at least in part, a show while we think through our next strategic move. I could see his belly move in a silent chuckle and an almost unnoticeable shake of the head as he wolfed down more of his massive breakfast. *Yeah, you know.*

We cleaned the kitchen and took our questionable tools back to my bedroom suite. *Can't think of a better place to begin.* Henry elected to work on the walls and ceiling; I assigned myself the floor and furniture. We tapped the handles of the knives on every square inch of floor, wall, and ceiling, then pried at every edge and corner with the blades. We pulled every knob and poked at everything that could be a secret button or lever in that room. *It may be a stall tactic to appease our captor for the moment, but I also have to be sure that if there is a way out, we'll find it.*

We tried everything that could be a secret to opening a doorway. *I feel foolish. Will this even appease the requirements of "playing nice"? Am I being overly optimistic? Are we going to find anything useful this way?*

The monotony of the task allowed us to think about how to practically and realistically free ourselves or subtly get information out. Precisely what information we needed to convey was beyond me. *At least we know we have the opportunity.*

We worked for hours without a word, just the constant tapping and prying of the mallet and knives, until Henry broke in, "Are we going to talk about what happened yesterday?" His request was reticent. Avoiding my gaze, he kept going about his work, waiting for my response. I hesitated to answer.

That was probably the most traumatic experience of my life; I don't want to think about it, let alone talk about it. Can't we pretend it never happened?

Evidently, I was lost in my head because Henry dove right in. "The numbers. Do you have a thought on what they might represent?"

That's an easier conversation than I thought you were going for. Thanks for easing me in. "It seemed like a counter of some kind, maybe viewers?" *I don't know.*

Henry didn't stop working or even look at me as we talked, so I kept working as well. *This makes conversation easier; I can do this.*

"I agree," he responded conclusively. "If I had to guess, it represents individual logged-in views." He paused for a moment as though searching for exactly the right words. "I don't think they could have accounted for each individual watching in the crowds. The counter was moving too quickly. I think it had to be a technology-based counter, tracking people watching online.

"It's unfortunate, but it's human nature not to be able to look away from a tragedy in motion. That's why traffic slows down when there's a car crash on the opposite side of the road. So, when our tragedy went online, people couldn't help but watch.

"He's probably found a way to keep his location from being tracked, as well as ours. I have to wonder if he's monetized the feed, and that's why he hasn't asked for a ransom. Or perhaps he's purely done this for attention. That's what I'm not certain of yet." Henry stopped working and looked down at the floor for a moment.

His posture sank abruptly, his head dropped, and his face puckered as though he'd eaten something sour. "What is it?" I asked.

Henry snapped up, back straight, shoulders back, and went back to work. "Nothing. We just have a lot of house to cover. I'd like to finish your en suite before we quit for the day."

Well, that was strange body language. If only we could talk without being overheard. We have to find a way to communicate.

We worked in silence for a while longer. My mind roamed from subject to subject as I worked my way over the hardwood floor of the closet, tapping rhythmically; the sound hypnotized me as I went. The massive planks wouldn't budge; nothing moved. *Everything's tight as a drum.*

I pondered the scores of people that had appeared the day before. *Some of them seemed genuinely concerned for us. Others seemed like people who couldn't look away from a tragedy in motion, like Henry said. How many people are watching because Henry is their favorite actor?*

My mind drifted back to Henry's body language. *He's such an astute person; what's on his mind? What has him worried?*

My mind strayed again as I began checking the drawers and shelves in the closet for triggers and levers. *I really misjudged Henry when we got here.* I cringed at the thought. *I had painted all actors with the same brush: self-interested, egotistical, shallow, even simpleminded.*

My sigh was audible.

Ugh. Did he hear me? I can't believe myself; I've judged a whole profession based on a stereotype. Henry is none of those things.

Henry poked his head into the closet. "I'm done in the bathroom. You almost finished in here? I'm starving."

Of course, you're hungry.

My embarrassment for having judged him prevented me from turning around.

"Almost done. Why don't you head to the kitchen? I'll catch up in a minute." Even with my back to him, I knew he could read my mind.

I finished investigating the last piece of shelving, still feeling Henry's perceptive eyes on me. I forced myself to ignore the feeling and slowly, methodically finish my work. When I was through, I carefully picked up my tools and turned to the door. He wasn't there. *How long has he been gone?*

I made my way to the kitchen and found Henry whistling away as he cooked, like a bulky Martha Stewart in his bright-yellow apron. I giggled every time he put it on; it was two sizes too small and had ruffles that encompassed the border like frilly frosting. Yet, there it hung, on the most unlikely mannequin, every time he cooked.

He appeared to have had several different dishes going at once. I had stressed myself out for nothing. He'd been in the kitchen all along. *Huh.*

"Can I help with dinner?" Not only did he look like he had everything under control, but he looked like someone who was juggling while spinning plates. He didn't need me to interfere with his rhythm. Still, I wanted to be useful.

"You could set the table." He gave me a half smile and gestured toward the dining room with his eyes.

Excellent. I'll help; you keep spinning plates.

While I set out the blue-and-white melamine plates on the brilliant-yellow Formica table, I couldn't help but glance around the corner as Henry moved around the kitchen like a figure-skater, seasoning one dish, stirring another, setting a timer for a third. He was far more extraordinary than the one-dimensional man I'd initially taken him for.

I popped my head into the kitchen with a wine selection. "What do you prefer to go with whatever it is you're making?" I held up bottles for him to examine.

He glanced over his shoulder. "Always sauvignon blanc with freeze-dried chicken." With a smile, he went back to his juggling act at the stove. I set the chilled bottle of white wine on the table with the appropriate glasses and put the cabernet away. Then, I stacked several serving dishes and brought them to the peninsula between the dining room and the kitchen. I had no idea what he needed, but I thought I'd be thorough and provide an exhaustive array of options to suit what was bound to be a culinary masterpiece. A tray, platters, several bowls.

I'm overcompensating because I feel guilty.

No. I'm excessively helpful.

"Thank you. Almost done." He hadn't turned around to see me.

Does he have eyes in the back of his head? The man has superpowers, I swear.

A timer went off, and Henry pulled a pan off the stove and emptied the contents into one of the bowls. *Mmm, perfectly cooked and seasoned rice.*

"You know, I could see your reflection in the splashback." Henry finished his sentence with a bellow of a laugh.

I turned my back to him.

My face is a billboard for my thoughts. I hate that!

Henry pulled himself together. "When I said 'thank you,' you looked surprised." I spun the stool around to listen. "I suspect it was because you didn't know how I knew you were there. The gold-flecked mirror over the hob." He tapped the foxed mirror used as a trendy '60s backsplash over the lemon stove top.

He chuckled to himself as he finished filling the bowls with his delightful concoctions. "And here's the last one, Mum's secret recipe for roast aubergine."

My attitude evolved from feeling guilty for misjudging him toward a balance between mild embarrassment, contentment, and slight confusion at his Britishisms that I wasn't in the mood to ask about, so I stopped reacting and quietly brought food from the kitchen over to the table in the dining room.

We devoured a sumptuous meal. Henry had an uncanny ability to turn what astronaut food we had left into a gourmet feast. We no longer had the benefit of frozen meat from the deep freezer after the power outage, so we were stuck with freeze-dried meat from the larder. It was . . . we'll call it different. We were limited in the garden as well. More than half the produce died from heat and lack of light. But somehow, Henry managed it. I overate to the point of being uncomfortable, a complete impossibility for Henry. *You're a bottomless pit, aren't you?*

We sat, unwilling to move. "That was magnificent, Henry. Thank you." He tilted his chair back on two legs and rested his hands behind his head, looking heartily pleased with himself. "Where did you learn to cook like that?" Henry's eyes widened before he carefully lowered all four legs of his wiry chair back to the floor and leaned forward on his elbows with a cocky smile. *What's this? He's going to spin a yarn for me now? This should be entertaining.* I settled into my chair for the ostensibly long tale I was about to get.

Henry's eyes focused behind me as his memory wandered into the distant past; a warm expression came over his face. "I was introduced to the kitchen when I was young, probably six or seven. Mum would have me fetch fresh vegetables from the garden for supper after school. She'd tell me stories or sing while I helped her prepare the evening meal. My brothers would rather play outside and were always late for meals. But I wanted to spend that extra time with just me and my mum. It was a time when the house wasn't crowded with people clamoring for her attention and a time that I had her all to myself."

Funny, that's a smile I haven't seen in any of your movies, Oscar. It's the smile of a sweet little boy who loves his mother superimposed on a grown man.

How about that.

"I learned how to care for every vegetable, plant, and herb we grew in the garden and how to prepare every meal she ever made. Father would never have approved. He thought that there was man's work, and there was women's work, and cooking was definitely women's work. Over the years, he never found out." A flash of boyish mischief crossed his face. I couldn't help but smile at his story—and particularly at the way he pronounced the "h" in "herb."

Consumed by new thoughts, his smile dissolved, and he looked down at his hands, fiddling with his napkin. He continued in a darker, constrained tone, "Over one particularly hot and humid summer—I was thirteen—she passed after a long, harsh battle with lymphatic cancer." Henry cleared his throat. "Cooking is my way of remembering her." My heart broke for him.

I leaned forward and held his hand. *What do I say?* He covered my hand with his, and we sat, comforted by the silence.

Moments later, I realized my face was wet. *Dammit! Henry can't see.*

I tried to subtly reach for my napkin with my free hand. The movement must have alerted him because he lifted his head. I adjusted to make it look like I was blotting the corners of my mouth. He snickered. "Nice try. You have mascara all down your face. Don't worry, I won't tell." He winked and stood up, clearing the dishes.

I dropped my forehead on the table. *I can't win.* I smeared away what mascara I could—probably making it worse—and got up to put the leftovers in the fridge.

Henry had started washing dishes, and I tried to take over. "You cooked; I'll clean."

Henry's smile was one of understanding. "I like doing dishes; it's relaxing. Why don't you freshen up while you decide what film you want to watch tonight? I think you could use a walk after a big meal, and I could use a moment alone after spilling my guts." He winked again.

Chivalrous to the end.

I shook my head at him. "If you insist. But you know I'll force you to watch more sci-fi when all you want to watch is a chick flick. Is that really how you want this evening to go down?" I swung my arms overhead in an exaggerated gesture as I walked off, hoping my humor would make him laugh a little.

"As long as you make sure it isn't action-packed; you know I hate those," he shouted back as I scuffed down the hall.

"No promises!" I called, trying my best not to laugh. I hoped I'd begun to lift his spirits. I didn't have to imagine that talking about his mom was hard. I knew from experience. I supposed that's why I looked like such a mess. My experience with my mom wasn't so idyllic as his. Maybe that was part of it. I envied him—*why couldn't that have been me?*

I shook myself out of my daze as I reached the bathroom. *I'm a disaster.* Mascara hadn't just run down the corner of my eyes; it left black streaks down the edge of my chin, and then I had smeared it across my cheeks. I would have been mortified if I hadn't spent the previous weeks as an unshowered, sweaty heap. I was hardly twenty-four hours into feeling human again, so I brushed it off.

I washed my face and barely applied some fresh powder, a little mascara, and ChapStick. *If he thinks I'm putting on an entire face worth of makeup to sit in a blacked-out theater, he has another thing coming.* I looked in the mirror. *Who do I have to impress? The entire world has seen me at my absolute worst. So, no one.*

I didn't make it back to the kitchen; Henry was already crossing the conservatory with glasses and wine—a gamay. At dinner, Henry had said he'd found it in the larder and that it would pair perfectly with my favorite movie candy from the theater bar. *We'll see about that.*

"You look refreshed." He smiled, but I covered my face.

"I meant it as a compliment. I actually prefer a more natural look. Some women wear far too much makeup. You look fantastic." That made me infinitely more self-conscious. "Did you pick a film?" He motioned toward the theater with the glasses, and I realized he never entered a room before me; he always gave the "after you" wave.

What an adorable walking cliché.

My mind popped back to the present. "Well, I thought we might move away from sci-fi tonight and watch an old favorite." He squinted at me, unsure of what to think. "Don't worry; I won't make you watch a musical or anything."

An unrestrained grin broke out across his face as we entered the theater. "Ha! That never even crossed my mind. You? Watch a musical? Never!"

That's insulting! "Hey, I have impressively diverse tastes in movies, thank you very much! They do. Include." I hesitated and stumbled over my words. "Some. Musicals." I shouldn't have added the qualifier, but I knew he would have tested my resolve. He held the glasses to his belly and laughed. The glasses clinked with the movement. *I have to shut him up.* "Would you rather watch one of my favorite musicals or the movie I had in mind?" I crossed my arms and stared him down.

Please don't say musical.

He stopped laughing, coughed, and waved me to my seat. "Proceed, madam." I breathed a sigh of relief.

He poured the wine at the bar, and I teased the movie while I navigated to my selection. "As I said, not sci-fi, more of an action flick. Do you like fast cars?"

His head popped up. "I do indeed."

Thought you might. "Do you like rare and valuable cars?"

He brought over the glasses of wine and the Swedish Fish I'd been nibbling on since our *Star Wars* marathon. My supply was dangerously low. "Even better," he responded as he plunked into the seat beside me.

I pulled the movie up onto the screen. "Blimey, I haven't seen this in years." *The movie monster is appeased.* I'd won the evening with my pick of *Gone in 60 Seconds.*

We enjoyed our flick, and he was absolutely right about the gamay and Swedish Fish. *What an oddly spectacular combo.* About halfway through, I collected the glasses and wrappers, moving them to the bar in the back. I returned to my seat during a particularly loud action sequence, sitting on my feet to give me a little extra height, and hooked my arm in Henry's, leaning in close to his ear.

"Don't worry, I'm not making a move. I've been thinking about how we might talk without being overheard. This was the best I could come up with. I wanted you to know so the option was available to both of us." I pulled my head away from his ear and tried to unhook my arm, but he stopped me by interlocking his fingers with my hand and holding my arm tight.

Henry lifted the armrest between us and leaned his head toward me, brushing his nose across the side of my forehead first. "It's a great plan," he began, "but you can't only look romantically interested when you want to talk; you have to follow through."

I must have looked like a trapped animal. My throat closed; my mouth dried up. Henry grinned widely before he put his lips right back in my ear. "Now you're stuck with me."

I didn't think this through.

All I wanted was a method of communication. *This is a step too far.* Henry still had my right hand interlocked with his right hand and pulled it closer. His left arm—which I had previously linked in my right arm—he freed up to sneak around me.

How did this even happen? Why can't I undo it?

We were pressed together, sharing one and a half seats with one of his arms anchored around my back and the other cinched around my waist, holding my hand. He was nuzzled in my ear as he talked. I was completely enveloped by Henry. When I pulled away, he sucked me in closer. *How is this even possible?*

"Sit still; this plan is genius." I could tell he thought it was an innocent game.

He doesn't mean any harm, Monti. It's a decent plan, really. It's the easiest way to talk with no one hearing us or suspecting that we're plotting.

I just . . . can't . . . do it.

It took some time for me to work up the courage to say something.

I'm going to offend him. He thinks this is hilarious, and I'm minimally embarrassed.

I finally took a deep breath and turned to tell him, but he turned, too. Our noses touched.

Too close.

I panicked.

I didn't intend to, but I yelled in his face, "Henry, I just . . . I can't!" I ran out of the theater.

He called after me, "Monti!"

I don't know if he followed. I didn't look back. I just kept running until I reached my room. When I got there, I slammed the door in a reverberating do-not-disturb sign.

I couldn't sleep. I sat up in the pink chaise longue, watching the artificial wilderness under the artificial moon through the artificial window.

Is it even night back home? Am I on the same continent? What am I going to say to Henry tomorrow? Worse . . . what will he say to me?

I can't believe I did that. Does he understand? I certainly won't explain myself. I never explain. I never get close enough to care what anyone thinks. He deserves better.

My restless attempt at sleep in the chair resulted in nightmares involving the unnatural, distorted gold mirror in the bathroom and the frigid, louring crypt. They startled me awake, leaving me dripping in cold sweat. That was the end of sleep for me. I marched into the bathroom and grabbed the heaviest object at hand, a noxious three-wick sandalwood candle. I stepped back and hurled it into the mirror. I would not allow it to disturb my sleep for one more night.

What in the world?

I put the candle down in the pile of glass shards on the bathroom counter, but my image was still portrayed behind the broken glass. I poked at the spot where the glass jar had impacted. A small shatter pattern and a strange black spot surrounded it, like someone had splattered paint behind the glass. I'd seen the pattern before when someone had backed into an OLED screen at my charity's office Christmas party.

Another screen. You've got to be kidding me!

There has to be a camera in here somewhere, and the Organic LED was used to display his malevolent manipulation of my face. My daughter's face. I should've known.

I clawed at the bulky wooden frame—top, bottom, corners, anywhere I could get a grip, trying to rip it off the wall—but it was firmly anchored in place. I adjusted my strategy and picked up my trusty candle to smash the OLED screen.

Wait. Even if I destroy the screen, there's still a camera. A camera in the bathroom. My stomach lurched. I needed to throw up, but it wasn't the time. I had work to do.

Where's the camera?

I waved my hand over the edge of the frame. When I reached a flourish at the top-center, the image froze. *There it is.* I covered the camera with a small towel, and the "reflection" in the gold mirror froze. I decided to leave the screen whole, so I would know that the camera remained decommissioned.

For my sanity, I needed to move on to the other object of my nightmares. No matter how many times I had closed the crypt door, it continued to open at random intervals, though it never seemed to happen when Henry was around.

A parasite eating away at the back of my brain—that door—I had to end it.

Barefoot, I stomped down the hall. A drowsy Henry poked his head out his door. "What's going on?"

"Go back to bed!" I barked at him and forcefully shoved him back into his room.

I crossed the threshold and marched heavily over the stone path, ignoring the large stones digging into my feet. I was on a mission. Reaching the crypt, I stared.

You've plagued me for too long. It ends now.

Wooden benches with iron-flourished frames lined the paths between the raised garden beds. There were eleven before Henry used some in his furniture tower. I took the armrest of the one closest to the crypt and tried to drag it toward the door. It was incredibly heavy and awkward; the feet squealed over the stones. I yanked and heaved, hardly moving it an inch. Then I fell over; the weight had vanished. Henry had made an appearance and lifted the bench for me.

"Where do you want it?" He was holding the bench—that I couldn't budge—in midair.

Good grief.

"I need that nightmare"—I pointed toward the crypt—"barricaded, or I'm never going to get a good night's sleep." I dropped my arm in exhaustion.

Henry kicked the door closed and pinned the bench under the handle. "Better?" He smiled, looking like a run-down dad who had chased monsters out from underneath a toddler's bed.

"Yes, thank you." He offered a hand to lift me to my feet; I didn't take it, and he took note.

"Are we finished breaking things for the evening?" He was trying to be cute, but he was too tired to succeed.

"You can go back to sleep. I won't keep you up any longer. I promise." As he walked ahead of me, head sagging, I knew I'd hurt him.

I have to get out of here. I have to go somewhere I can't hurt Henry anymore.

73971825

AGENT MARA THORNFIELD

The Art of War

J. Edgar Hoover Bldg., Washington, DC

SSA Thornfield burst through the double doors at the back of the Cyber and Criminal Services tactical hub. I was standing at the side of the stadium-style room in a huddle, listening to a series of reports—none of which gave me much hope. We were nearly five weeks into the case and weren't any better off than when we started.

I flipped through Agent Barone's file—an overly positive spin, despite the bleak circumstance—and watched Agent Thornfield barreling toward us out of the corner of my eye. She had that look of pertinaciousness I'd come to expect from one of my favorite recruits.

Agent Thornfield had worked hard in her time at the Bureau, harder than any of her peers. Perhaps she felt that she had to because she was a woman or because she was Latina. Being one of the first People of Color to make it to the Director level, I understood her drive. But she certainly didn't need to compensate for any shortcomings as an agent; she consistently excelled in every task she was given, every role she undertook.

Thirty-four days ago, I tasked SSA Thornfield with her highest-profile assignment to date: Operation "Libertas." Latin for "freedom." She coordinated with Interpol to identify an actionable number of possible locations holding The Host's victims, victims the FBI designated the "Guests." This moniker had to remain for in-house use only; we couldn't risk the media getting ahold of the term. Retribution over our hypocrisy would have been untenable. Personally, I abhorred our use of the term.

On the third floor, Thornfield's team sifted through construction permits issued worldwide since 1950. *If she's charging into Tactical Operations now, she's got something. Excellent.*

Not even five feet tall, she strode through the enormous room buzzing with activity like she was RBG. *Makes a mentor proud.* Maria Lanoff, one of our SWAT team members, gave a nod of appreciation as Thornfield cruised by. As the first female ever to be commissioned as an Enhanced SWAT operator, Lanoff knew what it had taken for Thornfield to make it in this FBI world still dominated by men. Both of these agents had thrived against odds.

Thornfield had a singular way of entering a group. None of the other agents saw her coming, so I continued my briefing in order to indulge in a fleeting moment of watching her perplex and discomfit them. Only half listening to Agent Delarge speak now, I watched over the top of his head to see Thornfield accelerate toward the group at a jog. Her curly hair, meticulously wrestled into a bun, protested for an early release with each leaping step as she barreled our way.

"Make a hole!" Her voice punctured the briefing.

Startled, the members of the circle retreated. Thornfield proudly presented a navy folder with the FBI emblem embossed on the front. All eyes firmly fixed on Thornfield. All voices silenced.

Small, but certainly not delicate. Enough moxie for an agent twice her size . . . and she knows it.

"Director Fenn, Operation Libertas is ready to execute."

Without acknowledgment, I leafed through the contents.

Good to go. Attaboy, Thornfield.

Pointing to Agents Delarge, Sutcliffe, and Thornfield, I gave the order, "With me." I led the agents down to an adjacent conference room. As we descended the three tiers of the operational center, I

THE HOST

summoned key agents from workstations on each tier.

The conference room doors closed behind us. As the youngest Supervisory Special Agent and the only woman in the room, establishing Thornfield's authority in the situation was a top priority. *If I have to make it awkward or uncomfortable to attain my goal, so be it.*

I approached my seat at the head of the table and spoke, intentionally refusing to look up from the folder. "When we formed teams to search for Ms. Cameron and Mr. Beecher, one of the approaches I authorized was Thornfield's strategically coordinated search for the underground bunker.

"Thornfield . . ."

Standing assuredly, Thornfield briefed, "As you know, my team has joined forces with Interpol to sift through all the blueprints for bunkers built since the 1950s. We have our target list; we're ready to go."

An eruption of voices broke out around the table. Spewing questions about her methodology, strategy, and results. Her fellow agents blanketed her proposal with layers of critique.

"How could you check records with North Korea and Micronesia, countries that don't cooperate with Interpol?"

"What about bunkers without permits?"

"Do you even know what bunkers to look for?"

"Are you sure you've had enough time to thoroughly review the millions of data points?"

Still leafing through the folder even though I'd finished reading it thoroughly, I leaned back in my chair, completely relaxed, ready to watch the Thornfield show.

Seizing the moment, she leaned forward and planted both palms on the table, her light grey suitcoat cuffed up her forearms, exposing the bangled band of her Apple Watch. She wasn't boastful or condescending, but she wasn't meek either. She stood her own.

"Gentleman," she interjected into the skepticism, "my teams and I have done our due diligence. Was this list easy to come to? No.

"In the 1960s, the world became gripped with fear of nuclear war, leading the populace to take extraordinary precautions. For example, the city of Dallas, Texas, built enough fallout shelters to accommodate 971,000 people—more than the city's entire population at the time. Most major cities in the US followed suit.

"Similarly, Switzerland mandated that every home and major structure have a fallout shelter that could garrison all of the people living or working inside it, a mandate still in effect. That is 9.8 million bunkers today in Switzerland alone. Sweden can accommodate 80% of its population, and Finland, 70%. China has over one million fallout shelters just in the city of Beijing.

"Private citizens across the globe continue to install shelters and bunkers—it's even become trendy, like the fifteen-story Survival Condo Project in Kansas, the Vivos xPoint complex in the Black Hills, and the Vivos Europa One. These developments consist of dozens to thousands of bunkers in one location.

"Conservatively, my team estimates that there are well over a billion bunkers and underground shelters worldwide today.

"Consequently, I had teams in three countries sifting through data. We only pulled the blueprints for bunkers over six thousand square feet, which we estimate to be the minimum square footage for the size of the rooms on the video feed. And a bunker of this magnitude and complexity, Agent Sutcliffe, isn't a handyman special. It would've been permitted; thank you very much.

"And to your point, Agent Delarge, Interpol may not have a relationship with North Korea or Micronesia, but that doesn't mean we don't have people who can get information when necessary. We've got it covered.

"Filtering by square footage left us with 0.01% of those bunkers. While that may not sound like much, over one hundred thousand blueprints required eyes-on assessment. My teams each had a battery of architects scouring the remaining blueprints to potentially match the configuration of the Guest House. From those, we have a solid list of possibilities."

Thornfield paused, allowing everyone to mentally catch up. I looked up from the folder to find every eye on Thornfield. I was pleased with how she had handled herself—exactly what I expected when I recruited her.

"How many remain?" I asked, already knowing the answer from the folder she had provided.

With a cocky half smile, she answered, "Eight, Director: two in the United States, one each in Brazil, Russia, China, India, Dubai, and South Africa. We have teams ready at each location, waiting for your go."

Calculating the use of a rare expression, I withheld the smile that sprung from deep within and was able to stop it at my professional mask. "And your justification for hitting all the locations at once?"

"Yes, sir. Sun Tzu. They must be breached simultaneously to minimize the risk of the unsub being alerted to our operation, should a failed breach occur."

"Well done, Thornfield. 'Attack where he is unprepared. Appear where you are not expected.'[7]" I stood and returned the file to her. "You have a go." Two strides later, I was at the door and addressed the room, "Run the op from Tactical Operations. Patch Interpol in from there."

Abuzz with activity, the swarm of agents headed for the door. Agent Sutcliffe whispered to Agent Barone on his way through the door, "Sun Tzu?"

Barone wiped a hand over his face before placing it on Sutcliffe's shoulder, "*Art of War*. You should read more."

There was an electricity about Thornfield, but she applied enough resistance not to betray her excitement. She expediently stepped out of Tac. Op. to message her department and retrieve her team.

Tech teams linked in liaisons at Interpol and the eight Enhanced SWAT teams waiting on location. Final checks were run on equipment, and within minutes, SSA Thornfield returned with her team.

Standing in the double doors at the back of Tactical Operations, Thornfield surveyed the room like a head coach exiting the tunnel at the start of the big game. The sloped floor of the oval room, with its layers of workstations, gave it a stadium feel. The agents rolling along curved counters scanning data-filled screens were her cadre of assistant coaches, coordinators, and analysts. The theater-sized screen at the front of the room was her real-time scoreboard, constantly updating with the livestream of the Guests and those of her tactical teams. This was her home field; this was her moment.

As she walked toward the top arch of the room, an alert from her pocket broke her concentration. She discreetly swapped her work phone for her personal phone.

Unusual for her to tend to personal business in the middle of an op, especially one with stakes so high.

I subtly moved to her side, and she slipped the phone back out of sight.

"My husband," she said with a shy smile and a soft voice. He always broke down her tough exterior, revealing her softer side.

"Agent Pieri, wishing you luck?" He had impeccable timing despite handling his own mission in the field. She nodded, then cuffed her jacket sleeves to the elbow, kicked off her heels, and braced herself on the polished walnut railing, shifting her focus back where it belonged.

To avoid confusing the chain of command, I moved to the side of the room and let her take the helm at the top arch. Her headset in place, and everyone properly connected; it was time.

"Go."

Color drained from her face as the word projected over the room, but she didn't concede to any nerves in her posture or expression. On eight of the nine screens surrounding the theater-sized image of the Guest feed, helmet cams from the Enhanced SWAT team operators hypnotized the room.

With an elegant precision and an almost impossible unison, the elite operators breached the eight bunkers across the globe. At each building, one operator advanced silently around the left, one around the right, and one guarded the back of each team. Finally, two breached the door.

The US, Dubai, and South Africa teams used discreet explosives that didn't alert the occupants to their entry. Our arrangements with local governments limited the Brazil, Russia, China, and India teams to unsophisticated battering rams—effective, but crude.

Once the breaches began, chaos dominated the comms. Messages flew back and forth. DC SWAT, including Crowley and Hamovici, had requested to liaise between the international teams and Tac. Op. leadership. While Crowley managed her DC team, Hamovici ran back and forth, delivering key snippets of comm chatter to Thornfield.

"10-24" rang out from multiple feeds. Hamovici, who could hear a pin drop in a crowded stadium, immediately ran to the stations where the feeds were being reviewed. While the room wondered who was reporting in, Hamovici initiated standard protocol to get the team leader on camera for their debrief.

South Africa reported first, followed by China. The tension in the room deflated upon hearing the reports that both locations had collapsed bunkers—no hostages, no Host.

On the top row of monitors, second, from the right, an image of utter confusion and distress splashed up on the screen.

"10-32!"

"10-32!"

"Gun! Gun!"

Gunfire pierced the comms. Tac. Op. went silent.

The thirty seconds that followed . . . felt like thirty minutes. Finally, someone shouted, "10-95, subject in custody."

Relieved, Thornfield snatched a headset to address the team lead directly. Relief gave way to disappointment. The man in custody was not the Host but rather the head of a paranoid family hiding from the world who had greeted the Dubai team with survivalist hospitality.

Minutes later, while the team lead in Utah delivered her report, another 10-24—assignment completed—broke in. Hamovici spoke to the India lead on a private channel while Thornfield engaged with Utah. Both units revealed bunkers that were pristinely kept and functional but completely unoccupied.

Running out of possibilities, Tactical Operations was on edge, waiting to hear from Montana and Russia. Eyes danced between the top left and top right screens, respectively.

A 10-24 came from Montana—an abandoned site.

Russian language spilled over the comms. An argument between the FBI and their Russian counterparts ensued. Without warning, the comms went dark. Thornfield glared at Hamovici. "Get them back online!" she barked.

Crowley and Hamovici rushed to the Russia workstation. Nothing. Not a squawk. Not even static. The line was dead.

Heads down, trying to reconnect Russia to Tactical Operations, a code jerked Hamovici's attention to the Brazil workstation.

"10-35. Drug ring on location! Seven subjects secured and in custody. Local LEOs contacted. Requesting DEA assistance."

Brazil had stumbled across a narcotics stash house.

Within minutes, it was over. The operation had failed. Frustration and consolation filled the room. Thornfield appeared crestfallen by the failure. I slipped through the crowd to offer encouragement, words shared with me by my mentor in this very spot. "Failure happens to all. Your team is looking to you. Congratulate work. Don't show your disappointment in the results. You can do everything right and still fail."

Her day would not be over any time soon. She'd have to deal with the State Department over Russia and the DEA over Brazil, and the shooting incident would create more paperwork than she probably cared to think about.

Working the room, I thanked people for their hard work in Tactical Operations. Before they signed off, I thanked people at Interpol for their partnership. From the corner of my eye, I saw Thornfield lift her chin, adjust her expression, and pick up the phone.

She'll be fine.

The live feed on the big screen crackled and flickered. The room silenced. Heads turned to the front. A message overlaid the streaming video of the Guests:

nice try director fenn
thought i'd leave a paper trail?

With those words, our FBI fortress had been breached. A new threat level caught us by surprise. My agents were people of action. With the FBI under cyberattack, this was not the time for retreat.

Agents dove back to their workstations, grabbing the nearest phone to rally additional forces and stop this invader.

More text flickered onto the screen:

let them play the game
or people get hurt

Chatter swelled in the room, and the command structure collapsed in the hurricane of conversations. *Seasoned agents should know better.* I had to bring order to the chaos.

Out of character, I boomed, "Quiet!"

do you know your enemy?
do you know yourself?

Is there a camera in here? I searched the room and found Thornfield's perceptive eyes on me. *I need to govern my expression.*

The text disappeared; the feed returned to normal.

"Director?" Thornfield had a way of trying to read my mind.

"Yes?" I spent more time trying to govern my expressions and my tone with her than with any other agent.

"Is he referring . . ."

I stormed away, oblivious to the agents talking to me and around me.

I have to get to the bottom of what this unsub knows and how he knows it.

"If you know the enemy and you know yourself, you need not fear the result of a hundred battles. If you know yourself but not the enemy, for every victory, you will also suffer defeat. If you know neither the enemy nor yourself, you will succumb in every battle."[8]

DAY 20

Sneezing

Morning arrived—unbidden and unwelcome.

74296841

Preparing to face the day, with no idea what to say to Henry, I found myself drawn to an old pair of thin green cargo pants I used to wear when cleaning out the garage or doing anything dusty. I dug around in the drawers until I found the white cotton top I always wore with them. Nice, lightweight, breathable clothes for working in. I felt better about the day, having found something of comfort.

Now, to face the penalty for my outburst. I advanced down the hall and toward the kitchen. *I feel like an inmate walking into a courtroom.*

The coffee pot virtually overflowed as the last drop plopped into the carafe. There was evidence of breakfast having been made and cleaned up, but Henry was nowhere to be found. *I could not possibly feel worse.* I dropped my hands on the counter, the slap echoing through the room. The sting in my palms registered as my forehead landed between them. I crumpled there, groaning to myself.

"You okay?" Henry's chipper morning voice drifted into the room.

My head jolted off its retro resting place. "Um, no. Didn't sleep much." *Okay, this is completely normal Henry.*

"Well, coffee is fresh and hot. I made extra because we have a lot of work ahead of us. I had an early start and didn't know when you'd be up, so I didn't make extra breakfast; no one likes cold eggs." I waved it off.

He's acting weirdly . . . normal.

Henry kept talking as he walked out of the room with his freshly filled bottle of water. "I'm making good progress on the gym today; I'm going to bash on in there. You may want to pick a room and run with it. I think we can turn this place upside down today." There was a smile in his voice as he went about his task.

No hurt feelings. No problem. I guess it was all a game to him. Huh. I was up the entire night, worried about nothing.

I drank my coffee and stared at the window scene, wondering where I'd most like to work. Halfway through my second cup, it hit me: *the library. I haven't spent any time in there. If I were on vacation, I'd have locked myself in there and never left. Might be interesting. Then again, I haven't had the best experience with books in this house. Maybe it's a bad idea.* I debated while I slowly sipped my coffee sludge.

It has to get done regardless. A creepy library is as likely a place as any for a hidden door or passage. I have to suck it up and give it a shot.

With that thought firmly lodged in my mind, I guzzled the last of my coffee dregs, grabbed my tools, and darted off to the room we had barely entered since we'd arrived.

I walked into an oddly shaped room with floor-to-ceiling bookcases. *If there's a secret lever or trapdoor, it'll be here.* The dimly lit room had library ladders to reach the books at the top of each of its twelve-foot bookcased walls. Between each of the eleven sections of bookcases was solid wood paneling with intricate-flourished wood carvings and a brass candelabra. On either side of the room were two leather armchairs with a tiny carved wooden table next to each, barely large enough to rest a cup of tea.

Recessed in the center of the floor, like a Russian nesting doll, was a classic 1960s sunken sofa in a dark-orange leather, arguably a favorite color of the house's original owners. Between four sections of the circular sofa were built-in end tables complete with cork coasters. A room transported in time, I half expected to see amber ashtrays and worn-down shag carpet.

Exploring every inch of this library will take a lifetime. I'll have to look at each and every book to see if it's a lever, pull each and every lamp and candelabra, tug at each bit of rug, move every chair and every table, tap every floor plank. If I don't want to be a senior citizen before I find the exit, I need to get going.

I suppose the best place to start is by the door. The real challenge will be not getting lost in all the books I want to read.

I was relieved to find that the library books didn't have the sinister undertones or hidden messages I'd expected. Like the replication of my wardrobe in the bedroom and my cosmetics in the bathroom, my captor also knew my taste in books. I wanted to read everything in the library, or they were books I'd already read and wanted to read again. There was an original leather-bound first edition of J. R. R. Tolkien's *The Hobbit* and a 1953 copy of Ray Bradbury's *Fahrenheit 451*. Not to mention an 1898 edition of *The War of the Worlds* by H. G. Wells. Some of the books were even out of print. *How did he get his hands on all of these?*

When the door to the library opened, I was sitting on the floor, thumbing through a first edition of Isaac Asimov's *Foundation*. Startled, I slammed the book shut, and dust flew into my face, making me sneeze.

"À tes souhaits!" Henry smiled down at me. I sneezed again. "à tes amours. Now, are you hungry? It's long past lunchtime." He motioned to the door with his head. I looked at my wrist for a watch that wasn't there, forgetting that we hadn't had clocks since we'd arrived. He laughed at me. "Must be disorienting in here without the sun?" He lifted me off the floor. "Find anything interesting?"

"Well, only if you count every book I've ever wanted to read consolidated into one room." His face twisted, reminding me exactly how intrusive that reality was. "I know. I know. Tempting or unsettling? At this point, I give up; I'm not choosing." Henry laughed, and I joined him.

How do you make everything easier, no matter how awkward I am?

Lunch was tuna casserole. Mum's recipe. He told me it was supposed to have crisps in it; I discovered those were potato chips. We didn't have any, so, according to Henry, it was lacking. I wanted to pass; the meal didn't sound appealing. But it was Mum's recipe, and he called it comfort food. Who could say no to that? I was reluctant to admit that even though it was heavy, it was pretty good. And . . . I went back for seconds.

The meal was occupied with discussions of the books I'd found. Henry asked about some of the titles he would choose for his perfect library. I'd come across a few, but not all. *The Book of Disquiet* by Pessoa and *The Labyrinth of Solitude* by Octavio Paz were a couple I remembered. "Don't lose hope; I haven't been through more than a quarter of the library yet. Maybe it isn't only catered to me. It might be for both of us after all."

He threw his hands up in protest. "I don't want the library to be about me at all; thanks anyway."

I laughed. "No kidding. Actually, I'd rather none of this place be about me." The thought made us both a bit dour.

"Okay. What is the craziest thing you've found in there so far?" Henry asked, trying to lighten the mood.

Hmm. I don't know. "Well, my radar for crazy has been skewed lately." His smile returned. "But I've been noticing that most of the books I've pulled out to inspect seem to be rare in some way. I haven't checked a lot of books because I have so much to get through, and I'm really trying not to let the titles distract me. But there are some provocative, even extraordinary, works in there. Most of the time, they've been leather-bound first or second editions. I think that's strange. Everything here is perplexing, so I don't know if that should move the needle or not." I took another bite.

You've got that look you get when you're piecing things together. I'll stop talking and leave you to your thoughts.

We cleaned up lunch and went back to work, each in our own strange corner of our time-warped prison. I spent the rest of the day working my way through the library, trying my best not to get distracted by the titles I was interested in. I pulled on books, sections at a time, to see if any one within the group was a lever, then I knocked on the back of the bookcase to see if there was a false panel behind the books. I tried moving each of the bookcases. I pulled on the sconces. I took a stab at everything I had seen in every B movie I'd ever watched. Nothing produced any kind of result.

I was a little more than halfway through when I was ready to quit for the day, and I plopped myself onto an orange leather cushion on the sunken sofa to rest my aching leg. On the built-in table beside me was a wooden box with a brass plate affixed to the lid. The plate was blank.

Odd. Nothing in this house is an accident. Every detail so far has been meticulous and purposeful. I picked it up.

Inside the box, which appeared to have been hand-carved and not particularly well crafted, was a stack of brass plates. There were more than a dozen of them. Removing the stack, I spread the plates across the cushion beside me. Each one was identical, mostly blank, the same series of numbers hand-scratched at the top.

—25 12 24 12—

What is that about?

While I scooped them back into the box, it struck me. *These look remarkably similar to the plaques in the crypt.*

As the realization sunk in, my grip on the box tightened until my fingers shook, and I snapped a fingernail off. I threw the box to the floor, scattering the brass plates, breaking a hinge, and twisting the lid.

I can't deal with this right now. I have to get out of this room. Opting to search for Henry, I left everything on the floor to deal with in the morning.

74813507

Henry had finished in the gym and had already started making dinner. "You finally done?" he called from the stove as I approached. The aroma was enticing. "Come wash your hands and get to work. These onions aren't going to chop themselves." I could hear the lilt of a smile in his voice. He liked making me chop onions and couldn't understand how I could manage it without my eyes watering. Henry's kitchen banter was exactly what I needed to take my mind off our captor being prepared for more burials.

I enjoyed cooking with Henry. Well, whenever he let me in the kitchen. Sometimes, he rendered the area off-limits, and sometimes, we disagreed on how the task should be accomplished. It created some entertaining arguments. That evening was relaxed and easy. I chopped onions, garlic, and various other vegetables that we were lucky enough to salvage from the garden. Henry cooked and seasoned and turned some otherwise unsavory ingredients into an edible delicacy. We got in each other's way on occasion—*impressive given the size of the kitchen*—but it wasn't a problem. I elbowed Henry, and he moved with a smile. If I was in his way, he lifted me by my elbows and relocated me to a more suitable area of the kitchen. It was comical, and laughter was a great way to cope after having been in that house for so long.

While we ate dinner, Henry regaled me with stories of actors bungling their lines and their stunts on set and of mistakes that made it into movies that fans didn't often notice. One story in particular surprised me. Henry shared it in passing as he did every other story, but the content caught me off guard.

"I don't know if you ever saw that film I shot about six years back in the Australian outback, but there is a funny story behind the head injury my character had in that one. They did a good job of working it into the script—it was an action film, after all—so it wasn't a big deal to have Steri-Strips on my face for the majority of the film. The truth is, I received the head injury from a stunt accident."

My mouth opened. Only slightly. I may have held my breath. Henry laughed at me; he always seemed to tell stories for the reaction.

"It's not a big deal. We have accidents all the time. The medics bandaged me up and sent me on my way. I had one fine stitch above my right eyebrow. No big deal. Didn't even hurt. We didn't realize until weeks later and several doctors down the road that I had severed a large nerve just above my right orbital socket."

He turned back, smiled broadly, and raised his left eyebrow as he so often did. I could feel my eyes widen and my body lean forward without my approval. He obviously intended to get the reaction.

"That's right. My signature look is technically a medical disability. I can't move my right eyebrow anymore. It's a workplace injury. The studio wanted the neurosurgeon to correct it, but I wasn't up for the risk. Besides, it's a great story. Your face is priceless!"

I couldn't respond. I wanted to be empathetic, but he kept laughing. My well of sympathy ran dry.

"The injury was in the script. I don't believe it. I can't believe it. You're pulling my leg."

"Nope, it's one-hundred-percent true. I cannot raise my right eyebrow. You will never see it move. And it's due to the injury during the initial stunt in that film. Word of honor."

True or false, he kept me laughing throughout the course of dinner. It wasn't just the stories; it was the way he told them. I laughed so hard my sides hurt. The more I laughed, the more motivated he seemed to come up with even more wild and audacious tales. And he succeeded—each one more outrageous and hilarious than the last. But I was getting too relaxed, too close.

When we finished eating, I stood to clear the table. Henry took the dishes from my hands and asked me to pick some wine and a movie. "Not another one of your chick flicks, now," he teased with an overly dramatic raised eyebrow and a half smile as he walked toward the kitchen.

After I cleared the rest of the plates from the table, I began putting the leftovers in the fridge. I spoke while my back was to him. "I don't think I'm up for a movie tonight. I'm going to turn in early.

It's been a long day." I was tempted to look over my shoulder to see his reaction, but I didn't dare, and he said nothing. We finished cleaning the kitchen without another word.

With our chores complete, we walked out of the kitchen and into the conservatory. Henry went on toward the theater, and I headed for the bedroom hall. He turned back and made one more petition in a soft, gentle tone. "Last chance. I think I'm going to go with *The Fifth Element*, and I may finish off your sweets if you're not there to stop me." I couldn't restrain the slightest smile.

Leaning in the doorframe at the entrance to the bedroom hall, I paused to reconsider. "You aren't going to make this easy, are you? Trying to entice me with a classic and threatening to eat the last of my Swedish Fish? I think I'll still have to pass. Enjoy them on my behalf, won't you?" I let out a silent sigh before I turned down the hall, and I could have sworn I saw Henry's head sag before I lost sight of him.

I felt loathsome as I walked toward the bedroom. *He deserves better. But I can't talk to him about it. Even if there wasn't a host of people watching. But here? With millions of people watching? No way. I've spent the better part of the decade hiding from people, avoiding contact, both physically and emotionally. I can't stop now.*

That's it.

That's why he picked me. It's part of the rat maze, his social experiment. Living in this house is the opposite of how I live at home. I don't come in contact with a living soul but once every two or three months and only when absolutely necessary. I never reveal anything personal. I communicate via email or text and stay locked in my house, where all my needs are met via delivery. Even my family members gave up on me years ago. My friends have all but disappeared. Here, in this house, the world is stalking me, watching every word, every move, every bite I take. I'm in a concrete fishbowl.

And then . . . there's Henry, always interested in me, always caring. Ugh, Henry. He doesn't deserve to be treated like everyone else in my life. He's different. He's better. Everyone else abandoned me years ago; he's still here even after I treated him . . .

I'm a horrible person. I have to get out of here. I have to get away from him. Somewhere, I can't hurt poor Henry ever again.

I sunk back into the fluffy pink fainting couch in my bedroom. It had become matted down with use. If I spent too many more nights on that damn couch, I was going to leave a permanent Monti-shaped impression.

I spent the night fixated on finding a way out. *If our captor is pushing us to search for an escape, there has to be one. He got us in. Someone has been coming into the house and leaving books, starting the fire, opening the crypt door. There has to be a way out. It's here. I'm going to find it.*

My determination was renewed.

I sat up most of the night, straining my brain on the subject.

Find the way out of the rat maze, Monti!

I got precisely nowhere. I could have sworn the sun began peeking over the mountains the moment I fell asleep. I could have been dreaming. Waking, dreaming, the whole night was one long blur of accomplishing absolutely nothing.

DAY 21

Acting

My shower was probably hot enough to boil pasta but didn't seem like it was going to wake me up. I'd probably slept all of fifteen minutes. *I wish we had an espresso machine. There's irony in being surrounded by so many top-shelf supplies and such lousy coffee.*

75382951

I dragged myself down the hall, wiping my hand across my face, hoping it would somehow help me focus. *Wishful thinking. Caffeine is my only hope to peel my eyes open this morning. I have to haul myself to the kitchen.*

Henry was barricading my path in the conservatory. *He's pacing. Not a good sign.*

He cut me off. "Monti, we need to talk." He rubbed his hands together nervously. "About the film."

I'm not awake yet. Is this really happening?

My eyes pleaded with him, but I tried to keep the whine out of my voice. "Henry, I didn't sleep much last night; I haven't had my coffee yet. Can we please do this later?" *How did I do?*

His hands balled into fists, and he squinched his eyes in frustration. *He's never been worked up like this.*

"No." He opened his eyes, calm but determined. "We're stuck in here, and we're stuck in here together. We need to talk about this. Don't shut me out."

He isn't going to let this go. I have to give him something. "I'm not shutting you out. I'm cranky and exhausted, Henry. We can talk. I just need coffee first." I maneuvered to walk around him and make my way to the kitchen.

He was having none of it. His arm shot out to block my path, his hand reached my left shoulder, and his unnaturally behemoth fingers wrapped almost all the way around my upper arm.

"Look, you isolate yourself and avoid letting people get close to you. I understand that. Letting people in is hard. You never know if they will be decent people or if they will hurt you.

"But after everything I've endured with you, I think I've proven that I'm not a horrible person. I'm worthy of a single grain of trust."

I didn't mean to, but I cut his speech off with a snort and an eye roll that may have incorporated my head. Henry's hand dropped from my arm, and his mouth fell open slightly.

"That's not why I isolate myself." I slapped my hand over my mouth. *Dammit. I never do this with anyone else. Ugh. He can tell I overshared, too.*

Henry ushered me into a seated position on a bench. Kneeling in front of me, he patiently asked, "What other reason could there possibly be?" My eyes darted nervously around the room, searching for an escape, or at least something creditable to say, anything but the truth.

Maybe I can admit to his reasoning for my isolation. It's a logical thought, and it would get me out of delving into my past.

As I searched for something to say, the sky behind Henry's head morphed into a gruesome figure. I didn't know what it was at first —some kind of face, but not a normal face.

Holy shit!

Our keeper had crudely stitched together a collage. This collage was comprised of pictures of dead people's faces—not whole faces, but a forehead from one, ears from two others, eyes from two more . . . Decay afflicted each of the twelve images. Cobbled together, they composed a single grotesque figure. For a split second, I wondered if they were the faces of the people in the crypt, then I had to fight to keep the bile from rising.

tell henry i'm here and he dies

75753864

I covered my mouth and looked down at my lap so Henry wouldn't notice my shocked expression or what I had seen. He gently stroked my cheek with the back of his hand. "It's okay. I'm not trying to start a barney here. I only want to talk."

"A what?" A fugitive tear escaped the corner of my eye.

He tenderly wiped the tear from my face with his thumb, and his voice seemed to soften even more—if that was possible. "An argument." I could hear his smile as he spoke, even though I still hadn't met his eye.

He's making it so much harder. This would be easier if he was a jackass.

I took a deep breath, preparing myself to deal with Henry, and lifted my head. His warm, gentle smile was instantly calming. With a quick glance over his shoulder, I saw that the text over the macabre face had disappeared, though the putrid figure remained.

"So, why do you isolate yourself?"

My attention moved away from the menacing image, back to Henry. "What?" Momentarily confused, I'd forgotten what we'd been talking about.

Your patience with me really is unending, isn't it?

"I suggested that you isolate yourself to avoid investing in people who might hurt you, and you laughed at me. So, I'm asking the question, why the isolation?"

I sighed and looked around, squirming in my seat. Henry planted a hand on either side of me on the bench. He continued to smile pleasantly yet remained resolute. "You're not getting out of this. I've been patient and a good friend. I haven't pressed once. This time, I'm asking, and in case you're wondering, I weigh twice what you do, maybe more; there is nothing you can do to make me move." He was doggedly determined to stay until I broke.

By the time he finished his speech, new text appeared over his head.

tell henry the truth or he dies
76108529

My jaw dropped; I couldn't help it. Henry's face shifted; he must have noticed that I was looking behind him because he slowly turned his head. "Henry!" I yelped, and his focus jerked back to me.

I have to talk fast to keep his attention. I opened my mouth as I collected my thoughts for a fast second, making my story as coherent as possible.

The text changed again:

the whole truth
76352419

"Fine," I blurted, louder than necessary, "the whole truth." *I can't leave anything to chance. I don't know what's hidden in this place. I can't risk Henry's life.*

I sighed deeply and ran my hands through my hair, resigned to divulge my tale from the beginning.

"Do you remember several years back? There was a couple in the headlines. I'm sure it reached the UK as well. They each bought lottery tickets, and each of them won a separate lottery on the same weekend? Collectively, they won over $2.7 billion. That's billion with a 'B.' The media dubbed them the luckiest couple in the world.

"You may remember the ensuing investigation into lottery fraud because the chances of winning the lottery in the first place are so low. Then, the chances of a couple both winning lotteries on the same weekend are about the same as finding life on Mars. The investigation captivated the world, and I think the majority of the public were disappointed that the couple was cleared of any wrongdoing."

He nodded slowly with a pensive expression, and I held my breath, waiting for him to catch on. It felt like an eternity passed, though it was probably only a few seconds. The numbers scrolled behind him like an odometer in a speeding car on the autobahn. My heart pounded in my ears with the silence.

76597139

"Wait, that was you?"

There it is. I nodded and tried to continue, but it took me a moment. The words were stuck in my throat like a chicken bone. I'd never actually recounted the tale before, not to anyone. Not a friend. Not family. There I was, telling everyone in the world whether I wanted to or not. I had to, to save Henry's life.

I smiled reticently as I remembered. I hadn't allowed myself to remember in so many years. I'd hidden it all safely away in the back of my mind where I couldn't reach it. "I was married once. To—inside and out—the best man that had walked this earth.

"Paul.

"Before the lottery, Paul and I led the life every little girl dreams of. Well, I had dreamed of. We lived in the suburbs of Upstate New York. We had two great kids—a thirteen-year-old daughter named Lily and a ten-year-old son named Ash. We had an oafy Great Dane and a two-story house with an enormous backyard where we had plans to put in a pool someday. We both had careers that we loved. Paul was an MIT grad and worked in cybersecurity. We met when he contracted with my PR firm in NYC early in my career. You know, I even drove a minivan with an honor-student bumper sticker. We lived the perfect Christmas portrait life.

"Then the lottery happened, and it all fell apart. What I thought was my perfect life was just a poorly stacked game of Jenga that toppled when the right piece was pulled.

"Six months after the lottery, there was a car accident. In a single moment, my entire family—the three people I loved most in all the world, even the dog—just gone."

I felt splinters of wood find their way under my fingernails as I gripped the bench. I didn't want to continue. But I had no choice.

"Three weeks after the accident—one week after the funeral—our family home, our sanctuary, burnt to the ground. Every scrap of memorabilia from our life together was left in cinders.

"The investigators never found the cause of the fire. I never found resolution. I can still smell the burning timber and plastics, the firefighter's foam. I honestly think the fire here was intended to bring back that trauma, to remind me of what I lost."

The lump in my throat felt like I'd swallowed a porcupine, but it wasn't important; I had to ignore it. I had to move on.

"I had nothing left of them after that. Nothing but the money. I loathed that money. Did you know I received four marriage proposals before my family's funeral even took place?" My face reddened as my abhorrence resurged.

I have to stop; I can't tell him the rest.

I gripped the bench, my nails breaking off into the wood underneath. As I stared at the stones beneath my feet, Henry took one of my hands, silently reminding me that while I once had to endure alone, with Henry, I was no longer alone.

I'm gonna have to finish.

I looked up, not at Henry, but past him. I fixed on the face, the abomination our captor had chosen to represent himself. The numbers turned with fury. The phrase loomed above them:

the whole truth
76842958

"I . . . " My voice cracked. I cleared my throat and began again. "I tried to take my life after that.

"Two separate attempts."

My eyes blurred with tears, but I kept focused on the scrolling numbers as a propellant, forcing me to make it to the end.

"Obviously, I wasn't successful." Henry didn't seem to appreciate my macabre sense of humor. His face maintained its steadfast concern. He tightened his grip on my hand. "I just didn't want to exist with the pain of what I'd lost or to live in a world with people who only valued me for that damned money." I had to stop again. But the numbers felt like a ticking time bomb threatening Henry's life.

Finish, Monti, finish!

"After months locked up alone in my tiny apartment—not once glimpsing the light of day—I made a decision. My children were gone, and I wanted nothing to do with the money; I had to get rid of it. I would use it to help children who didn't have families to care for them. I'd live out the remainder of my days improving the world for those children. I was a lost cause, but maybe there was hope for them; maybe I could give them the future that was taken from my children.

"That's how I got involved with each charity I work for. That's why they are my mission. I'm particularly involved in the group that rescues children who've been trafficked. I just can't deal with a world that would do that to kids." I shifted my focus back to Henry and clasped his hand tightly between mine. He needed to accept my story as it was and not ask questions.

Move on, Henry, move on.

"I isolated myself after the funeral, not because getting close to someone might hurt." *The idea of it is absolutely comical.* "I'm so broken. No one can hurt me anymore.

"I don't want to get to know anyone because I'm afraid to care. I can't allow myself to care.

"Henry. I almost didn't survive losing my family. Losing the love of my life. If I lose anyone else, I won't survive."

My voice barely managed to croak out the last couple of words. I gasped for a breath. I had to finish.

Finish!

I shouted to force out the last of it. "So, please forgive me if I try my damnedest not to care about you. It is the absolute hardest part about being trapped here. Now, can I please be done talking about this?" I wasn't asking Henry. I was shrieking at that sadistic face behind him.

The levee broke, and tears flooded down my cheeks. I could barely see, but I lifted my face to the ceiling to find that the sky illusion had resumed. An ocean wave of relief knocked me over and suffused me. The tears stopped just as suddenly as they had started, and I shoved Henry's arm out of the way and vomited in the grass beside him.

Henry sat beside me on the ground and held me for a long while.

He had no idea what I had just gone through, what he'd almost been a victim of, and I never wanted to tell him.

I was shaking from the experience. Henry stroked my arm. He must have thought I was cold; it was probably some form of shock. As I recovered, I felt distanced from my feelings; they turned down, almost off. I didn't want to, maybe couldn't, feel them anymore.

I sat in the grass with my head on Henry's shoulder, watching an eagle soar overhead; he still had his back to the dome when the butchered face flashed up again, though only for a moment.

well done

77087139

My whole body shivered once more, and Henry wrenched me away to look me in the eye. "I am so sorry. I shouldn't have pushed. That really messed with you." He clenched my biceps with his mammoth hands. "We need to get you warmed up; you are freezing." He lifted me to my feet like a rag doll. "We'll have a cuppa and get you into bed."

The last thing I wanted was time alone with my thoughts. I pushed him away. "No, I'm fine, honestly. Maybe . . . " I wasn't sure what I wanted to say next. I looked at the ground and covered my face with my hands.

The images from the screen raced through my mind. *I don't want to be alone right now, but I still don't want to be close to anyone. Can I even trust this lunatic to keep his word? Is Henry actually safe? Are either of us?* Too many things fought for a place in my mind all at once.

Henry put a supportive hand under my elbow. "Hey, you don't have to decide anything this second." His voice was steady and comforting.

I moved away from the support of his hand—*I can stand on my own two feet, thank you*—and closed my eyes. "I don't want to be alone." *Well, that's out there.* "Do you mind working in the library with me today?" I lifted my head and looked up through one uncertain eye, not knowing what I'd find.

His magnanimous smile waited for me as I peered up at him. "Of course. Maybe I'll find a good book to read tonight. The musical I watched last night was rubbish." I couldn't believe he could make me laugh at a moment like that, but he did, and we walked to the library side by side.

77146250

In the library, Henry pulled one of the big leather chairs over to the section of books I was working on so I didn't have to stand. Then he pulled a small table over for the gigantic cup of tea he made. "Here, lavender and chamomile with a touch of honey. Relaxing. It'll do you good."

It was incredible; I had treated him so poorly, and when he found out why, he began waiting on me hand and foot. There was no explanation.

"Do you have everything you need? Can I get you something else before I start this section over here?"

He really is too attentive.

"I'm fine, really. I just need to occupy myself with work," I answered absently, already distracted with the next section of books, back to my routine from the day before.

"What in the world?"

That was fast.

Henry was surprised by something he'd found. When I turned to see what it was, he wasn't at a bookshelf but kneeling on the floor in the center of the sunken sofa, his hands full of the brass plates I'd left spilled on the floor the day before. "What are these?" He held up a handful for me to see.

I leaned over the armrest of my chair, not wanting to engage the topic. I pointed to the upturned box behind him with its lid half-twisted off. Henry began to neatly replace the plates one by one. "What happened?"

I shook my head. I wasn't about to explain, and he knew it.

"Are these the same plates from the crypt? He's prepared for more deaths, more burials, isn't he?"

I had no response.

Henry put the box on the table where I'd found it the day before and tried to twist the lid back where it belonged. Then he plopped on the armrest of my chair and examined the plate he'd brought with him. "What do you suppose this series of numbers means? It's the same series I memorized in the crypt. It's hand scratched into every plate in the box."

Henry drummed his fingertips on the back of the plate as he thought aloud. "If the number is used for multiple graves, it can't be connected to any one person buried there. It either applies to every person in the crypt, or it's all about him. I'm inclined to think it's the latter. What could he want to say with a number? And why would he want to keep saying it repeatedly since 1998? What does he gain by continuing to say it going forward?"

I hadn't thought of it like that. It just appeared to be a kind of serial number to me. But you're right. Every grave since 1998. He's saying something. But what?

Henry continued to tap the plate against his fingertips while I massaged my temples. *Your line of thinking is giving me a headache.*

"Right then." Henry slipped the plate into the pocket of his cargo pants. "This thought is going to need some time to percolate. Back to work. Monotonous tasks clear the mind and allow space for the solution to surface." He gave my shoulder a compassionate squeeze on the way by—an uncharacteristic violation of my personal space—and moved back toward his bookcase, tugging at random books and candelabras along the way. He gave me a half smile over his shoulder when he reached his destination, and I looked back uneasily.

Throughout the day, I was physically feeling better from my encounter with the cadaverous face, but I was progressively feeling worse about Henry.

It has to stop.

He was being saccharine sweet: refilling my teacup when it was more than half full, constantly brushing hair out of my face, and touching my cheek. He walked by every two minutes when there was no earthly reason to do so and made the most ridiculous puppy-dog eyes, sighing when he passed by.

The constant, over-the-top pampering made my blood pressure rise; my skin was hot to the touch. It wasn't long before I had to say something. *It's going to come out all wrong. I've never been good at this. Years of not talking to people isn't going to help.*

Dropping the stack of books I held, I abruptly left the library to collect my thoughts. *I have to figure out what to say. There's no winning here. No matter what I do, we both lose. How can I respond in a way that we'll both lose the least?*

I paced back and forth along the path in the conservatory. As I turned to make my fifth or sixth pass, my face slammed into Henry's chest.

"What is going on?" He held my shoulders and looked down at me, bewildered. I pushed his hands off my shoulders.

If we're having this conversation, I am not about to be pinned down.

I resumed pacing. "I haven't thought through what I want to say, so this isn't going to come out right."

This is a horrible start. "I've never told anyone that story I told you this morning. Ever."

He took a huge step toward me and tried to talk. I put a hand up to stop him and took my own step back. "I believe that you understand the gravity of my story, but I think you missed the point." Confusion and hurtfulness crept into his face.

It is killing me to cause you pain.

Stepping closer again, I picked up one of his massive hands and held it between mine. "Listen, you rightfully feel that my sharing something so deeply personal brings us closer. That's a normal part of the human experience."

He squeezed my fingers, bursting to say something. *That's not like you. You don't interrupt.*

I didn't give him a chance. "Henry, you missed my purpose in sharing entirely." I stopped there and stared him down.

The sparkle in his emerald eyes dimmed; his grip on my hand loosened and slid to the fingertips of my left hand. He pursed his lips. "Oh," he said, and took a couple of breaths, waiting for me to say something, but I wanted the truth to settle in.

"You really don't . . ." he continued. I nodded and nudged him on. He had to be the one to say it. He had to say it out loud. It couldn't be left unclear, unsaid.

He took a short, sharp gasp. "You really don't want to care about me. Do you?" He was hurt. I could see it on his face and behind his eyes, no matter how hard he tried to hide it.

It took everything I had to keep a stolid face. "I don't. I can't."

At that, he dropped my hand and stepped back, putting his hands in his pockets. "Then. Don't worry about me." His eyes were glassy, and a slim-but-brave smile crossed his face. "I'm just a friend, here for you when you've been kidnapped. That's all, okay?"

I tried to smile, but my bottom lip refused to stop quivering. It was agonizing knowing that I had wounded him. "Thank you," I responded.

He sat on the bench, leaned back, and looked at the manufactured sky above. "No thanks needed, ever. That's what friends are for."

I can't stand it. I have to get away.

I sprinted down the stone path and into the dining room, burying my head in my arms as soon as I reached the table. After a few minutes, I sat up straight, trying to pull myself together. As I faced the window scene, it morphed from our standard mountain view to the repellant, festering face I'd seen earlier. I scrunched my eyes tight and took in a deep breath, preparing myself for whatever I was about to encounter. When I opened them:

don't let viewers know i'm here
or someone moves into the crypt
77201783

I sat motionless, trying to stare at the screen as I had so many times before, as though I were looking at mountains and wildlife. Inside, I was incensed with this rotting face and his demands. The text changed:

our audience deserves a show
77243165

I was certain my face was letting on that I wasn't just looking at scenery. It was taking all my willpower to keep it expressionless. Then, my eye began twitching. I couldn't make it stop. I leaned an elbow on the table and rested my hand over my twitching eye.

win her back for them

or one of you dies

77261573

I didn't intend to, but I reacted to that! *The face isn't talking to me; it's talking to Henry!*

He won't realize that I've seen it too. I tipped my chair back on two legs, forcing my head to continue facing the window. The door at the end of the hall was open, and I could see out of my peripheral vision that the same image was on the dome in the conservatory where Henry was watching it.

no one can know we've had this little chat no one

77292368

It all disappeared. The sky resumed in the conservatory, and the mountain scenery resumed in the dining room. My hands were shaking; my eye was twitching.

That was partly for me and partly for Henry, and I can't tell him I've seen it. The viewers have to believe the romance is real, and so does Henry. And now there has to be a romance.

Oh, come on! How am I supposed to allow him to win me over? Believably. I'm not an actress. And Henry is excellent at reading people. Not to mention, I just rejected him in front of millions of people. What the hell am I gonna do?

I dropped my head into my folded arms on the table, wishing the day was already over when Henry walked into the room as though nothing had happened: no fight, no chimeric face threatening our lives, issuing impossible tasks. Nothing.

"You hungry? It's been a long day. I thought I'd start supper."

His poise was mind-bending. Transfixed, I followed him into the kitchen.

"I can help unless you plan to kick me out of the kitchen." I gave him a half smile to test the waters.

"Nope, if you're willing, I'll put you to work." He slipped a ruffled yellow apron over my head. I was floored.

Bold move, given our most recent conversation.

He noticed my shock. "I'm sorry, did that cross a line? I was trying to be helpful."

Bridging the gap between awkward DTR and death-threat video chat would be tough. *This is probably the best opening I could ask for, so . . .* "Look, I don't want things to change. Let's not be weird, okay? Can we go back to the way we were before? The apron is fine, really. Before . . . I just didn't want to suddenly be, I don't know . . . launched forward because I overshared. Does that even make sense? We don't have to undo the friendship we've built."

Ugh, why am I so awkward? Did that even work?

Henry spun me around and tied the apron behind me. "Yeah, that works for me, as long as you chop the onions."

Okay then. Henry reached in front of me, grabbed the bowl of root vegetables we kept on the counter after they'd been picked, and gave me marching orders on what to wash and cut. I was profoundly taken aback. It was as though the last hour never happened. I didn't know what to do; I saluted him like a soldier and went straight to work.

He was so confident in every action, every word, every facial expression boldly self-assured. I doubted my ability to tell what was real and what was acting. After all, he was the most awarded actor of his generation. *Hmm.*

We cooked, ate, cleaned, and I found myself struggling to pay attention to what I was doing and saying. I wondered if everything Henry said or did was genuine or contrived. At one point during dinner, I even questioned if he had seen the message. I couldn't tell if he was acting that far out of the ordinary. *Has he been acting all along?* My brain was so twisted up in a knot that I couldn't think of what to do or how to respond. I had to constantly remind myself of the message. *If I screw up, Henry's life is on the line. I have to stay focused.*

We finished the dishes, and there was a lull. It hadn't yet reached awkward, but it was well on the way. Henry neatly folded the tea towel he was drying his hands with and put it away. "I noticed you set out a book to read in the dining room. You probably want to finish that tonight, don't you?"

"Holy H. P. Lovecraft, Batman. I did no such thing, and I have no intention of reading whatever quote was left there to unhinge us." I stomped over to the dining room table, grabbed the book, and hurled it on top of the fridge with the other books left around the house to beleaguer us.

Henry calmly walked over and slipped the book off the top of the fridge, standing more than slightly closer than normal, and effectively pinned me with my back to the fridge.

"Hmmm." His voice rumbled in the back of his throat as he read the highlighted text. Standing so close and being so tall, his head curved over mine like a candy cane. I couldn't tell if it was cozy or disquieting. I wanted to step back, but there was nowhere to go. I pressed myself flat against the fridge to avoid contact with Henry, but he just leaned in closer.

I pushed the book up to his nose so I could see the cover and read the title. *No Country for Old Men*, Cormac McCarthy.

Familiar, but not something I've read.

Henry moved the book back evenly spaced between us and peered over the top. "Do you want to know? I think you want to know."

I don't need you to taunt me with books as well. You aren't going to let it go, are you? "Fine. What does it say?"

One eyebrow baited me over the top of the book as he read.

"By the time you figured it out it would be too late."[9]

He stuck his nose in the fold of the book and looked over the top of the pages for a reaction.

"Are you kidding? Nope. I'm done with the books." I yanked it out of his hand, giving his nose a paper cut, and tossed it back on top of the fridge.

We need to get back to our newest assignment. "Movie anyone?"

Henry took a step back and smiled, seeming pleasantly surprised. "It'll be hard to top your musicals, but I'll give it a shot."

A cocky half smile lit up his face as he headed toward the hall. "Maybe it's time we tried a chick flick. You know, to balance out our diet." Without a doubt, I looked like I had smelled something foul. Whatever face I made, Henry belly laughed louder than he had since we'd arrived. It was conspicuously disproportionate to my facial expression.

Acting laugh?

I began to inventory his laughs in my head. I didn't know if I could tell the difference. He stopped laughing and tilted his head at me like a German shepherd.

Crap. I'm making a face, aren't I?

"What are you thinking? Have you decided?"

Yeah, you're wondering what I'm thinking, but you're not wondering what I want to watch, are you?

He knows something's up. Does he know I'm questioning his general sincerity? I have to get out of my head. Say something, Monti!

"I've decided, unequivocally, that we are not watching a chick flick. Other than that, I'm going to need a few minutes." Passing Henry on my way toward the hall, I paused. "Hey, Oscar?" I looked back over my shoulder. "Do we have anything around here more interesting than wine?"

His face sparked with anticipation. "What do you have in mind?"

Nothing, in fact; absolutely nothing. I should think before I open my big, fat mouth. Think, quick. Think. "I don't know, maybe ingredients for a decent margarita or a martini. Just something more adventurous than wine for a change."

His eyes brightened, and he held up one finger before darting out of the room. *He's a bulky guy, but when he wants to move, he's fast.*

It felt like only an instant before he returned with a slim blue bottle of Milagro Tequila and a tall white bottle of Belvedere Vodka. "No margaritas, no martinis, but we have shots." He held out my options with a puckish smile.

I searched the cabinet where the wine glasses were and shouldn't have been surprised to find a set of shot glasses. I pulled out the hand-blown, blue-tinted glasses and showed them to Henry. "Why not? It's been a helluva day!" We carried our spoils to the theater and took our seats.

We poured, clinked, and drank before we bothered to pull out the tablets to make a movie selection. "We should probably figure out what we're going to watch." Henry took my glass and the vodka away.

"I was thinking we could watch one of your films tonight." I grinned and snatched the bottle and glass back.

With a stern look, Henry put his foot down. "Um, no. If we're drinking vodka, we are not watching any of my films. Final answer. Give me that tablet." He scrolled, and we drank for over half an hour.

At some point, the armrest between us was lifted. *When did that happen? That was a stealth move.*

After a while, we needed to put the vodka away; we were no closer to choosing a movie, and I was getting close to not being capable of watching one at all. "We have to choose something." *Am I slurring?*

Henry agreed. *He's not nearly as intoxicated as I am—probably because he's a Sasquatch—so unfair.*

Instead of picking a movie, I sat and contemplated his accent. *Is it getting thicker with the application of vodka, or is it my imagination?*

"Think fast." Henry's finger waved in my face. "All-inclusive favorite sci-fi franchise of all time. Go." I stared at him, not quite sure what to say. "Quick, quick, this is supposed to be your gut response." He motioned for me to answer.

Why is he so close to my face?

I closed my eyes. "Okay, okay, my all-time favorite sci-fi franchise? No question. *Star Trek.*" I squinted back at him. *That's a deeply personal question.* I didn't know if he would approve or laugh me out of the theater. Nerds are profoundly territorial of their fandoms.

"Excellent, then I know exactly what to watch." He didn't judge or condemn; he simply put on one of his favorite *Star Trek* movies. It happened to be one I also enjoyed, and we finally sat back to watch.

We ate stale theater candy, drank more excellent vodka, and shouted obnoxiously at the screen while we enjoyed the movie. Much to my surprise, Henry didn't make a move. We just enjoyed the flick and the company. Loud and boisterous, we laughed and shoved each other when our favorite lines and movie moments occurred. It was truly a memorable evening.

About halfway through the movie, Henry removed the vodka from the equation; I'd clearly had more than enough. Half an hour after that, he took the candy away, too. I'd thank him for that later.

When the movie was over, I stumbled back to my room; Henry followed out of concern that I'd injure myself—not unwarranted. I fell into bed, fully clothed. I could see Henry's silhouette leaning in the doorway, hands in his pockets, his relaxed and natural self. "Goodnight, you." He pulled the door closed.

"Wait," I called out into the darkness. He opened the door and stuck his head back in. "Don't close the door. Please?" He opened it wide and leaned back in the doorway, crossing his arms. I had almost no self-control left after the gross quantity of alcohol I'd consumed. I was afraid I'd say something I'd regret, so I rolled over, hoping he'd give up and go away.

Don't get attached.

I held my breath but felt my mouth open even though I didn't want to say another word. "I like to know that I can hear you, and you can hear me."

Get a hold of yourself.

At least he's gone now.

"Okay," Henry responded. Then I heard his footsteps down the hall.

No more alcohol. Period.

AGENT GRAYSON HOLT

Swimming

J. Edgar Hoover Bldg., Washington, DC

My favorite part of the day.

I moved unobtrusively throughout the halls, peering in the windows of each team's conference-room door. I wanted to gauge the success or struggle of each operation.

Most Executive Directors officed on the seventh floor and had their agents work autonomously in some other part of the building. I preferred to get involved and provide support where necessary. Operational reports were no substitute for seeing my agents, talking to my recruits. While I never wanted to intrude and slow their progress, personal presence kept me immersed, up to speed, and available.

Reaching the third floor, I stopped to look in on Agent Thornfield and her team. Operation Libertas, the search for the Guest bunker, continued forward. I had kept a close eye on her after the breaches. The defeat she'd been served hadn't smothered her fire; it fanned her flame. As I passed out of view, I allowed myself a measured smile. Thornfield thrived under the pressure, and given enough time, she would find that bunker.

The next room housed Special Agent Miles Sterling and his team. I remembered scooping him up out of his undergraduate class at Carnegie Mellon. We caught him tunneling into Homeland's secure network on a dare from a dorm room wearing a bathrobe. We decided his talent would have been wasted in federal prison. I didn't know if Homeland was more upset about the breach or that he joined the FBI instead of them. Either way, Sterling thrived in cybercrimes.

Despite never having finished his undergraduate degree, he was the best. With his talents, he could become an expert in the

Bureau, even train green agents. While Sterling hadn't yet shown any inclination to develop his leadership skills and become a full-blown Supervisory Special Agent, I was nevertheless thankful to have his skills where he was.

I peered in the window, inspecting Sterling's four-man team. Each one flooded by the light of their five screens. Their heads darted from display to display, analyzing and synthesizing, while pounding furiously at their keyboards. They were in their element, but to me, their workspace was the antithesis of an FBI bullpen. Food wrappers and empty soda cans were strewn across the table and floor. I couldn't work in a space like that. To an outsider, it was chaos. To them, it matched the speed and fervor with which they worked. I certainly wasn't a twenty-something cybercriminologist.

Sterling's team was responsible for tracing the live feed from the Guest bunker. His team had people working in twelve-hour shifts twenty-four hours a day. They were intensely focused and seemed to be making progress. I didn't break their concentration and moved on.

All my rising stars—so young, so bold, so full of energy. There are moments I feel like I'm old and out of touch. Cybercrimes didn't even exist when I started as an agent.

The fire that burns within me has evolved since I was a tenacious, young agent—from the spark amidst kindling so easily blown out to the bed of coals that feeds a blaze. I wonder, though, if they see me that way, or do they see a fire blowing out?

Time is a funny thing. I began as an agent who needed to make a statement with every case, leaving my mark on the agency and in the world. I'd become a Director, incorporating every agent into fulfilling that need. That hall was my mark. *They are the future.*

My usual determined pace became a nostalgic stroll, and I turned the corner, reaching my next team led by Supervisory Special Agent Grayson Holt. Operation Libertas was his first op with the shiny new title, and he was not only eager but anxious to impress. I decided to go ahead and step into the conference room to see how things were progressing with such a high-profile case. As I reached for the handle, Holt exploded out of the room. The heavy wooden door swung out, smashing my hand.

"Director Fenn!"

Finding me on the other side of the door rattled Holt. Seemingly oblivious to any injury he may have caused, Holt waved a collection of papers and FBI folders wildly in my face. And though I was only inches from him, he shouted, "Director, we found him! We found him!"

I clutched my hand as the throbbing in my finger suggested that it was broken. The pain was insignificant next to what I had just heard.

"Define: 'We found him'?"

Holt straightened his lanky frame and smoothed his vibrant tie. Once collected, he began again, though only slightly less frenzied than before. "We traced the signal. He had it masked and bounced it around, creating a chain of over a dozen proxy nodes hiding the origin point. One by one, we back-traced the chain, raiding each facility hosting a node—with the cooperation of international police, of course. The proxy nodes had equal inbound and outbound traffic, but we now have the origin point with only outbound traffic. We've found him, sir. We have a location. He's here. He's in DC!"

Agent Holt assaulted me with the collection of embossed folders. He seemed to be physically vibrating with excitement, visibly trying to control it. *I have to coach him on that, but now is not the time.*

He wasn't like my seasoned agents. Holt never wanted to join the FBI. It was merely a legitimate occupation where he could put his skills to use. He was a hacker—and he was exceptional—even if I had wondered lately if he had met his equal with this unsub.

"Sir?" Holt's tone seemed anxious for a response. My prolonged silence must have been too much for him.

The data and analysis were sound. It was time to move.

"With me." I marched down the hall, Holt on my heels.

He dealt with ones and zeros on a day-to-day basis, not seeing much of what happened outside the four walls of his office. He compiled information and handed it off. Holt had never, not once, seen the part of an operation after disseminating the information. This would be a first.

Holt followed me into Tactical Operations. Holt had never entered the nerve center for fieldwork. It thundered with activity —monitors everywhere, people frenetically moving about and collaborating, the livestream of the Guests front and center. Of course, every conference room streamed the live feed, constantly reminding every agent of whom they were working to free. In my four decades with the Bureau—really in its history—we have never mobilized so many resources to free two individuals. Our inability to find Ms. Cameron and Mr. Beecher had been so public and so constantly televised that the FBI had to devote every resource to prove to the world that we weren't incompetent.

While Holt had seen the feed of the Guests on any number of monitors in any number of rooms, the sheer reality and enormity of Tactical Operations obviously overwhelmed him. I had walked him into the center of the hive, and he immediately stepped back and shrunk away.

He'll have to adapt, and quickly.

I advanced station to station, mobilizing resources to engage Holt's analysis. Holt followed tacitly, almost invisibly behind me. Orders were given and followed; Holt watched like a hawk. It was good for him to see how the operation unfolded, to soak it all in.

Not an hour and a half later, the final pieces were in place, and we landed at the helm of the room. I placed my hand on Holt's shoulder. "There's the drone." I pointed to a large monitor across the room displaying a drone image of an old brick warehouse.

"Is that the target?" I projected my voice to the drone operator across the room.

"Yes, sir," the agent operating the drone called back from a station on a lower level of the room.

"One of DC Chem's old warehouses. They went under in the '80s. According to city records, the building should still be abandoned. This is the location where the proxy chain ended. The IP address of the malicious traffic came from here. All evidence says this is the origin point, sir."

"Excellent." Holt's intel seemed accurate. I turned to Holt and placed a hand on each shoulder. "Have you ever been in the field?" I asked, already knowing the answer. He wasn't a field agent, but I intended to stretch him beyond his monitors, stress ball, and ergonomic office chair.

He shook his head, fear perceivable in his eyes.

Time for you to discover what I'm convinced you're capable of.
"Well, Holt, there's a first time for everything."

I turned back and addressed the room at large, "Mount up!" Our Enhanced SWAT teams—sixteen operators, four teams of four—grabbed their gear and headed for the door. I steered Holt toward the door after them so as not to interfere while the teams moved with practiced stealth and precision. Awestruck and out of place, Holt got himself into my sedan without a sound.

Four black government SUVs arrived at the warehouse. My sedan followed behind, Agent Holt's eyes fixed out the window, looking both terrified and intrigued as they widened and began to dart from place to place, surveying our new surroundings.

Upon our arrival, Holt and I watched as the four teams moved swiftly and coordinated in a silent ballet from their vehicles into invisible positions around the perimeter of the building. Most of the windows in the three-story red brick building had been broken out during its lengthy season of abandonment. The concrete that was once a parking lot had cracked and heaved and had long since been reclaimed by Mother Nature. The facility had probably been built in the '50s and repurposed a dozen times over before the city invisibly, soullessly gave up on it.

"In position, sir. On your order," SSA Crowley, the operation leader, quietly announced over comms.

Agent Holt's long, slim body slid down in his seat slightly, his eyes peering out the bottom of the window. It was not behavior I found acceptable in an agent. But I had thrown him into the deep end without proper training, so I withheld the reprimand.

Sink or swim, Holt.

"You have a go." I gave the order with no perceptible emotion, both out of habit and as an intentional example to Holt. I watched him wonder how to control his mounting anxiety. *Considerable responsibility weighs when your decisions impact lives, Holt. This is the first time you'll have to witness the ramifications of your work; it's logical that you'll feel that weight. The burden will only become heavier, the nights more restless, as your responsibility increases and your choices impact more lives—as they should, as they have for me.*

Commotion erupted over the comms, terminating my internal thought. A chorus of agents shouted warnings. "Get out!" An explosion ripped through the warehouse. Then another.

"Dear God! My people!"

I leapt from my vehicle, and a third blast caught me midair, throwing me against the car. Holt stumbled out of the sedan. *What is he thinking?* "Back in the car! You're no good to me dead!" *This is not the time for on-the-job training.* Holt froze, glued to the side of the car, unable to return to its refuge.

I shed my suit coat and charged the ten yards toward the flaming shell of a building in search of my teams. The main entrance was off to the side of the building, and the door hung by a single hinge, exposing a long entry hall. *They would have cleared the front hall first; I'll have to follow their most likely path.*

How far into the building did they get before the explosions began?

I found Agent Barone deep in the entry hallway. "Barone!" I called to him.

"Boss, I can't see!" he shouted back, wandering deeper into the building. I rushed to his side.

"Barone, it's an op with zero visibility. Hand on my shoulder. Follow me."

"We can't leave. I got separated from my team. Lanoff, Pieri, Hamovici. We have to get them out. I can manage." Barone turned to head back down the hall, determined to help his team.

I stopped and held Barone by the shoulder, knowing the pull he felt to go back inside. "Vincent, we have to get you out. I will get back in here and find them. You can count on it. Tell me what you know. Where and how did you get separated?"

"Boss, they were clearing the room at the end of the hall. I was to hang back and watch their six in the corridor behind. I was scanning where we had come from when the first explosion happened. Then I turned toward the end of the hall to see what had happened, and I caught the full flash of the second blast. I haven't seen a thing since."

"That's all I need to know. I'll find them. Let's get you to the medic." I led him back down the hall toward the exit, and he started to chuckle. Then he got louder, and it became a full-blown laugh. We were almost out of the building. "Barone, are you okay? This is not the time to be laughing, operator."

"I'm sorry, boss. I can't help it."

"What is it?"

"I'm the team medic." He broke down again, almost in tears, and lost his grip on my shoulder. I took hold of him as we exited the warehouse and headed for the closest SUV.

"Well, boss, I suppose we'd better hope EMS gets here on the double. I'm an excellent medic, and I've worked in the dark before. But pitch blackness and bombing injuries are a next-level kind of challenge I'm not sure I want to attempt." Barone snickered as I rested him in the open gate of the SUV. He always had a sunny disposition and a sense of humor about any situation. But I never expected him to be cracking jokes about losing his sight. *It better be temporary.*

"You'll be fine here until EMS arrives. I'm going back for the others."

"I'm good. I'll take care of anyone else that makes it out. Go!"

Now he's ordering me around? He'll be fine.

I raced back into the building and through the entry hall, choking on smoke, dodging fallen debris, trying to get deeper into the building to find someone else—anyone else. I turned a corner and reached a large room. One of the devices must have detonated there. It looked like the wall had come down, and the temperature was significantly higher.

"Agent Lanoff!"

She was halfway across the room with her ankle trapped under debris. I had to climb over fallen bricks and upturned warehouse barrels while still trying to remain low enough to avoid inhaling too much smoke.

When I reached her, she seemed to put on a brave face for my benefit. I needed to ease the stress. "If you needed a vacation, all you had to do was put in for time off. No need to go to this extreme."

"Yes, sir." She seemed to appreciate the distracting humor in the midst of her intense pain. Not every agent does.

I finished my assessment of the beam, determined that it was safe enough to move, and carefully lifted the fragment off her. "It's a compound fracture, Lanoff." There was bone protruding through the flesh of her ankle. "You won't be able to put your weight on it. Let me help you up. Arm over my shoulder; we'll do the three-legged race like the games at the FBI summer barbecue. Let's go."

"Ready when you are, sir. You know me, first in line for anything." She offered a wry smile. I could tell she was in pain, but she'd never admit it.

"That you are, Lanoff. That you are."

I carefully lifted her off the ground and pulled her arm over my shoulder. We struggled through the warehouse and toward the exit. Before we could reach the long hall, flames leapt out at us, forcing me to shield Lanoff with my body, searing my entire left side.

Reflexively, I dropped Agent Lanoff. She yelped.

Instantaneously, I felt the pain from the burn. It was penetrating, unmerciful. But when I moved to clutch my left hand and arm that had caught the worst of the flames, I noticed Lanoff reaching for her ankle. *I can't think about myself. Not yet.*

I set my own pain aside and reached down for Lanoff. "Come on. We can do this. Not far now."

Despite the pain, she hobbled down the length of the corridor with me. One of the few remaining windows shattered behind us. I wasn't even sure if either of us was struck by glass. There was so much heat, so much pain, neither of us could tell.

When we finally made it out, ambulances had started to arrive.

She'll be properly taken care of, but I have to go back. One. Two. There are still three agents unaccounted for.

"Hamovici and Pieri are still inside!" Lanoff called from the back of the ambulance, reminding me to find her teammates. I was already running back in; I waved in acknowledgment. Crowley, the mission leader, was missing, too. I had to get them all. Every last one.

I was running out of time. The flames had reached the roof by the time I entered the building for the third time. I'd never felt oppressive, choking heat like that in my life. I ran through the hall where I'd found Barone. Having traversed it several times already, I was able to negotiate the debris more quickly despite the thickening wall of smoke. I moved deeper into the large room and passed the fallen beam that had broken Lanoff's ankle. I called out for my three missing agents, but the only response was the roar of the fire and the crash of building segments.

I turned to retrace my steps, but the fire had devoured the passage behind me. I had to find another path. There was another hall. I didn't see any flames, only smoke. I kept low.

Pieri lay unconscious halfway down the hall. *Where am I? I have to get him out of here. Thornfield will never forgive me if something happened to her husband on my watch. She's a force to be reckoned with. Her temper is hot, and her resentment cold. If I don't bring him back unscathed . . . I can't think about that. I have to bring him back. Safe. Safe and whole.*

Seeing no burns or debris, I suspected smoke inhalation. I grabbed his arms and began to drag him in the direction I best determined to be out. Each step was plodding and arduous due to the intensifying smoke and heat. Flames swallowed the hall behind us and followed us down the corridor, moving faster than we could. I almost dropped Pieri when flames spread through an open door and caught my shirt on fire as we passed. I had to brace him against my legs to smother my burning sleeve. There wasn't time; we had to move.

Greedy arms of flames reached out for Pieri. I thought I dislocated his shoulder with my vigor at heaving his slack and unresponsive body when I finally saw an open door.

We made it out.

I had to catch my breath before dragging him around to the front of the building. Somehow, we had ended up toward the back of the right side of the building. Fortunately, two firemen found us before I tried hauling him around to the front. He was in good hands, and I needed to move on. But when I handed him off, the fire department restrained me from going back.

There were two more missing. Two decorated agents, Special Agent Hamovici and Supervisory Special Agent Crowley, didn't make it out.

I dragged my broken body to the front of the building, thinking about these agents, what they had meant to me. *Crowley had only been leading the Enhanced SWAT teams for about nine months, and she was damn good at it. Her husband had taken leave to be with their kids so she could focus on the new position, too. What am I going to tell them?*

A window exploded overhead, enunciating the danger that still raged inside. Forbidding me to forget even for a second.

And Hamovici. He was married to his work. First one in, last one out. He had a unique set of skills I've never seen in another human being. I didn't even know who he had listed as next of kin. We were his family.

Why won't they let me back in? It's my life to sacrifice, my choice.

The fire department said the flames had consumed too much of the warehouse, and my agents likely hadn't survived the initial blast.

Likely? That's not good enough. Two people I am personally responsible for are gone.

Egregious.

Unjustifiable.

I sat in the back of the ambulance, the EMT irritated with me because I was not about to let her treat me until every one of my agents had been seen to first. She obliged, though under protest; I didn't give her an option. My shirt appeared to be seared to my skin, but the medics couldn't do anything about that until we reached the hospital anyway. *Best that they see to my agents first.*

The reflective surface of the stainless-steel cabinet in the back of the ambulance allowed me to self-assess my injuries: severe burns over my hands, left arm, left shoulder, and head. *Interesting, I'm not in much pain.* My left ear was mangled, and my hair was melted. I tried to touch the left side of my once perfectly symmetrical face. I was unrecognizable. "Looks like my days of being a devastatingly handsome SOB are over," I mumbled into the mirrored stainless-steel surface, thankful there was no one there to hear me.

Returning to her problem patient, the EMT announced that every agent had been seen, and most were en route to the hospital. She perfunctorily forced an oxygen mask onto my face before she began triage. I tried to offer my own diagnosis, but she summarily refused my input.

I pulled up the oxygen mask and demanded to see Agent Holt before leaving for the hospital. *This experience could ruin his path toward future fieldwork and his growth as an agent overall; I have to speak with him.*

The EMT restrained me, strapping me to the gurney like a prisoner. I struggled against her to lower my mask and speak to Holt when he arrived at the back of the open ambulance. "Do not let this stop you; let it spur you on. You can find this monster." That was all the EMT would let me say. I watched Holt pick up his pace as he jogged back to the sedan, seeming bolstered by my confidence in him.

The EMT wasn't gentle. She forced me back into a supine position, tightened the straps, and repositioned the mask. She leaned over and ratcheted the strap over my shoulders, her name patch inches from my face.

Janice.

Click, click, click, snap! *Argh! Too tight.*

Janice, the rankling impediment to getting back to my case, didn't see that I'd kept a hand free from her bindings, and I wasn't going to let her in on my little secret. After compressing my rib cage, she fiddled with medical equipment behind my head while I watched my sedan pull out of the parking lot, assuaged that Holt would continue the search.

Without warning, the sedan door opened, and Holt jumped out of the moving car before it screeched to a halt. He scrambled toward me, his scrawny limbs flailing wildly as he waved a tablet in my direction, his face panicked and pale. Holt dove into the back of the ambulance, startling Janice, who protested vehemently.

Ignoring Janice, Agent Holt thrust the tablet in my face and blurted, "Director. The first part of the message. It was addressed directly to you!" Superimposed over the live feed of the Guests, the next lines appeared:

you interfered
people got hurt

Between being strapped flat on a gurney, Holt's shaking hands holding the tablet, and an IV drip of morphine, I couldn't take it. I had to seize control, to fight to stay alert and focused.

With my free hand, I tugged at the IV line in my arm. No-nonsense Janice pulled my hand away; the morphine drip had taken my size advantage away from me. *I've lost too many battles today.* Incensed, I ripped the tablet away from Holt and held it over my own damn face, forcing my eyes to refocus.

The text changed:

leave the game alone
or lose more lives

Infuriating. Enraging. I lost good agents today, all for a malignant game a sociopath wanted to play.

Untenable.

Reaching my limit, I launched the tablet out of the back of the ambulance. Agent Holt stared back at me, wide-eyed. He didn't appear to know how to respond to my uncharacteristic outburst.

Still all business behind me, Janice subtly took a syringe out of a drawer and administered a sedative into my IV line. *She's a sneaky one.* "Alright, Mr. Fenn, we're going to have a nice calm ride to the hospital now." I scowled at her as she shooed Agent Holt out of the ambulance.

Lifting my head as much as I could, I addressed him one last time before the drugs wouldn't allow me to complete a coherent thought. "Don't give up. You find him. You find that son of a bitch."

I knew Holt could find him. Holt had been molded by that fire just as I had. My head dropped, and I drifted off before Janice even shut the ambulance door.

DAY 22

Falling

Standing in my closet wearing nothing but a towel, wet hair dripping down my back, I thumped my head against the wall. *I have never spent so much time overthinking an outfit in my life. Lots of women have this problem every day. C'mon, Monti, you're not one of those women. There's a purpose for the day. Narrow it down. There's weather. Well, maybe not here. Then there's mood to consider. It takes all of five minutes.*

Why is this not one of those days?

77380142

This is insane. I have to move on. But do I adjust how I've been dressing? Will Henry notice? Would that help or hurt our cause? His life is hanging in the balance.

I stood with my wet head resting on the wall of the closet, soaking the plastered wall. The ridiculously large pink towel made me look child-sized, and a migraine-hangover stood between me and a decision.

"That isn't the usual method for relieving a hangover." I hoisted myself into an upright position. Henry was in the doorway, perky morning person that he was, presenting an oversized mug of coffee. "This might help, though." His smile, reassuring as always.

I mumbled "thank you" through my sips as I tried to imbibe the caffeine. As he walked out of the closet, I noticed that Henry had raised the caliber of his wardrobe. *He usually wears a T-shirt and cargo pants. Polo and khakis today, Oscar? How very interesting. I'm not the only one overthinking this. Then again, you think thoroughly through everything, don't you?*

A smile accompanied a glance over his shoulder as he disappeared into the morning sunlight of my room and then down the hall.

He'll read into any changes I make. Right, stick to exactly what I've been wearing. Maybe fractionally cuter pants? He won't notice that, will he?

I finally made it out of my room, trying not to dwell on my closet crisis. On my way past Henry's door, I noticed that a book had been carelessly tossed on the floor in the doorway. *That's strange; Henry exists in military neatness. He wouldn't leave a book on the floor.*

The cover read *Onyx* by Jennifer L. Armentrout. When I picked it up, a page fell out.

I'm not the only one getting creepy messages. I dropped the book and picked up the loose page. True to form, there was a highlight.

> "That's the funny thing about trying to escape.
> You never really can.
> Maybe temporarily, but not completely."[10]

Well, that'll throw anyone off. Why didn't he put the book on top of the fridge with the others he's hidden there to preserve my mental health? Of course, throwing books at walls has proven cathartic for me. Maybe he needed some therapy, too.

I tucked the torn page back in its place and left the book on the floor exactly as I'd found it. *Henry can deal with this little chestnut in his own time and in his own way. He has more important things to worry about.*

I half expected a banquet to be laid out when I got to the kitchen, but Henry was already cleaning up his breakfast. *I guess he isn't going to be obvious.* So, I refilled my coffee cup; caffeine was all I needed anyway.

Henry washed his dishes while I sipped my medicinal effusion of caffeine, trying to soothe my pounding head. I fished in my pocket for Excedrin and attempted to extract the pocket lint from the fistful of pills in another attempt to relieve my migraine-hangover.

"That's a different necklace than you typically wear. It's rather lovely. What prompted the change?" He didn't lift his head or look at me; he just kept washing dishes. I, on the other hand, was stunned. My fistful of pills and pocket lint spilled onto the counter next to my mug as I looked down.

How had I drifted so far from my routine? I held the pendant in my hand and stared at it. I'd been so focused on not being obvious with my outfit that I hadn't thought at all about my jewelry choice and veered far enough from my norm that it caught Henry's attention. *What am I thinking? Everything catches his attention.*

"What is it?" While I was absorbed in my thoughts, Henry had finished his dishes and made his way around the counter to join me. He slipped the delicate piece of rose gold from my hand and examined it. "That's right extraordinary. Does it have a special meaning?" He heard the catch in my breath despite my every effort to even it out.

I'm stuck; I have to tell him.

"I didn't even realize I had put it on this morning." *I can't look at him.*

I went as far as to get off my stool and turn away as though I wanted to walk while I told the story. I didn't actually go anywhere; I only stared at the pendant hanging at the bottom of its long, delicate double chain.

After a deep breath, I gathered my courage and held it out for him to see. "My daughter gave this to me for my birthday. The last one before . . . " I tried to smile, but my lips wouldn't cooperate.

"It was made by pouring molten rose gold over an actual rose leaf. They heat the metal to a precise temperature. Most of the leaf burns away, and the metal adheres to the remaining veins and the stem. The effect is fragile, unique, rather breathtaking. She said it reminded her of me." *It physically hurts to remember her. I don't want to talk about this, to think about this.*

"I kept my jewelry in a fireproof safe. It was among . . . " I had to pause for a second and swallow the lump in my throat.

"My jewelry was among the few things that survived the fire. I haven't worn it in . . . well, in years. I don't know what made me put it on this morning."

Holy shit!

"This isn't a replica! This is mine! From my house!" I looked back down at the intricate veining in the leaf, remembering my sweet little girl proudly presenting it to me.

Then, I just couldn't. I hid my face, determined to stop thinking about her, about the invasion of my home, my personal space. I didn't have the emotional strength to deal with the waves of grief on top of everything else.

Strong, solid arms enveloped me. He didn't say a word; he simply held me. I didn't want to at first, but for a short moment, I allowed myself to rest my face hidden in my hands against his chest and let him squeeze me almost to the point of not being able to inhale. Somehow, he knew before I did that that was exactly what I needed to get a hold of myself.

I can't break down right now.

My fortitude returned, and I took a restorative breath, removed my hands from my face, and rested them on Henry. When I looked up, there was his reassuring smile. "Right then. I think we need some comfort food. What do you think?" I noticed a glint of mischief twinkling in his eye.

"Is food your answer to everything?" As I spoke, he gently released me and made his way back into the kitchen.

"Well, now that you mention it, yes. Yes, it is." In a way, he seemed surprised by the revelation, though not displeased. He fished around in the cabinets, looking for various cooking tools as he spoke. "Well, whenever something wonderful would happen, I cooked with my mum, or she made us something good to eat. If I had a grueling day or something shattering happened, I cooked with my mum, or she made us something to eat. If I was bored or my brothers were cruel, and I didn't want to play with them—"

I interrupted, "You cooked with your mum?"

His smile sparked. "You've got the idea. I don't think there's a problem that can't be solved with good cooking or a celebration that is complete without it. Umm. Hold that thought." He dashed out to the larder.

He was trying to distract me. I looked back down at my necklace, still deeply disturbed, but I noticed that Henry and his kitchen antics had made some improvement on my state of mind. Henry returned in moments, his arms full of intriguing ingredients. "What are you making?"

"You'll see when I'm done. I'm not confident it'll work with what I have here, so I don't want to tell you quite yet." He raised an eyebrow before he turned his back to me and began mixing and pouring like a mad scientist.

"You know, I can see what you're saying." I decided to continue the conversation as he worked. "It seems like society centers our activities around food. We meet for business around meals. Family gatherings are around meals. Holidays, celebrations, weddings, funerals, even sports and movies—just about every event I can think of involves some form of food. I suppose we should embrace it and make it a healthy social habit."

Henry looked over his shoulder and waved a wooden spoon at me. "Exactly!"

It wasn't ten minutes before his concoction was in the oven. "Well, that'll be a while. Should we get to work?"

I was disappointed to return to reality. It had been a refreshing fifteen-minute break from the turmoil that had become our lives. "Yeah, I suppose we should." There was zero enthusiasm in my voice.

Henry took note. "Did you want to work alone in the library today, or would you prefer some company?" His voice was insecure but slightly hopeful.

I met his eyes with a faint smile. "You know, I think I would enjoy the company today. That is, if you don't mind putting up with me?" His eyes brightened.

Are you perking up because you actually want to spend a day with me or because you think you're making headway with your task? No matter, it's not only your assignment; it's mine, too.

"I don't mind at all. I'd enjoy the company as well." He grabbed the ancient yellow kitchen timer and sauntered off toward the library ahead of me.

We spent the morning rather pleasantly. As we searched the library for hidden passages or some secret way out, Henry pointed out the books he encountered that were on his must-read list or his favorites list. We both called attention to the rare and unusual books we happened upon. More than once, we made note of the ridiculous nature of what we were doing. It felt like we belonged in an episode of *Scooby-Doo*.

That morning was more idyllic than any other had been. We laughed and were occupied. Henry surprised me with brownies for breakfast. They were unlike any brownies I'd ever eaten because we had no fresh eggs. Still, any chocolate for breakfast was winning in my book. I may have smeared gooey brownie on the pages of a rare first edition, but we were going to keep that between us and however many million people noticed it on the livestream.

When the time came, we decided to eat lunch in the library. A change in routine gave us the illusion of being away from the constraints and disincentives of captivity, even if only for an hour. After lunch, we weren't ready to get back to work. We enjoyed the vacation from forced prison labor, and bit by bit, our lunch hour morphed into a lunch afternoon.

Digesting on the sunken sofa in the center of the room, my back on the seat cushion, feet hanging over the top of the couch, and dirty plates scattered in the center of the floor, Henry continued to entertain me. I wasn't inclined to budge. It started with a discussion of books we'd found throughout the library that we wanted to read or that stood out. But the conversation had turned to Henry's soapbox of movies that were more exceptional than the book and movies that were inferior versions of the books they were based on and should never be seen or talked about ever again. Riveted, I rolled over, clutched an orange throw pillow, and stretched out across the matching leather sofa.

I ate leftover brownie while Henry stomped around the room and stepped over the back of the couch, lecturing about movies and books, most of which I had never heard of. Entertained and enthralled, I wanted to watch and read them all, no matter which list they were on because they'd gotten such an extreme response from a normally reserved and quiet man. I spun around, wide-eyed in my seat, following him as he paced in circles around the sunken sofa when he stopped mid-sentence and shifted his attention back to me. "I'm so sorry. You don't care about any of this at all, do you?"

How could you think that?

"What? I've been fascinated this whole time. I've been tempted several times to get a pen and paper to make a list, but I was afraid you'd stop." He eyed me unpersuaded. I sat up straight in my seat, put on my most angelic face, and lifted three fingers in the air. "Scout's honor."

"Well, I should probably descend from my soapbox regardless." He chuckled and leapt over the back of the sofa to plop himself in the seat next to me. In the process, his Sasquatch foot knocked the wooden box filled with brass plates off the end table and onto the floor.

"Ugh. Those again." I bent over to pick them up. "This psychopath has a knack for spoiling the rare moment of peace, doesn't he?" I was irritated that our glimmer of fun had been squashed.

"Wait." Henry reached down and took the last brass plate from my hand before I could put it away. He tapped it against his fingertips and stepped over the back of the sofa again.

What are you doing?

Tap, tap, tap.

Henry perused the bookshelves while he rhythmically tapped the brass plate against his fingertips. "What are you looking for?"

Tap, tap, tap.

"Not sure." He let the plate brush against the bindings of the books as he passed. One by one. Thwap. Thwap. Thwap. Slowing to a—thwap—stop.

Do you see something?

I leaned over the back of the sofa for a better view.

Where are you going?

Henry pulled out an oversized, cumbersome white book and launched himself back onto the sofa, landing next to me. He showed me the cover. *Introduction to Number Theory* by Open University.[11] *Strange reading choice.* He looked in the table of contents, flipped through the pages, and stopped at a bookmarked page.

"I came across this earlier. It has a weird bookmark with sheep on it. Something in the back of my mind said it was important. I didn't make the connection until the box spilled." Henry used the plate to underline the heading on the page. "Affine ciphers. I think the number may be a code. Look, the same wavy highlight as the taunting quotes we keep getting."

Sure enough, the chapter title was highlighted. "If we're really supposed to use this cipher to decode something, what makes you think that it's that particular number we're meant to decode? And for what purpose?"

This is preposterous.

Henry laid the book down open to the page with the cipher and took the box from my hand, dumping the plates onto the cushion between us. "This number is important to him for some reason. It *means* something. I don't know about you, but I need to find out what.

"As far as the purpose . . . Everything we've experienced in here has been a power play. His goal is control. Every time we push, every time we try to regain some kind of control, he has to seize that control back. I want to know. I need to know what it is he has to say. Whatever it is, he's been trying to say it since he killed Mum and Dad in '98."

Well, that's deeply disturbing.

"Okay then, affine cipher." We read the chapter together. It was fairly straightforward. Each letter in the alphabet was replaced with a number. A was 0, B was 1, C was 2, and so on until Z was 25. Then, the number standing in for each letter was fed through the cipher to encode. In order to decode, we needed both the correct multiplicand and summand parameters to fit into the equation. That was the key to completing the cipher.

"I can do the math, but how do we find the two numbers to fit into the equation? Where do we even look for that?"

Henry slapped the book shut and looked at me as though I'd asked him to walk on water. "I bloody well thought I was doing well to come up with the affine cipher. I'm gonna need a minute or two to find your parameters."

We stared at the book lying in the pile of plates, waiting for an epiphany.

I scanned the room, hoping something would jump out at me.

Henry poked around in the empty box of brass plates.

What are you expecting to find in there? The box is empty.

Resting his elbows on his knees, Henry absently traced the scar the chemical burn left in his palm the first day we met. I flopped back on the couch, giving up. We'd come up empty.

I lay on the couch, silence shrill in my ears.

"Right then." Henry broke the stillness, startling me. "I'm going to have to let this one percolate."

I let out a sigh as I stood and headed for the door. "You know, we should watch one of the movies from your list of unwatchables tonight." I closed the door behind me before he had a chance to answer.

"Hold on there, where do you think you're going?" I could hear his voice booming through the closed door.

I knew it would instigate a fight, so I tried to get some distance between us before I hollered back, "I'm starting dinner." I didn't plan to, but a giggle slipped out along with my response.

Henry jogged after me. "Hey, now, that's my territory!"

I had skills; being faster than Henry was not one of them. His stride, twice that of mine, caught him up to me by the lettuce bed in the conservatory. I tried to look innocent. I failed.

"If you think you're going to steal my one contribution to this insane asylum, you have another thing coming." He was standing over me, trying to appear intimidating, but I could tell he desperately tried not to laugh. He did not succeed.

"Oh, yeah?" I tried to shove him playfully. He didn't budge; in fact, he didn't move at all. We both burst into laughter. "Come on. You can't even pretend to let me push you a little?" He was laughing so hard he couldn't answer. He just shook his head. When he collected himself, he resumed his imposing stance and refused to move, trying futilely not to smile.

I was about to give up and tell him that he was welcome to do all the work even though I was a fantastic chef . . . but I didn't get a chance.

Over Henry's shoulder, the clumsily pieced-together bits of decaying face returned.

don't tell henry

79655602

Trying not to change the expression on my face, I attempted to feign that I might try to escape to the kitchen as a distraction. Henry obliged and playfully stopped me, taking the focus off my distressed face.

make him kiss you

or . . .

79946106

The necrotic patchwork face on the dome disappeared, but my heart leapt up into my throat. I lowered my head. There was no way I could hide the expression on my face. I turned my back to

Henry. What am I supposed to do? I'm not an actress. Anything I attempt will end dreadfully.

I felt a gentle hand on my shoulder, followed by his tender, patient voice. "What just happened? Did I do something wrong?" My heart broke.

He's such a gentleman. How can I . . . ? But I have to.

I put my hand over his and took a breath. "No, you haven't done a thing. I was only thinking." I broke for a moment.

I can do this. I can say something to manipulate. Maybe a coy look, a provocative touch. I can make it happen.

But the thought of being disingenuous for the entertainment of a madman. The result of wounding one of the few pure and decent men in the world made me physically ill.

Delaying is too dangerous a risk. I have to go through with it. I wiped my eyes and turned to face him with a hair flip.

I'm so bad at this.

Henry knew right away that something was off. He gave me a side-glance, though he didn't say anything. *I can't look him in the eye.* I began fiddling with my necklace and staring at my hands.

He was strong, but his hand on my shoulder was gentle. "I don't know what's wrong, but I'd like to help if I can."

Of course you do. You're that guy.

Henry's hand slipped tenderly from my shoulder to my hands and cupped them as I tugged nervously at my necklace. He guided me to sit on a bench and sat next to me. "Now then, how can I make your life less stressful right now?"

I looked up at his earnest face, and without even thinking about it, I reached up and barely brushed his cheek with the side of my thumb. Before I could pull my hand away, he pressed it flat against his face—his hand covering mine—and closed his eyes. I could feel the heat from his face and hand radiate through my fingers. He leaned forward until his forehead reached mine.

For a long moment, the house and all its madness fell away. I didn't sense anything around us. Only him and me.

The responsibility for the life in front of me weighed heavily. Yet, crushing Henry's soul to possibly prevent physical harm tormented me.

I can't do it. I can't lie. Not about this. Not to a man so fundamentally remarkable in so many ways.

Before I realized I'd made a decision, I heard an almost inaudible rasp. "I can't."

It had come from me.

When I recognized what I'd done, I vaulted off the bench, ran toward the tree, and turned around. I shrieked, not at Henry but toward the cameras. All of them. "I can't! I won't!" Henry didn't understand the distinction of whom I was yelling at and stood up.

Only a section of the dome changed, the section to which Henry's back was turned as he watched in utter disbelief. The rest of the dome remained sky-like, but behind Henry, the distorted, vile face returned with a message:

last chance
the crypt has a reservation for henry
80105833

The message disappeared as quickly as it had arrived. Henry was rightly confused by my declaration. He didn't see the message over his head and began walking toward me. I put my hand up, hoping he'd stay put.

"No. This is it. I'm done."

I was about to turn and walk away when a deafening mechanical screech came from overhead. The panel of screens above Henry's head blinked and blackened. No sky, no morbid face, nothing.

The section of screen shifted, accompanying a popping sound.

Henry stopped walking, and his gaze followed the sound. I ran toward him as fast as my legs would carry me—not nearly fast enough. "Henry!" I shrieked. His eyes met mine, and he recognized the terror on my face. He tried to move out of the way, but the screen was already plummeting from the ceiling, loose wires sparking as it dropped. I ran toward Henry and looked up to realize that not only was a section of screen coming down, but chunks of the concrete above it were falling as well.

I dove at Henry, tackling him to the ground. We tumbled over a planter, narrowly missing the largest pieces of debris.

Shards of broken screen components caught us both in the legs. A three-foot boulder-like piece of concrete landed directly between

Henry and me, scraping my arm. Somehow, we both managed to remain whole.

After extricating himself, Henry traversed the fallen debris and tried to pull pieces of screen off me. "What the bloody hell was that?"

"Punishment for not following instructions, I suspect." *No more questions, please. I'm tired of it all. Let it go. Are you capable of that?*

"Okay, that's it." Henry was resolute. "He's not going to divide and conquer us anymore. I will not keep things from you, and you will not keep things from me. We are getting through this as a team. From now on, we are a single unit. Agreed?"

Nope, definitely not leaving it alone. His expression was firm but, somehow, not demanding. He wasn't forcing me to spill my secrets; he was coming alongside me, wanting to get through this together.

Huh, I've been alone for so long, I haven't had anyone to share life's struggles with.

Overwhelming feelings. Can't deal with that now. Set it aside, Monti.

As we sat in the rubble for a moment, catching our breath, I became acutely aware that my foot was wet. We were leaning against a planter, crowded by pieces of shattered screen and blocks of concrete ceiling. My left foot was pinned between concrete and a section of the display that had tumbled down on top of us. I reached over to move the display piece so I could see why my foot was wet. Pain raced up my leg. "Ahh!" I dropped the fragment back onto my foot. Pain shot up my leg again.

"What is it?" Henry carefully stepped over my leg and lifted the heavy corner of display off my foot. A sliver of metal was embedded up the length of my calf, and blood trickled down the wirelike piece of technology and dripped into my shoe. It was strange; it didn't hurt as long as I didn't move.

"That's no good; we need to get you out of the dirt so I can clean that." I wasn't worried until I noticed the pallor of Henry's face. I tried to stand, wrenching my ankle to unpin it. The movement caused a pain sharp enough to make me think I might pass out. I fell backward into the grass.

"Seriously?" Henry was not impressed with my attempt at independence. He carefully lifted me out of the debris field and carried me off to the dining room.

"We should rename it 'Henry's personal OR.'" I didn't mean to say it out loud, but the pain had reduced my verbal filter.

"Let's avoid needing it again, shall we?" Henry tried to look scolding, but I could see the humor in the green of his eyes.

Even though he was careful, every step he took sent pain shooting up my leg. After carefully placing me on one dining chair with my leg propped up on another, Henry left to retrieve his medical supplies. *If he's going to stitch me up again, I need a distraction.* Having been through it twice before, I considered the process akin to torture. Henry was sufficiently skilled at first aid, but being on my end of the needle was remarkably unpleasant.

I drummed my fingernails on the table and looked around the room, finding nothing to occupy my mind. *We were trying to figure out that cipher earlier; maybe I could work on that. A brainteaser might be just the thing to keep my mind off Henry's needle ripping through my flesh.*

"Here we go. I'll even use the anesthetic this time." Henry held up his supplies as though he were offering a carnival prize.

"Gee, thanks. Before you get started, can you grab that cipher book and the code? I'm going to need something to focus on besides pain. I'd like to feel like I'm accomplishing something while you jab at me." Henry didn't look interested in fetching things for me, but I think he wanted my cooperation, given the circumstances.

He set the supplies on the table and jogged off to the library for the book and code. His return was far more expedient than I either expected or wanted; I'd hoped it would take longer, having found no other excuse to delay the stitching process.

"Happy? Can I start now?"

You're rather irritated, considering I'm the one about to be sewn!

"Have at it, Nurse Ratched." He began by sliding the long, stiff metal piece out of my calf—a piece shaped like a twisted wire, though not as flexible. I braced myself with the table in one hand and the edge of the chair in the other to keep from passing out. The intense pain left crescent-shaped fingernail marks in the blue pleather of the chair's cushion, surprising since I broke most of my fingernails off in the wooden benches the other day.

"Hang on, the worst is over." One reassuring hand clasped my knee as he debrided the wound with the other.

That's it; I'm going over.

"You can do this; stay up, come on." I focused on his voice and gripped the table, white-knuckled.

Henry's hand left my knee, and he dug into his supplies for

something else. I dropped my head onto the table to collect myself.

"Hey!" My head jerked up as needles jabbed me one after the other along the puncture. "What are you doing?!"

"Lidocaine." He was far too happy about it.

"What?" This was by far the most painful treatment I'd received yet. He had pitched pain-free stitches.

"This is the anesthetic. It'll take a minute." He held up several empty syringes and smiled, proud of himself. I groaned, deciding to focus on the code instead of my throbbing leg. It took me a moment to focus my eyes, but after a minute, I managed to read again.

"Alright, we have a series of numbers we need to decipher from the plate: 25 12 24 12. And we think we have the right cipher." I flopped the enormous book open to the page where the bookmark with the sheep had been placed.

"Now we're looking for the numbers that unlock the cipher. The multiplicand and summand." Henry leaned back in his seat and nodded in agreement. *Does he actually understand the math? Are you even listening?*

"We can try random numbers and see how it comes out, but there are an insane number of variations." *Is it worth the shot in the dark?*

I didn't know where else to begin, so I tried the cipher with a 3 and a 1. I came up with "XKWK." "Well, that's nonsense."

I got a distracted, "Mhmmm." Henry was focused on his stitching. *At least that lidocaine stuff is working.*

"Maybe a larger number will work. What do you think if I fit a 9 into the multiplicand and a 6 into the summand?" I asked, thinking of the best random numbers to try next, knowing that statistically, people are more likely to choose a multiple of 3 when selecting a random number. *Maybe my wealth of random and useless knowledge will pay off.*

Henry gave me a distracted "uh-huh."

As I worked the math out long-hand, I chuckled, thinking back to my middle-school self, arguing that I'd never have a real-world application for long-hand arithmetic. Never in a million years would I have anticipated this particular scenario.

"Ow!" Apparently, Henry missed a spot with the lidocaine.

"Sorry about that." He kept stitching.

Yes, deeply sorry. I can tell.

I finished decrypting the cipher. *FSCS. Well, that's gibberish as well.*

"Henry, we have to find the right numbers to fit into the equation. That last quote said that by the time we figured it out, it'd be too late. So, there's an answer here somewhere. What are we missing?"

Henry stopped what he was doing and thought for a minute. "It's probably hiding in plain sight." He looked around, pondering.

I sighed. *Why did I take on such a daunting task? What is wrong with me?*

"You know . . . " He paused midsentence, dropped the needle still attached to my leg by the thread, and wandered around the dining room.

"What are you doing?"

"It's struck me as odd over the last few weeks that there are eleven seats and eleven place settings at this table. It's unusually long, and I've never seen a table with an odd number of chairs before."

I hadn't noticed, but you're right.

He moved over to the sideboard where two candelabras sat and touched each of the eleven candlesticks on one of them before looking back at me.

Without saying anything, Henry swiftly moved to the end of the hall and peered out into the conservatory. "Hey! Try 11."

"What? Why? In which spot?" I shouted down the hall at him, "What did you find?"

"Just try it; I have a theory." His eyes grew wide as he rushed back in and reached his Sasquatch arm to swipe the pile of books down from the top of the fridge.

"What are you doing?!" *I don't need to deal with all the creepy quote trauma right now.*

He splayed the books out on the floor. "Hold on."

What's he looking for? He tossed books across the kitchen floor as he sifted through them, and then . . . I guess he found it.

Henry pulled a bookmark from one of the books, a red one; I didn't catch the title. He sat beside me at the table and pulled the bookmark from under the cipher text I'd been referencing. They were similar, though not the same.

"Look." Henry laid the two bookmarks side by side. They were photographs, not printed bookmarks like you'd find in a store. They were taken on the same sheep farm; I could tell by the old barn in the background. "This one has eleven sheep. This one has two. I think the second number in the cipher is a 2."

"That's a stretch, don't you think?" *You're grasping at straws.*

"Well, the number eleven seems obvious. It's blatant now that I've noticed it. In there, in the conservatory, there are eleven halls, eleven paths, eleven benches—"

"Alright, alright," I cut him off. "What about the number two?"

"The bookmarks are what make me think the number two is correct. One has eleven, and the other has two. But I also got to thinking about when he started this. When he killed Mum and Dad. Two. When he's handing out the cipher now, with us. Two. Monti, the other number has to be two. Either way, it can't hurt to try."

He slid the two bookmarks over for dramatic effect, almost daring me not to try the number combination. *Now I have to.*

Henry returned to the hall and looked at the eleven spokes on the wagon-wheel-patterned paths, waiting for me to work out the math. "Two trees in one," he muttered as I worked.

"What?" I stopped. I couldn't listen to him and do complicated math at the same time.

"Nothing, keep going." He waved me off.

I worked as quickly as my brain would allow, fitting an 11 into the multiplicand and a 2 into the summand parameters of the equation. Even though it had been years since I'd done that kind of math, I managed it in a reasonable amount of time. I held up the page and scrutinized my results. "I don't know if this makes sense either. Does 'VICI' mean anything to you?"

"So, it was intentional." He spoke more to himself than to me. "Eleven doors, eleven paths, eleven benches, eleven sheep. Two murders, two captives, two trees, two sheep."

Henry sat back in the chair he'd been sitting in to finish stitching my leg. "Well, if it's what I think it is, that's a reference to Julius Caesar, who imprinted the words 'Veni, Vidi, Vici!' on a placard. 'I came, I saw, I conquered!' He paraded the placard around the known world, announcing his triumph over Pontus in 46 BC. By quoting Caesar, this man is trying to say he's conquered?"

We looked at the word I'd scrawled on the page. It was decoded, but what it meant was still a mystery. I flopped the book closed and hung my head over the back of the chair, my hair hanging freely behind it. "What a waste of time and brainpower." Henry finished stitching my leg and mopped up the blood.

He verbally processed the cryptic message as he cleaned the mess off the table. "This predator has been leaving this message on every grave since 1998. Why? What is so important for him to feel that he has dominance over? And what does it get him now, decades later?" Henry slammed the box of leftover medical supplies on the kitchen counter, obviously frustrated.

"I can't fathom what happened with all those people he buried in the other room." Just the thought made me shudder. "But I know he's been fighting with us for submission. He wants control or obedience. Well, both. Maybe he fought with them, too, and the plate declares that he won? He conquered?"

Henry's eyes narrowed at me. "I'm not ready to play that game. He's been manipulating us to create drama for his audience and to increase his viewership. I won't kowtow because he claims to be a conqueror." Henry scowled and stomped off to put the box of syringes, needles, and thread back in the larder. I wasn't sure how his declaration would go over. I cringed at the window image, waiting for another demand to appear.

Nothing happened.

"And another thing," Henry shouted back at me across the conservatory; the cavernous space carried his voice, but he didn't finish his thought.

He didn't get the chance.

A mechanical screeching I'd heard not long before echoed through the house again, followed shortly by the popping of concrete releasing from the ceiling. I jumped out of my chair, but my injured leg refused to support my weight. Before I could hobble across the dining room or even get close to the short hall to reach the conservatory and see what had happened, a ground-shaking crash told me that another panel had dropped from the ceiling and large pieces of concrete had fallen on top of it.

I clung to the walls to support myself as I made my way down the hall and into the conservatory. "Henry?" I didn't see him anywhere. "Henry!" I hopped closer to the newly fallen panel; the stones in the path prevented me from getting there as quickly as I wanted.

"Here." His head, along with one arm and shoulder, were sticking out from under the mostly whole display panel. He'd been knocked face-down in the grass. I fell to my knees next to him, trying to determine where he was injured.

"Are you hurt? What happened?" I yanked and pushed at the panel. But it hadn't broken apart like the first one; I had guessed that the grass cushioned its fall. With the panel covered in concrete, it was too heavy to budge.

"I . . . I can't move. I'm not sure." He turned his head toward me in the grass, looking battered and winded. As I tried to use my lower body weight to push the screen off him, I noticed blood oozing through the gauze in my leg, again, dripping into my shoe, and it struck me . . .

We can't win. We'll never find the way out.

I tried with renewed zeal and passion to lift the fallen screen and free Henry. "Ahh. Stop!" he cried out in pain, and I fell backward into the grass.

Shit. He's probably got a broken rib, maybe internal bleeding.

We're going to die here.

I ground my fists into my eye sockets. Waves of realization crushed me.

I can't let him add Henry to the names in the crypt. I can't let Henry be conquered.

Not Henry.

I smashed my fists into the grass beside me.

Maybe . . . Maybe we just need to submit. Is that what this has been about all along?

I struggled to my feet and looked around the room at each place we knew there were cameras. I looked him in the eye. *He's watching.*

I know you're watching. "Alright. You win." I wailed at the walls and threw my hands in the air.

"What are you doing?" I could hear the pain in Henry's voice. He grabbed my ankle with his free hand, but I kicked it away. The pain was sharp.

"I refuse to let him finish killing you," I growled at Henry under my breath.

"We submit. You've won. You are the conqueror," I shouted at the ceiling, standing on my one good leg, arms raised in surrender, and waited. For a long, silent moment, nothing happened. I glared down at Henry.

"No. I won't submit to this lunatic. We can't." He coughed painfully, and the tiniest droplets of blood appeared on his lower lip. "Not after everything he's put us through. He can't win. You can't let him." He clutched my ankle; tears welled in his eyes. "Don't give up, not now." Not only his words but every inflection in his voice, every fiber in his body, seemed to plead for me not to give in.

I stretched out my injured leg and squatted down on my good one, taking the hand he had around my ankle into my own. "I can't let him destroy you. He's won. I won't fight anymore. Not if that means that you die." My tear fell onto his hand and rolled down the back of it. He squeezed so hard I thought my hand might fracture.

What are you gonna choose?

Henry let go of my hand and slammed his head and fist into the grass like a hammer. I lost my balance and fell backward. A visceral roar rose from deep within him, a sound I'd never heard from a human before. When it finally reached his mouth, it tried to form words. "Argh! Fine." He scrunched his eyes closed. "You win. We submit. No more fighting back." By the time the last phrase gurgled up and had left his lungs, all Henry's will seemed to have deserted him, and a last drop of blood dripped from his mouth and off his lip.

"Henry!" I cried out and reached for him. But before I got there, the power went out, and the house blackened completely.

"Henry?!" I couldn't find him in the dark.

The hum of the house wound down into an eerie silence. Above us, blinding white letters on the blacked-out dome appeared:

vici

80650144

I couldn't see Henry. I'd moved too far when I fell away from him, and I had lost my bearings in the dark. I continued to reach for him in the darkness, but all I found was damp grass and empty space. He didn't answer my frantic calls, and then . . .

Blackness.

DAY 24

Suspended

Disorientation is the first symptom when you regain consciousness after being drugged. The world spins. Sounds don't make sense. Skin tingles like it's waking after a long sleep. You feel like you're moving despite profound efforts to remain still.

Where am I?

I closed my eyes and tried to focus. The crush of sound hit wave after wave. *Is that a mob?* Arguing, shouting, shoving. People trying to bring order. High-pitched beeping. I couldn't make it all out. *It sounds close, yet far away . . . Am I out?*

Slowly, I managed to open my eyes. *I'm not in the house. Is this a hospital?*

A scratchy blue hospital gown adorned my battered body. I had an IV in my right hand and machines strapped everywhere else. The dimly lit room had a wall of opaque windows with people swarmed on the other side like locusts over a field. I made out a shadow of two people trying to control the crowd outside the room. There was such a commotion outside the door: shouting and shoving. *What's going on?*

The door opened, presenting a man in a wheelchair. My senses were so hazy. *I'm not up for this; I feel like a stranger in my own skin.*

A nurse parked him by my bed and told me to call if I needed her, then she ducked out of the room. *Do I know this man?* I didn't recognize him; his head and hands were bandaged. I tried to sit up, but the room moved without me.

"Don't get up." His low and comforting voice, reminiscent of James Earl Jones, continued, "You've been through quite an ordeal, and the doctors tell me that you have residual drugs in your system.

They need to work their way out before you jump up and take down your next trafficking ring."

I couldn't argue with that. "So, who are you?"

"My name is Lucian Fenn, Director of the Cyber and Criminal Services Branch of the FBI. I've been searching for you for six weeks. The FBI has been working night and day toward your recovery, watching since the day you were taken."

A Director from the FBI? Unexpected.

"Wait, six weeks? That's not right."

"Yes, ma'am, six weeks. Your captor used multiple psychological techniques, typically deployed by the military, to mislead an individual's perception of time. It may take several weeks for you to reacclimate to a twenty-four-hour day.

"Forgive me for interrupting your recovery, but I wanted to personally tell you how relieved I am that you are alive and free. And I promise that we will not stop hunting until we have found the man responsible."

I tried to respond without venom, but I was without control of my filters. Out came all my bitterness.

"What? I was imprisoned, manipulated, and tortured like a lab rat. With six whole weeks, you still couldn't manage to find him?!"

Without taking offense, the Director continued, "We've been close. We thought we had him at several points. I lost two decorated agents, and several more are being treated for burns and injuries from explosions in a warehouse where he set a trap."

When I realized what he said and took note of the appearance of the man before me, I couldn't help but ask, "Sir, were you involved in the explosions? Did people suffer and die trying to rescue"—I almost couldn't finish—"me?"

The Director put his bandaged hand over mine, careful not to interfere with its IV line and the medical devices strapped to my wrist and finger. "Ma'am, every agent understands what they're signing up for when they take this job. Knowing what they know now, they would each choose to do it all again. We are here to protect every citizen of these United States. Don't ever confuse this: you are not at fault; he is."

Rendered speechless by the man before me—the price that had been paid while I thought I was the one suffering; I would never allow myself such self-pity again.

"You may have felt alone in that bunker, but we were all there with you. And now, as you resume your life and try to recover from your ordeal, know that teams of agents—know that I—will continue to fight to bring justice to you and to Mr. Beecher."

"Mr. Beecher? Henry! Is Henry okay? He's trapped. He's hurt!" I leapt from my bed as soon as I remembered that I had left Henry crushed under that panel, under concrete. *He's bleeding internally—maybe dying.*

The Director stopped me and eased me back into the bed. "Don't worry, Ms. Cameron. He is in the hospital as well and has already had surgery and been treated for his injuries. He'll be fine. I'm sure you'll be able to see him soon."

"Surgery?"

I didn't have time to absorb what the Director said before he gingerly gripped the wheels of his wheelchair and turned himself around. It had to hurt his hands to maneuver himself, though a man like that didn't seem likely to complain. When he got to the door, he knocked gently with the toe of his perfectly shined wing tips. "It was truly a pleasure to have met you in person, Ms. Cameron. Godspeed." With that, the door opened, and a nurse wheeled him into the barrage of reporters clamoring for a photo or a sound bite.

"Wait. But what about Henry?" I asked, but the crowd had engulfed the Director. He was gone.

I lay back in bed, trying to make sense of my situation, hoping the vertigo would subside. I didn't make any progress, and it wasn't long before the crowds outside my room grew louder again. There was more shouting and shoving, and the door opened. *Henry.*

Henry!

"Are you okay?!" The door slammed behind him, and the people resumed their previous levels of commotion outside my room.

"I'm getting there. A dislocated shoulder, a broken arm, and a few broken ribs. I'll manage."

Henry crossed the room and sat on the edge of my bed. He looked as though he were tiptoeing past a sleeping dragon. He walked with such care I wondered how much pain he was hiding. *What injuries aren't you telling me about?*

He barely sat on the edge of the bed in such a way that I thought he would slip off at any moment. He stared at the floor for a long second before his penetrating gaze landed on me. "Have you had some time to adjust to the outside world, or have you only now woken up?"

I couldn't fathom how to respond. I looked around the room, at the people pressed against the glass, and finally back at Henry. "We're really out?"

He smiled and stood, gingerly modeling his designer hospital gown. His was green, and they apparently struggled to find one that fit him as the short sleeves seemed to cut off the circulation in his biceps. He went on to model his IV pole like he was Vanna White, though his glimmering Hollywood smile was tainted with pain. "We're really out."

Despite the show, I wasn't ready to believe it. Henry sensed my skepticism and rejoined me at my bedside. "You were right. He wanted our submission, to know that he had conquered. You saved our lives. You saved me." He rested his hand on mine before he continued, "He drugged us again; they said it was probably a gas pumped into the house. You and I inhaled the same amount, but being so small, ma puce, it's taking longer to wear off of you.

"Doctors on a late-night shift found us unconscious on the grass in the park outside the hospital. I'm told we aren't far from your home. As the crow flies."

I looked toward the window. Even with the blinds down, I could see through the slats enough to tell exactly which hospital it was. "We're back in New York City. We could walk to my building from here."

Henry gave my hand a little squeeze. "You freed us. You did it."

"But that makes no sense. None of it. None of this makes any sense. Why did he let us go? He was what . . . ? Done toying with us because we gave up? I don't buy it. Something else is going on.

"And why us? I'm nobody. You, I get. You brought a huge audience. I don't understand. At one point, I thought I had it figured out, but now? No. I don't get it. None of it."

He placed his hand over mine. "It doesn't have to make sense. We're out. It's time to move on."

Leaning over to the nightstand, he grabbed the remote and turned on the television. He crowded into the bed beside me, and we watched as the news was broadcast from outside the hospital.

The anchor was mid-report. "The celebrating continues as we wait for the second day after Henry Beecher and Monti Cameron were suddenly released from captivity and deposited in front of Bellevue Hospital in New York City. Onlookers have gathered in squares around the world to celebrate their freedom just as they watched the pair, hoping for their safe recovery. Now millions wait, hoping for a glimpse of the freed captives."

We watched in disbelief. It felt like we were back in the house watching crowds on the dome again as the image on the TV flashed from one gathering to another, scores of people in cities all over the world now watching our hospital gate on giant screens, waiting for us to appear. They were crammed into plazas, drinking, dancing, shouting, and celebrating. It looked like a cross between New Year's Eve and Mardi Gras. I buried my face in Henry's shoulder, completely overwhelmed, and he turned the TV off.

"I'm sorry; I didn't mean to upset you." He gently ran his fingers through my hair. Even though he'd never done that before, it felt familiar, almost as though that was how it was always supposed to be.

"It was too much like the house, I think. It looks like people are legitimately happy for us, though." I tried to sound less overwhelmed than I felt.

Henry attempted to change the subject. "I don't suppose you know what you'll do now that you're free?"

I was still bewildered by our new reality; I shook my head and blinked. "You?" I asked in return. *Please don't make me talk.*

He looked down and stared at my hand as he began to lightly trace my fingers with the tip of his. "Well, I thought we might pick up privately where we were forced to start off publicly." His voice was hesitant and unsure. I took a sharp breath in to respond, but he cut me off and jerked his hand away. "Don't."

He stood up, collecting his thoughts. "I can guess what you're about to say." Henry wouldn't look at me, or couldn't. But I could see him nervously tracing the scar on his palm again. "It was real. For me, at least. Do you remember?" He paused and swallowed. "I told you about the list I made as a schoolboy? The list of the perfect woman that has kept me from forming a lasting relationship?" His back was to me as he dug in the chest pocket of his hospital gown. I leaned to the side, trying to meet his eye, but it was no use.

I answered as delicately as I could. "Yes."

Henry pulled out a tattered, yellowed piece of notebook paper that had been opened and folded so many times that it had holes at the corners of the folds. He walked back guardedly and laid it on the bed next to me with trepidation, pressing his hand over the paper so I couldn't look at it or pick it up.

He sat next to me, fixated on his hand covering the list. "It's you." The words barely snuck past his lips. With a kind of sleight of hand, he lifted my fingers and slipped the paper into my palm, tenderly kissing my knuckles. His eyes were welled with tears, though none fell. With that, he left the room.

I had no time to respond. I was left alone, holding a fragile piece of paper with a list in juvenile handwriting. I carefully unfolded it and read:

- She won't mind that I'm a nerd.
- She will like me for who I really am, not who people want me to be.
- She will stand up for people who can't stand up for themselves.
- She will care about a person's character, not about their money.
- She will take care of others' needs before her own.

She will love with all of her heart or not at all.

Tears flowed down my face as I read the list. *This isn't the list of a fifteen-year-old boy. What must have happened to him as a child that this is what he came up with?* The thought that our experience in the house made him check these boxes paralyzed me.

I'd hidden from the world for years because I was devastated by losing my love. Henry promised a new love. With his offering came a choice.

Should I choose the pain of rejecting his love and the emptiness inside me growing larger with each passing day? Or I could choose Henry and risk losing another love and have that pain consume me once again, this time completely.

I gripped my hair, feeling it release from the roots before I let go.

What am I supposed to do?

Before I met Henry, I thought I was safe, content in my solitude—my emptiness—hidden away from pain because it wasn't possible to find love again, to find a match for such a difficult and imperfect person like me a second time.

I guess I was wrong. I certainly don't deserve him. But now that the choice is here, how can I possibly let him go?

My mind was made up before I'd reasoned it out. I jumped out of bed, still dizzy from the drugs. I forgot about the IV and medical contraptions hitching me to the bed, and was yanked back into place. I didn't realize I had to disconnect most of the things attached to me and pull the IV pole with me wherever I went. I frantically looked around the room for clothes; once I found them, I discovered that getting dressed around an IV line was no small endeavor; it appeared that it would require the nurse call button and a small army of people.

A nurse named Christopher arrived. Christopher vehemently objected to the idea of my getting dressed, and my attempts to persuade him were unsuccessful until he caught a whiff of my desperation.

The whole world had watched what transpired in the house between Henry and me, and that audience had included Christopher. "Did something happen? What happened?!" Christopher confessed to calling in sick more than once because he was watching us. He was dying to know if something had happened off-camera or, more importantly, since we'd been released.

"If it will motivate you to help me, I've changed my mind."

"About wanting to care?" Christopher prodded as we played tug-of-war with a pair of my jeans.

"Yes."

"You do know that was a devastating moment?" Christopher put his hands on his hips, still holding the ankle of my jeans, scolding me for crushing Henry.

"And you realize this is my real life, not reality TV? Will you help me?"

"Yes!" He let the jeans go, and I toppled backward onto the bed, unstable on my leg and reminded sharply that the stab wound in my ass wasn't healed.

Christopher was a whirlwind. I never figured out how he got me dressed around all the wires and tubes, but before I knew it, he was clipping off the IV line, unplugging cords, and slipping on my shoes.

"Between the leg injury and the medications in your system, you won't be particularly steady on your feet. I'll help you get there."

"Thanks." I could have ended up with a hundred different nurses in the hospital. I was fortunate to get the superfan.

Christopher put my arm over his shoulder and helped me to a door at the side of the room. "What's this?" I was confused. We were supposed to be going to see Henry.

"This room is part of a suite, two rooms connected by this door. If we enter the hall from the second room, you're less likely to be noticed and won't have to deal with the gaggle of reporters."

Good thinking.

As we walked the short length of hall to Henry's room, I listened to Christopher chat about Henry and me. "I was a big fan of Henry's before all this. And when tragedy struck, listen, I have been rooting for you two since day one." Christopher made me laugh. Putting a face to a fan made having them easier to absorb.

When we reached Henry's hospital room, Christopher gave me two thumbs-up and a full-faced wink of good luck before he snuck into the adjacent room of Henry's suite to give us some privacy.

I need all the luck I can get, Christopher.

Henry stood at the window glowering. I'd focused so much on getting to his room undetected that I hadn't thought about what to say or do when I arrived.

What now?

"I feel fine. I don't need anything." His tone was abrupt and despondent.

"You don't sound fine." His head lifted at the sound of my voice, but he didn't turn around. "I read your list. I'm not sure I qualify for all of these or any of these for that matter; maybe we should have them do a CT scan while we're here. I think that display hit your head harder than we thought." That got a chuckle and a turn out of him, but he remained by the window, hesitant and uncertain.

I held out the list, my hand shaking as it reached into the void between us. I tried to smile and keep the mood light, but I had to fight back tears. "I'm afraid I'll disappoint you; those are some high expectations there." My voice cracked.

Henry's eyes bore into me as he crossed the chasm dividing us and liberated the paper from my hand, letting it fall carelessly to the floor.

"You couldn't disappoint; you've already surpassed every expectation. From here on, everything is new. No expectations, no lists, just getting to know one another outside that bloody house." He lifted my hand toward his lips, stopping a hair's breadth before they touched. He stroked my fingers with his thumb. "What do you say to a new beginning? Shall we start over?"

The tears welled in his eyes, making the green sparkle as he looked down at me. I was tempted to wonder if he was acting or genuine, but I had learned, and I finally knew better. I let the thought go. I didn't have to force it away; it drifted freely, never to return.

Bewildered by the idea of starting over without the world watching, words escaped me. I nodded almost imperceptibly, but he noticed. He always noticed.

Henry placed my hand on his chest, tucked just under the strap of his sling. As I focused on the strength of his pounding heart, he brushed his hand across my cheek and around the back of my neck. When he kissed me, the room around us dissolved and the rest of the world with it. The last month vanished, and all that remained was the two of us suspended for those few precious moments outside of reality.

DAY 1 TAKE 2

Comfortable

New beginnings are full of promise. This beginning, void of the pressures of constant surveillance, I sat in my own living room in all its modern glory. No '60s décor, no orange suede, no furniture upholstered in the matted hide of a fluffy pink Muppet.

I sank into my white leather love seat, cozy in front of my fireplace. I smiled at my modern stemless wine glass, with wine of my own choosing, from my own tiny and intentionally understocked pantry. I looked around and reveled in my complete and utter seclusion. No eyes secretly observing from an unknown vantage point. No one else, however amiable, in the apartment with me.

Perfect, untainted solitude.

Will it be an adjustment, returning to my old life? I don't think so.

I smiled at the thought of the endeavor. I wasn't entirely returning to my old ways. I'd remain in my reclusiveness as much as possible and hide from the world again. But the world was far more aware of and interested in me. I stood and crossed the apartment to peek out my window and see if the photographers were still positioned across the street, waiting to get a photo of me.

There they are. The FBI made it clear they had to stay at least one hundred feet from the entrance to my building. They weren't more than an inch or two further, but I didn't mind.

It's a nice change to be filmed by cameras I can see, and to have photographers with faces.

A shiver ran up my spine. I determined to shift my mind to more pleasant thoughts, but instead, my eye found a growing stack of letters on the counter, more than half of them unopened. Publishers, agents, ghostwriters—dozens of them. All lined up, begging me to tell my story. *Will I indulge them? Do I want to go back and recount every detail of our time in the house? I don't know. Not yet, anyway.*

A new relationship was a lot different from my old life. I never thought I'd give love a chance ever again. Yet there I was. I'd take it at my own pace and in relative privacy. No one artificially manipulating its path, and we didn't have to let the relationship unfold in front of the world. Well, not every moment, at least. There was a lot to figure out between a Hollywood superstar and a hyper-introvert. *Can we really make this work?*

Only time will tell.

As I sat on the couch pondering and enjoying the idea that I finally had all the time and privacy I wanted, my tablet lit up. It was Henry. I couldn't restrain the smile, and why should I? It was good to see his face. Even though he was on the opposite side of the country, it was nice to share a glass of wine and a chat.

In New York, I was three hours ahead of him. He was eating a late dinner in a hotel in LA, and I was up well after midnight reading by the fire. It was our time to catch up despite the time difference and having returned to our previous hectic schedules. There was nothing special in the conversation, nothing particular to talk about. But it was Henry. It was comfortable. It was perfect.

1503

EPILOGUE

Cenotaph

Priority one, my first day back at work: visiting the plaques for Supervisory Special Agent Crowley and Special Agent Hamovici. I had called and visited their families. Though, in my condition and under the circumstances, it probably made things worse. Crowley's kids were five and three years old. Seeing a burn victim when their mom had died in an explosion was not reassuring. And Hamovici's elderly mother—his only living relative—did not want to see his boss among the living when he was not.

So, there I stood, in my finest suit and freshly shined shoes. The hall was empty, plaques glistening in the morning light through the skylight above. My most respectful posture didn't feel good enough—it was the best I had to offer. I stood past the point where my body cried out for my cane and then a chair before I gave in and left the hall to return to work. I didn't want to leave, but I had to get back to the case. I had to find him.

It had been months before I was cleared to return to work. Agent Barone wasn't so lucky. The doctors determined that he would never regain his sight. Though, he had a remarkable attitude about it and was being headhunted by several companies, despite the disability. He said he would take some leave and let his wife and kids pamper him first.

Lanoff would require several surgeries before her ankle was in working order. She'd already had two. The doctors said she'd be able to return to duty, but the chances of her getting back onto SWAT were questionable. My money had always been on Lanoff. If anyone could make it back, it would be her.

Three months and my lungs had recovered enough from the smoke inhalation that, with the help of physical therapy, I no longer needed the wheelchair. My burns weren't completely healed; a few were still bandaged, and the ones that weren't were hideous. People would have to find a way to cope with my new appearance.

I was still Director Fenn: the same leader, boss, and mentor as before.

Thankfully, the majority of my face was undamaged, making interactions easier. The burns on the left border of my face didn't allow my eye to close completely and left the edge drooping—a disconcerting sight. So, I wore sunglasses regardless of being indoors or out. As an added bonus, tinted glasses made it easier to read people without being noticed. *Win-win.*

My head and hands were more unsightly. I had little hair left, and what remained of my left ear was mutilated. My left hand had required grafts that were still in process, and the results thus far left me with a patchwork of scar tissue and mismatched skin tones. Fortunately, the doctors managed to save all but one finger. Even more interesting was that people seemed to stare more at my right hand, where Agent Holt had broken my fingers with the door. The middle finger was shattered and required a rod. People seemed to stare because my middle finger was always straight, and occasionally it appeared inappropriate.

Despite all this, I desired neither pity nor sympathy. I did, however, expect the same measure of respect I had prior to the explosion. Nothing should change because of my appearance.

The Cyber and Criminal Services Branch had to continue normal operations; there was a country to protect. To do that, I couldn't let them see this failure get past my armor and fester. I had experienced defeat in the past, and not in small doses. But this one was more public, more personal than any I'd experienced. I couldn't back down.

Before I officially got back to work, I had reassigned four covert teams to rooms on a classified subfloor of the building. Reporting directly to me, Operation Libertas had to continue. My teams would find the Host and put him in an underground bunker for the rest of his life.

They have to.

At the end of my first day back, I checked on my teams to see how they were progressing. Holt's and Sterling's teams chased the technology. Southerland's team worked the psychological profile. Thornfield's team followed non-technology leads.

I poked my head in the door. "Thornfield. How's Pieri doing?" She looked surprised. I usually reserved personal questions for one-on-one situations. But this group knew what had happened at the warehouse. No need to keep the question private.

"Well, sir, progress is slow. He's at home and still on oxygen. He needs the wheelchair to get out and about or the walker in the house. Physical therapy is painfully demanding. But he's determined and hard-working. The doctors say he'll make a full recovery if he keeps giving it this level of effort."

"That's wonderful to hear. He's a good agent, a good man."

"Thank you, sir." Thornfield smiled and leaned back in her chair.

I scanned the room. "Well, team, how's it coming?" *The investigation is again in its infancy; I don't expect much progress. Nevertheless, these are my star players, and I am going to be kept in the loop.*

"Well, sir," Holt began in a measured tone.

He's mellowed over the last few months. Fieldwork and explosions will do that to an agent.

"I think we've got something."

After the lethal results of Holt's previous findings, I was both skeptical and cautious. My eyes narrowed at Holt as he continued.

"There's a new feed."

Agent Sterling angled his monitor toward me. There it was: a split screen of two live camera feeds, Ms. Cameron in her home on the left side and Mr. Beecher in his home on the right. A number in the bottom right-hand corner of each image leapt off the screen, immediately catching my attention.

"This feed is different from the last." Agent Sterling pointed to the monitor. "It's on the dark web, it's harder to trace, and it doesn't appear to be intended for mass consumption this time."

Holt turned to me hesitant. "Sir, if we allow the feed to continue, it may be the back door we need to locate the Host."

I could see that Holt was appalled with himself for thinking it, let alone uttering it aloud. *If we warn the Guests and remove the cameras, the unsub will disappear and strike again. This is the only way to track him undetected.*

There is no alternative.

"Find him." I barked the order, slamming the door behind me to make the point: their course of action was peremptory and unerring. Their path was justified.

The feed remained.

The hunt continued.

21915

THE HOST

—10 02 03 24 01 12 15 16—

this is not the end
this is not the beginning of the end
it is the end of the beginning[12]

-your Host

[1] Peter Swanson, *The Kind Worth Killing* (New York: William Morrow, 2016), 257

[2] George Orwell, *1984* (New York: Signet Classics, 1949), 255

[3] Paul Brickhill, *The Great Escape* (New York: W. W. Norton, 1950), 236

[4] Peter Swanson, *The Kind Worth Killing* (New York: William Morrow, 2016), 257

[5] Ella Dominguez, *Grace Street* (N.p.: Bondage Bunny Publishing, 2014), 180

[6] Harlan Ellison, *I Have No Mouth and I Must Scream* (New York: Open Road Media, 1983), 27

[7] Sun Tzu, *The Art of War*, trans. Lionel Giles (Seattle: Amazon Classics), Ch.1 #23, p. 4

[8] Sun Tzu, *The Art of War*, trans. Lionel Giles (Seattle: Amazon Classics), Ch.3 #18, p. 7

[9] Cormac McCarthy, *No Country for Old Men* (New York: Vintage Books, 2005), 249

[10] Jennifer L. Armentrout, *Onyx* (Fort Collins, CO: Entangled, 2012), 124

[11] Open University, *Introduction to Number Theory* (Milton Keynes: The Open University, 2015), 61, 62

[12] *Millennium*, directed by Michael Anderson (1989; Gladden Entertainment), 1:40:50

ACKNOWLEDGEMENT

This book would not have been possible without my IRL bestie in Fla and my writing bestie, Tammy Blakley. Both have made me a better person and writer, there when I need support, a laugh, or to be pulled out of the mire.

Jody Wenner, a fantastic author and an even better friend. Always there when I need writing help or tech support.

Genalea Barker pushes me to be better and do hard things—and Sarah Miller who constantly makes me laugh.

Leslie Conner, C.L. Geisler, David Gwyn, & Deana Lisenby, who push me and the boundaries of my work.

My Twitter accountability and creativity groups, who knock it out of the park every day, motivate and stretch my writing.

#MomsWritersClub with Sara Read & Jessica Payne & #ThrillsAndChills with Kelly Malacko & Tobie Carter.

Davin Roberts & Jenny Lewis are constantly checking in on me and supporting me.

Kerri Jackson, the first to believe in this manuscript.

ABOUT THE AUTHOR

T. C. Westminster

Some of my closest author friends joke that I live in a bunker, much like the one in the book. The reason is I don't often leave the house. I live with chronic illness and a neurological disorder that involve extended periods of intense pain. During those periods, I have learned to distract myself with stories. These stories and characters have kept my spirits up when my body has failed me. It is these stories I share with you.

Outside of writing, I homeschool my gifted children and do my best to keep up with my adventuring family despite my physical limitations. They're even willing to cart me around the wilderness in a wheelchair when necessary, so I don't miss out. We go the extra mile for an experience.

Made in the USA
Middletown, DE
27 May 2024

54797175R00205